# THE FALL
## OF THE
# READERS

VOLUME IV IN
THE FORBIDDEN LIBRARY

DJANGO WEXLER

KATHY DAWSON BOOKS

KATHY DAWSON BOOKS
Penguin Young Readers Group
An imprint of Penguin Random House LLC
375 Hudson Street, New York, NY 10014

Text copyright © 2017 by Django Wexler
Illustrations copyright © 2017 by Alexander Jansson.

Printed in the United States of America
ISBN 9780399539206

1 3 5 7 9 10 8 6 4 2

Design by Jasmin Rubero
Text set in Lomba

*For Readers Everywhere*

# CONTENTS

# PART I

# PART 2

# PART ONE

## Chapter One

# MIDNIGHT SNACK

In the darkness behind the mirror, something stirred.

It was an eye, cat-slitted and silver. Though it hung alone in the emptiness, Alice knew it was enormous, as big across as she was tall. It focused on her, the great pupil narrowing, and in its gaze she felt something inscrutable and alien.

And yet she felt no fear. Instead, staring back into the abyss, she felt . . . warmth. Kindness. *Love.*

A voice in her mind, strange and familiar all at once.

**Alice.**

She sat bolt upright in bed, sheets tangled around her

feet. Her cheeks were slick with sweat, and her heart pounded.

She was in the room that her master Geryon had given her when she'd first arrived on his estate, a dingy third-floor bedroom fit for a servant. It felt like home, now, if anywhere did. She knew every crack of the peeling paint, the smell of old wood and freshly laundered sheets, and the endless creaks and groans of the ancient building. Two stuffed rabbits, all that she'd been allowed to carry away from her father's old house, sat on the windowsill like sentinels.

She didn't have to stay in this room if she didn't want to. Geryon was right where Alice had put him—bound inside *The Infinite Prison*, lost in an endless sea of mirror images. There was no one to tell Alice where to sleep, where to go, what to do. It should have been freeing, but she felt more hemmed in than ever. Instead of Geryon's orders restraining her, now an iron cage of *responsibility* squeezed her ever more tightly.

There was no chance of getting back to sleep. Alice waited until her heart slowed, then swung out of bed and stretched her aching legs. A surprisingly loud growl from her stomach reminded her that she'd missed dinner, again.

*If I'm going to be awake, I might as well get something to eat.* It was still hours before dawn, but in Geryon's house the kitchen never closed. Alice shuffled into her slippers and opened the door to her room, carefully.

The house, which had felt empty for so long, now had several dozen inhabitants. The rooms immediately around hers were taken by the other apprentices, the friends who'd thrown in their lot with her after facing the Ouroborean. She passed their doors quietly: Isaac, her oldest friend, who'd once stolen the Dragon's book for his master. Dex, inveterate optimist, who'd fought beside her in Esau's fortress. Jen and Michael, younger than Alice, devoted to each other, the former fierce and the latter cautious.

Down the corridors were others, magical creatures from Geryon's library who'd begged her for shelter. As the labyrinthine Ending, the library's guardian, fought back the attacks of the old Readers, the once-peaceful library had become a war zone. Some of the inhabitants had retreated to their books, but many creatures in the library didn't have that option because their own worlds had become hostile, and had nowhere else to go. These refugees—sprites, the mushroom-people called Enoki, and stranger things—had taken up residence in the empty bedrooms of Geryon's manor house.

The kitchen was built on the same massive scale as the rest of the house, with acres of long wooden tables and ovens big enough to roast an ox. It was normally empty, since all the work was done by efficient, invisible servants who moved only when you turned your back. Tonight, though, Alice wasn't the only nocturnal visitor. Isaac sat at one of the long tables, in front of a jug of milk and a plate piled high with pastries.

"Knock-knock," Alice said, coming through the open doorway. Isaac looked up with exactly the guilty expression she'd pictured, which made her grin.

"Oh," he said. "It's you."

"Who were you expecting?"

"I honestly don't know." Isaac sighed. "Half the time I still wake up expecting to find my master—my *former* master looking down at me."

Alice's grin faded. He looked tired and pale, worn out, the same things she saw in her own face when she looked in the mirror. Wearing only a nightshirt and trousers, without his voluminous trench coat, he seemed smaller than usual, more vulnerable. His brown hair was growing out, flopping in unruly curls down the back of his neck.

"Are you going to eat all of those," she said, "or can you spare a few?"

"Please." He pushed the plate toward her. "I can't seem to get this place to understand that I just want a snack."

Alice sat beside him. Another cup had appeared on the table the moment she looked away, and a fresh jug of ice-cold milk. She poured, and took a pastry. They were flaky and warm, filled with raspberry jam.

If Geryon had died, all of this—everything that made the house *work*, the hidden creatures who fixed the food and did the laundry—would have ground to a halt, like a watch with its mainspring removed. She'd seen that in Esau's fortress, the gradual unraveling of a Reader's domain after their power vanished. By trapping her old master alive, she'd kept the house running. She'd also hoped to conceal what had happened from the other old Readers.

That part, unfortunately, hadn't worked.

"You look like you've had a long day," Alice said as Isaac drained his cup and reached for another pastry.

"You might say that." Isaac yawned. "Michael and I were working with the swamp sprites on our plan to evacuate the house in an emergency."

"It's not going well?"

"They don't seem to be able to grasp the concept of moving in a straight line," Isaac said. "And they kept turning the ground underneath me to mud, which isn't as funny the fourth or fifth time."

Alice winced. "Sorry."

"I thought they were getting it by the end," Isaac said, staring at the pastry. "But I just . . . I don't know."

"What is it?"

"Is it really going to make a difference?" He looked pained, as though the words were a betrayal. "It's all well and good to make plans to keep people safe, but in the end what is it going to actually accomplish? It won't keep the old Readers from coming to squash us flat. It won't—" He broke off, shaking his head, and looked up at Alice. "I'm sorry. I'm just tired."

Alice's stomach churned. The problem, of course, was that Isaac was right.

A month ago, she'd trapped Geryon in *The Infinite Prison*, hoping the old Readers wouldn't find out. But they had. Alarmed, they had unleashed the Ouroborean, an ancient weapon, in an attempt to destroy her. With the help of her friends, she'd defeated it, and afterward, she'd told the apprentices and magical creatures that she intended to stand up to the old Readers, to pull down their whole poisonous order once and for all. Only days later, the attacks had begun. The other labyrinthine forced open some portals into the library to bring the creatures of the old Readers through.

Since then, defending against these attacks had occupied all of Alice's attention. The refugees from the library had to be protected, and she'd organized them to help as much they were able. Ending did her best, but the other labyrinthine assaulted her constantly, and she had to conserve her strength. The task of hunting down attackers —beast-like monsters, for the most part, driven into a rage by cruel magic—fell to Alice and her friends. She'd worked hard to make sure everyone knew what to do when an assault came, and so far they'd had only a few injuries among the library creatures.

But it couldn't last. *It's not like the old Readers are going to run out of monsters.* They would keep coming until Ending's strength failed, and something *really* nasty managed to get through, or until Alice and her little squad of defenders were worn down and tired out. *We're not going to win.*

She'd hoped . . . *I hoped for a lot of things.* More *time,* first and foremost. *There has to be a way to take the fight to them, but it's no good if we can barely protect ourselves.*

Some of her thoughts must have shown on her face, because Isaac put his hand on the table between them, stretching toward her.

"Hey," he said. "It'll be okay. We're holding our own."

Alice put her hand on his, and their fingers interlocked. She made herself smile. "I know."

"I didn't mean to complain," Isaac said. "It's—"

There was a thump from the doorway. They both looked up, and Alice's mental grasp automatically went to the threads of magic at the back of her mind, which linked her to her bound creatures. The Swarm for toughness, Spike for strength, and—

"Soranna!" she said, letting the power slip away.

The girl was leaning heavily on the door frame. When she pushed away from it and took a stumbling step forward, Alice could see she was filthy, her rough clothes caked with dirt and sweat. A bandage was wound around her thigh, and one side of her shirt was brown and crusty with dried blood.

Alice was vaulting the table before she knew it, sweeping past the stunned Isaac and hurrying to the girl's side. As Alice took hold of her arm, all the strength seemed to go out of Soranna. Alice half carried her to one of the benches, and Soranna leaned back against the table, eyes closed and breathing hard.

Soranna was another of the apprentices who'd been with Alice in Esau's fortress and the fight against his labyrinthine, Torment. Alice hadn't seen her since—she hadn't been among the group that had come after Geryon's imprisonment, and Alice hadn't figured out how to contact her. Now she was here, and hurt badly.

"Soranna, what happened?"

"I'll get . . . someone," Isaac said, lurching to his feet.

"Dex," Alice said. "No, get Magda the bone witch, if you can find her."

"Got it." Isaac looked relieved to be given a task. Before he could leave, though, Soranna opened her eyes.

"They're coming," she said, her voice a croak. "Have to . . . tell Alice."

"I'm here," Alice said. "Who's coming?"

Soranna blinked and turned to look at her, a smile spreading across her face. She coughed, and winced as if in pain.

"Sunhawks," she said. "My master . . . sent. Sunhawks."

"Ending would have called us if something got into the labyrinth—" Alice began.

"No!" Soranna grabbed the collar of her shirt. "*Not* through the labyrinth. They're coming through the *real* world. Take you . . . by surprise . . ."

Her eyes rolled up in her head, and she slumped back. Alice hastily checked her breathing and found it steady.

"They can't send monsters through the real world," Isaac said.

"Why not?" Alice said, looking down at Soranna.

"The humans would see them," Isaac said. "It's the oldest rule of the Readers, not to draw attention."

"I think the Readers have thrown away the rulebook," Alice said. "Go find Magda, and then sound the alarm. We need to get everyone into the library."

"But—"

Alice looked through the window to the back garden. Above the brooding bulk of the library and the dense mass of trees that surrounded it, the night sky was a field of stars streaked with irregular clouds. But underneath those clouds, moving fast, were two points of bright orange light.

"*Now,* Isaac!" Alice shouted, and he ran.

## Chapter Two
# EVACUATION

D EEP IN THE HOUSE, a gong began to sound. It might once have been used to call the residents of the house to dinner. Now it served to raise the alarm, rousing all the creatures who'd taken shelter.

It was time. The plan was the same one Michael and Isaac had been practicing with the swamp sprites: Get everyone to the library. They'd rehearsed it a couple of times, or tried to. The idea of training was foreign to the sprites and the Enoki, while Lool, the clockwork spider, had insisted on computing the best route instead of actually following the group.

Alice was miserably aware that even their best performance had taken fifteen or twenty minutes to get everyone out of danger. Given how fast the sunhawks were moving, they might not even have ten. She could hear clattering footsteps and muffled voices upstairs. Soranna still slumped on the bench, unconscious, and Alice wavered, wanting to direct the evacuation but not willing to leave her friend hurt and alone.

Fortunately, at that moment there was a hollow clatter in the doorway, and Magda the bone witch arrived. She was a large woman, covered head to toe in bones: She wore them around her neck, woven into the elaborate bun of her hair, and threaded onto wires as a long, trailing cloak. They clicked and rattled continuously as she moved. Since Alice had declared war on the old Readers, Magda had been one of her most dedicated supporters, and her impressive presence had done a great deal to keep the other creatures in line.

More importantly, for the moment, she was close enough to human to know something about medicine. Alice beckoned her over, and Magda's breath caught at the sight of Soranna.

"By Ushbar!" she said. "Isaac said you needed help. She's had a hard time."

"Something's coming," Alice said, gesturing to the window. "I need to be out there. Please take her to the library and do what you can for her?"

Magda nodded and clapped her hands together, like a teacher calling a class to attention. The bones on her cloak shivered, then rose up with a tremendous rattle, long strings of them stretching out like multi-jointed limbs. Hands unfolded at the ends, bony fingers opening to slip under Soranna with surprising gentleness.

"I've got her," Magda said. "Go! They need your help. Send old man Coryptus to me if you can."

Alice nodded and raced from the kitchen. In the main hall, creatures of all kinds were already heading to the back door, where Isaac was waiting to hurry them across the lawn toward the library. Several different varieties of sprites, elfin humanoids with eyes and hair in a rainbow of colors, were pushing and shoving at the base of the stairs, while a clutch of wide-eyed Enoki children were backed up behind them.

"That's enough!" Alice shouted, wading into the fray.

She wrapped herself in Spike's thread for strength, picking up the sprites and forcing them apart where she had to. Mostly they separated themselves at the sight of her. There was awe in their eyes, and they rushed to obey when she directed them to the exit.

"Thank you," said one of the Enoki women. Like all her kind, she looked mostly human, except for the mushrooms that grew up from her hair, back, and shoulders. The fungi came in as many varieties as human hair or skin color, and this one was a pretty red with white spots.

"I thought they would never move," the woman went on. "Do you know what's happening? Is it safe to go outside?"

Alice sighed inwardly. The mushroom people were friendly, but timid to a fault, refusing to fight or even argue.

"You'll be safe once you get to the library," Alice said. "Hurry!"

The younger women nodded and began herding their charges out. Another trio of sprites came down the stairs, swamp sprites whose muddy forms made a mess of the carpet, followed by the harpy girl Ephraster and her two young siblings. Alice waved them past, then charged up the stairs while they were clear for a moment.

At the top, she met Coryptus, a bent-backed old man who walked with a cane and was practically covered in luxuriant purple mushrooms.

"What are you waiting for?" Alice said.

"Just making sure nobody gets left behind," he said in a voice like a badly greased hinge. "Got to see to the little ones."

Alice nodded. "When you get to the library, find

Magda. One of the apprentices is hurt, and she asked for your help."

"Nosy old biddy." Coryptus sniffed. "Well, if she *asked*, I suppose I might be willing."

Alice didn't have time for their rivalry. She ran up the stairs, while a few more creatures ran, slid, or flew past her before she got close to her own room. The other three apprentices were waiting, ushering the last of their charges toward the stairs.

Dex—a little older than Alice, and tall with dark skin and frizzy hair that she tied back into a messy tail—was grinning broadly, in spite of the panic all around. As far as Alice could tell, Dex was utterly fearless, a trait that occasionally got her into serious trouble.

Michael and Jen—who had served their master as a team and remained inseparable even after turning against him— made a good pair; Jen was ragged and wild, prone to rage, while Michael was prim and careful, with round metal glasses that made him look a bit like an owl.

"Sister Alice!" Dex said. "We heard the alarm. Has something escaped the library?"

Alice shook her head. "They're coming overland, not through the portals. Is everyone off this floor?"

Michael nodded. "One hundred three, I counted."

"It's going to be a pain sorting them all out again when this is over," Jen griped.

"We can worry about that later," Alice said. "You two go help Isaac get them into the library. I'm going to get a better look at what we're up against." She grimaced. "Find Emma too, and bring her with you." The servant girl would stand by calmly as the house burned down, if no one ordered her to do otherwise.

"I will accompany you," Dex said. "To the balcony?"

Alice nodded. Michael was already headed downstairs, and Jen followed. It was gratifying, in a way, that even the most headstrong of the apprentices was willing to follow Alice's orders. *I just wish I knew the right orders to give.*

She and Dex ran to the end of the hall, where a pair of double doors opened onto a seldom-used balcony facing the back garden and the library. The latch squealed as Alice tugged on it. With Spike's strength, the rusty hinges moved with a reluctant groan, revealing a few feet of water-stained tile rimmed by a dangerously rotten wooden railing.

Down below, a multicolored throng was streaming across the lawn. Alice saw Lool, the clockwork spider, her eight brass legs working like pistons and letting off frantic bursts of steam. Sprites, Enoki, and stranger creatures hurried across the grass.

The two sunhawks were much larger now. She could see that they were bird-like—broad-winged and hook-beaked—with feathers ranging from pale yellow to dark red, covering them in rippling patterns that looked like flames. Their eyes glowed like the sun, and they were *huge*, the size of an elephant, each easily big enough to grab a human in its beak.

One of them dove, wings folded tight, plummeting in silence toward the caravan of creatures on the lawn. Isaac was there, waving the line forward, and he hadn't looked up. Alice gripped the railing and screamed a warning.

Isaac spun and saw the danger just as the sunhawk leveled out of its dive. The light from its eyes flared to unbearable intensity and slashed out toward the ground, twin crackling beams of orange that traced a path through the surrounding forest toward the lawn. Everything they touched burst into flame as though it had been doused in gasoline, leaving a trail of trees blazing like torches. The line of destruction broke out onto the lawn, angling toward Isaac.

Isaac stood his ground, even as the creatures behind

him started to panic and flee. He brought his hand up and summoned a wall of swirling white snow out of thin air, which solidified rapidly into a frozen barrier. The flames met Isaac's sheet of ice in a tremendous cloud of steam. When it cleared, Isaac and the fleeing creatures behind him were unharmed, the path of devastation continuing some distance beyond them and into the forest on the other side of the lawn.

"Sister Alice!" Dex said. "They've seen us!"

The second sunhawk dipped one wing, changing its angle, then went into a dive like the first. Lances of burning energy slashed from its eyes, cutting across the forest and aiming straight for the house. Grass exploded upward in great gouts of flame and flying earth.

*Nowhere to dodge up here.* Alice grabbed Dex around the waist, concentrated Spike's power, and jumped. With the dinosaur's strength in her legs, she cleared the railing easily, describing a lazy arc toward the still-steaming turf where Isaac stood. Before impact, Alice wrapped herself in the Swarm thread, which lent her flesh a tough, rubbery quality that made her very hard to hurt. The combined strength and durability let her absorb the landing with a crouch. Dex, under her arm, gave a delighted laugh.

Behind her there was a splintering crash and a roar of flame. The energy beams raked across the house, searing a dark track up one wall and along the shingles of the roof. The building was mostly stone, but small fires had started here and there.

"Are you all right, Isaac?" Alice asked, while she set Dex back on her feet. "That was good thinking."

"Thanks," Isaac said. His face was pale, and he looked a little shaky. "I wasn't sure it was going to work."

Alice eyed the sunhawks, which were beating their wings hard over the forest to gain altitude for another dive. "Any chance you can do it again?"

Isaac blew out a breath. "Maybe once more, but I'm not going to be good for much else. It takes a lot of power."

Alice nodded. "Better get everyone into the library, then. They're not going to be able to burn *that*." In addition to whatever magical protections Geryon had provided, the library was a stone fortress of a building with only a single small door.

Isaac took a deep breath and ran across the blasted turf, pursuing a pack of panicky sprites who'd broken away from the line. Michael and Jen were still by the house, trying to convince a cowering group of Enoki to make the run across open ground to the safety of the library.

"There's still too many in the open," Alice said. "We're going to have to draw the sunhawks after us."

"I agree," Dex said. Alice felt her tugging on her threads, and she was suddenly wrapped head to toe in silver armor, the power of the creature she called the caryatid. "How shall we get their attention?"

## CHAPTER THREE

# SUNHAWK DOWN

ALICE STOOD ON THE library lawn, a five-foot spear in one hand, and stared up at the giant bird diving toward her faster than a freight locomotive. *This may not be the best plan I've ever come up with . . .*

The spear was made of what Dex called moon-stuff, the product of one of her creatures. She could shape it into simple objects, and it was marvelously light and practically indestructible. With Spike's strength behind her, Alice figured she could throw the thing quite a long way. Whether it would be far enough, she had no idea.

The light from the sunhawk's eyes, crackling and snapping like fireworks, turned the lawn into a morass of torn grass and flash-baked mud as it sliced toward the hurrying mob of creatures. The sunhawk was still several hundred feet off the ground, but Alice thought this was the best chance she was going to get. She pushed off, sprinting in huge, bounding steps, bringing the spear forward as hard as her magical strength could drive it. The silvery weapon left her hand at a fantastic speed, *screaming* through the air in a high, fast arc.

Too high, Alice saw, a pit opening in her stomach. The spear peaked above and behind the enormous bird before falling toward the forest. It got the sunhawk's attention, however, and the creature swung around, beams of fire slashing toward Alice. *Which means this worked, sort of.*

She wrapped the Swarm thread tightly around herself, and her body dissolved into a mass of furry black balls, each with two legs and a long, thin beak. It took a moment to adjust to her new point of view, seeing out of a hundred pairs of eyes two inches off the ground. But Alice's control had improved enormously since her first tentative experiments, and it was no trouble at all for her to spread the swarmers out like an expanding starburst, depriving the sunhawk of its intended target.

The sunhawk's fire washed over where she'd been standing, and she felt a sharp burst of pain as several of the little creatures that made up her body were incinerated. *I was right not to stand my ground.* The sunhawks were *fast,* and the swarmers' toughness offered little protection. She brought her myriad bodies back together, reforming into human shape beside Dex and Isaac.

"Ow." She put her hand to her side. Damage to her transformed self didn't leave wounds, but it took its toll in energy and pain. "That didn't work." *And* she was in her bare feet, as usual. Her shoes had probably just gone up in smoke.

"You kept it away from the others," Dex said as the sunhawk glided back out over the forest and began flapping upward again.

"And I think you made the other one angry," Isaac said. "Here it comes!"

The second bird stooped in, ignoring the fleeing sprites and Enoki and coming straight for Alice. Isaac raised his hand, and once again snow fountained out of the ground, forming itself into a semi-circular shield around the three of them. The fiery rays sizzled across it, then passed overhead and on toward the house, where crackling explosions marked their progress. The snow burst outward into wisps and steam, and Isaac groaned and dropped to one knee.

"I'm fine!" he said as Alice bent beside him. "Just . . . used up." He gasped for breath. "Sorry."

Alice found her hands clenched in frustration as she watched the second sunhawk positioning itself for another attack. "We can't get *up* to them! Dex, do you have anything that can fly?"

Dex shook her armored head. "Sister Jennifer has a bird of prey, I believe, but it may not be large enough to harm these creatures."

*Jen's hawk!* Alice had almost forgotten. She hadn't seen the girl fight much, but she'd summoned a large bird when they'd gone up against the Ouroborean. The sunhawks were a lot larger. *But maybe . . .*

"Dex, can you make a *net* out of moon-stuff?"

Dex clapped her hands. "Brilliant as always, Sister Alice! I can. But it will take some time."

"Do it. I'll find a way to distract them."

Alice sprinted toward the house, where Jen and Michael had finally coaxed the last of the refugee creatures out the door and were herding them across the lawn. Fire had taken hold, and even some of the stones had cracked. Part of the roof had caved in, and Alice could see tongues of flame licking up from underneath.

Everything she owned was in there. Everything she'd brought from her former life, the rabbits and a few clothes and books, mementos that seemed almost alien to her now. Everything she'd been given or made for herself since coming here—

*Enough. The Infinite Prison* and the other magical books were in Geryon's suite, protected by powerful magical wards. Nothing that was really important would burn. Alice tore her eyes away from the growing conflagration and grabbed Jen.

"Alice?" Jen looked over her shoulder at the sunhawks, who were coming around for another pass. "Is Isaac going to be able to keep them off—"

"He can't," Alice said shortly. "Dex is working on something, but she needs time. If you transform into Avia, can you fly?"

"Of course," Jen said, then paled. "You want me to—"

"Not to fight them," Alice said. "They're too big. How much can you carry?"

"Not a lot," Jen said. "Flying's tricky."

*She ought to be able to lift the net.* The moon-stuff was lighter than silk. *But it won't be ready . . .*

"Can you carry *me*?" Alice blurted.

Jen shook her head. "Avia's a big bird, but you're still way too heavy."

Alice ran through her alternate forms. Spike weighed a ton, the devilfish was big and couldn't breathe air, and she couldn't turn herself into fewer than fifty or sixty swarmers. The Dragon still wouldn't respond, and—

*The tree-sprite!* She ordinarily used its power to control plants, but the creature itself, without its bark armor, was a tiny thing. Alice wrapped its thread tight around herself and began to change, shrinking into the tiny, stick-limbed sprite, her skin turning the bright green of new growth.

"How about this?" Alice said. As the sprite, her voice was high and mouse-like.

"Maybe. Even if I can, what do you want me to do?"

"The closer one! Get me onto its back," Alice squeaked. "Then go over to Dex and help her with the other sunhawk. Hurry!"

The sunhawks were both closing for another attack. Jen looked like she wanted to argue, but they were out of time. She took a deep breath and closed her eyes, her body shifting and flowing like water. Her arms lengthened, becoming mighty wings, with a brown-and-gray pattern on their feathers. She flapped once, then settled on the ground, raptor's eyes regarding Alice inquisitively.

From the tree-sprite's perspective, Alice was looking *up* at the bird, and she had a sudden empathy for a rabbit under the gaze of an eagle. At a motion of Jen's beak, she stepped forward and grabbed one leg, the soft, downy feathers of the bird's underbelly all around her. Alice's stomach lurched as huge wings chopped the air, pulling them skyward.

The first sunhawk's blistering gaze licked out, blasting through the trees and cutting a swath across the lawn. The magical creatures fled before it, looking like scurrying ants from Alice's increasingly elevated point of view. As the sunhawk shifted its fire from point to point, those ants began to vanish in the blaze of light, one by one. Alice's throat went tight.

"Jen!"

She wasn't sure if Jen heard her tiny voice, but she could see what was happening, and she redoubled her efforts. She pulled above the sunhawk and matched its dive. Soon she was directly over it, and Alice could see the long feathers of its wings, the huge muscles shifting underneath with every wingbeat.

Convincing herself to let go, to *fall*, was harder than she'd expected. It was all well and good to know that she could probably use the Swarm to protect herself, but *probably* wasn't *definitely*, and in any case the blurred, distant landscape triggered a primal terror that wasn't susceptible to rational arguments. Grimly, Alice forced her tiny hands to open, and let the tree-sprite thread go as she tumbled toward the sunhawk.

The change to human took only a moment, but that was nearly a moment too long. Alice hit the creature's back before she'd settled into her real body, and only a reflexive grab kept her from sliding off. Its huge feathers were warm to the touch, and the flesh beneath them was positively hot. The sunhawk banked, irritated, and Alice hastily drew on Spike's thread to give her strength, clinging with fingers and toes.

*I've distracted it, at least.* The sunhawk was spiraling upward now, reducing the Library and its lawn to a tiny clearing in the green mass of the forest. Below, Alice could see the second sunhawk chasing a speck of brown and white—Jen.

Wrapping herself in the Swarm's rubbery skin, she began crawling forward. She'd landed close to the sunhawk's tail, a few feet back from where the great wings beat in a steady rhythm. Its body was surprisingly scrawny under the feathers. It screeched at her, the first sound she'd heard it make, and pulled up sharply in the air, forcing her to hang on for dear life. Its head came around, trying to look over its shoulder and see what was irritating it.

Another few seconds of crawling and she was atop

its shoulder. Alice wrapped her arms around one wing, linking her hands together, and braced her feet against the creature's back. It shrieked, and she dug in her heels, pulling the wing in the wrong direction with all of Spike's immense strength.

Something broke with a *crunch*. The sunhawk rolled over, tumbling out of the sky. Forest and clouds exchanged positions, over and over, and Alice fought back a wave of nausea. For the second time in a few minutes, she forced herself to let go, and pushed off the sunhawk into free fall. At the same time, she wrapped the Swarm thread around her as tight as it would go.

A moment later, the forest around the Library was subjected to a brief, unseasonable rain of swarmers. The little black creatures had the consistency of tennis balls, and when they hit the ground they *bounced*, sometimes ricocheting off several trees before coming to a halt. It took Alice a few breaths to collect her thoughts, with her body spread throughout the woods. Several of her could see where the sunhawk had come down, tearing up quite a length of forest and starting even more fires. It was clearly not getting back up again.

*That's one*, Alice thought. Tiny black legs blurred, carrying her over the roots and stones, back toward the house.

## Chapter Four
# BAIT

$A$LICE REACHED THE LAWN and returned to human form. In the moment it took her to get her bearings, something *screeched* from the direction of the house, and a line of turf only a few feet away detonated with a roar. Instinct made Alice throw herself to the ground, rolling behind a hummock of disturbed earth and raising her head cautiously to see what was going on.

The second sunhawk was on the ground beside the house, by the door to the kitchens. Or where that door *had been*, anyway—most of the wall had been smashed, and stones and rubble were everywhere. The huge bird moved awkwardly, and when she looked carefully, Alice could see silvery strands wrapped around its left wing, binding it tight to its side. *Dex and Jen trapped it!* With its wing pinned, the sunhawk couldn't fly.

It was still alive, though, and its glowing eyes sent short bursts of orange light across the lawn, blasting smoking craters from the ground and setting fire to the trees. Alice couldn't see any of the other apprentices, until a pair of steel blades flashed through the air and struck the sunhawk in the throat. This seemed to irritate without causing much damage, and Alice saw the small figure of Michael running full-tilt across the lawn. He dove into a hole just as the beams of fire licked out.

Jen circled overhead, still in hawk form. Alice wrapped threads around herself for strength and toughness, then sprang out of her hiding place, running for the spot where Michael had taken shelter. The sunhawk shrieked, and Alice dove to the left, to avoid a blast of flame. She rolled, jumped, and skidded down the crater wall, dislodging a small avalanche of dirt.

Michael was pressed against the side, his normally well-coiffed hair wild and glasses slightly askew. He sounded as calm as ever, though obviously relieved to see Alice.

"You made it."

"Somehow," Alice said. "Is everyone okay?"

Michael swallowed. "Some of the library creatures got caught in the open. I didn't see what happened."

Alice remembered the ant-like specks, vanishing into the orange glow. She gritted her teeth. "What about Isaac and the others?"

"Dex took Isaac into the trees," Michael said. "Jen's still up there. I've been trying to stop this thing, but I can't hit it hard enough."

"Can you get it in the eyes?" Alice said.

Michael shook his head. "Not unless I get a lot closer." He looked sheepish. "I'm not as good a shot as I ought to be."

"I'll draw its attention, then," Alice said. "That should get you close enough."

"All right." Michael straightened his glasses, hand shaking only a little. He looked at once both very grown-up and very young. "I'll try."

*Here goes nothing.* Alice scrabbled in the dirt until she found a good-sized stone. It wasn't one of Dex's spears, but it would do. *I don't need to hurt the thing, just annoy it.* She peeked over the lip of the crater, then pulled herself over, bare feet sliding in the warm earth. The sunhawk was looking up toward Jen, which gave Alice a moment to wind up and whip the stone at it as hard as she could.

This time, she managed to hit it, the rock *thunking* off the side of its skull. The sunhawk's head snapped around, orange rays reaching out for Alice, but she was already moving. Running with Spike's strength had taken a long time to get used to; she took huge, loping strides, almost jumping over the ground, landing hard enough to sink into the grass before pushing off again. It made her *fast*, faster than a galloping horse. Now she tore across the lawn in a curving path, outrunning the line of flames that blossomed behind her.

Out of the corner of her eye, she saw Michael scrambling forward. Alice turned her next jump into a dive, landing in another crater and letting the flames pass overhead. She came up with two more rocks and hit the sunhawk, then started running again, drawing its attention back the way she'd come. Ahead, she saw Michael concentrating, a dozen shining blades hovering in the air around his head. As the bird turned to face him, the flying knives shot forward with a *hum*. They struck home, biting into the thing's eyes, and there was an explosion of light and flame.

Michael shouted in triumph. Alice started to cheer with him, but the sound died on her lips. Michael had half turned, looking for her, and behind him the sunhawk was still moving. Its great head came forward, its blackened eye sockets trailing smoke, its huge, curved beak open wide.

Spike gave Alice strength, but even that strength had limits. She was moving the wrong way, away from Michael, and she had a great deal of momentum. She planted one foot, trying to stop, but that only turned her run into a slide, tearing up a strip of grass. Michael looked back toward the sunhawk, his eyes going wide as it lunged. A scream tore free of Alice's throat—

And a streak of brown and white hit Michael in the side, just as the massive beak snapped closed. The boy was thrown to the ground by the impact, sprawling in the dirt just in front of the sunhawk. Alice recognized Jen, still in bird form, trapped in the sunhawk's beak. The monster shook her wildly, like a cat with a captive mouse, then snapped its head sideways and hurled her against the half-shattered wall of the house. The bedraggled ball of feathers hit the stone and fell limply to the earth.

"Jen!" Alice screamed.

She ran directly at the sunhawk. Unable to see or use its beams of fire, it snapped wildly, missing her by yards. She jumped, landing high on the creature's chest, clutching its soft belly-feathers in both hands. It twisted beneath her, but she was able to climb higher, getting her arms around its throat. As it reared up in panic, Alice broke its neck with a quick twist, as though it were a chicken in a farmyard. She jumped free as the sunhawk collapsed, hurrying over to where Jen had fallen.

Michael was already there. Jen was back in her human form, lying on her side in the dirt. There was no blood on her, no obvious wounds, but she wasn't moving. Alice fell to her knees beside her, hands raised, not sure what to do.

*Breathing. Is she still breathing?* She looked hard, and was able to convince herself that there was still a slight rise and fall to Jen's chest. There was so much she still didn't know about Reader powers—Jen had been hurt while she was in another form, and Alice knew from experience that meant pain when you changed back, but what would happen if you almost *died*?

"I . . ." Michael's glasses were gone. Without them, he looked like a different person, wild-eyed and frantic. "Alice—"

"We'll take her to the library," Alice said. "Magda's there, and Ending. They'll know what to do."

As she passed into the library through the narrow bronze door, Alice looked over her shoulder at Geryon's house.

It was still ablaze, and more of the roof had collapsed. Flames glowed through the first-floor windows.

Inside, the library seemed endless, bookshelves standing in serried ranks like soldiers at a review. The appearance of solidity and changelessness was a lie, Alice knew. For all that the shelves were covered in dust and cobwebs, the master of the labyrinth could reshape them to her whim, connecting one place to another with a thought. That master was Ending, Geryon's labyrinthine, although thanks to Alice's connection with the Dragon, Alice still shared some of those same powers.

Today, Ending had created a large clear space around the door where the dazed refugees could spread out. Most of those who'd made it inside were sitting in small groups, but part of the crowd was pressed close to the door, trying to get back out. In their way stood Coryptus, the old Enoki, and Flicker. Flicker was a fire-sprite who'd shared Alice's journey to the Palace of Glass and the fight against the Ouroborean that had followed. He looked mostly human, a slim boy of about her age dressed only in ragged shorts, with eyes that glowed a deep red from edge to edge and long hair whose color constantly flowed and shifted, as though it were a window onto living flame.

"You've got to stay put," Coryptus said to a wailing

sprite with skin the color of a cloudless sky. "And that's that."

"But Selys is still out there!" the sprite said, eyes dripping huge, greenish tears. "She could be hurt!"

"Alice and the others are fighting," Flicker said. He had his black spear held horizontally, blocking the doorway. "They'll protect everyone they can, and the more people who stay here, the easier that'll be."

When Alice touched Flicker's shoulder, his skin was as warm as a rock left in the sun. He glanced over his shoulder, and his eyes widened.

"Alice! Are you—"

"You can let them out," Alice said. "The danger's past, for now." She raised her voice. "See if you can round up anyone who hid in the forests! Bring them here, where it's safe."

Coryptus and Flicker stepped aside, and the crowd of nervous creatures surged through the doorway, shouting the names of friends or loved ones. *They're not all going to find who they're looking for,* Alice thought with a sick nausea. Some of the refugees were probably injured; others had disappeared altogether in the sunhawk's fires.

When the door was clear, Alice went back into the

anteroom, where Michael waited with Jen. They lifted her together and carried her inside.

"We need Magda," Alice said to Coryptus.

The old man pointed wordlessly. Alice and Michael carried their unconscious burden in the direction he indicated, and Flicker trailed nervously behind.

Magda had made an impromptu bed for Soranna out of blankets taken from the house, and sat beside her with a bowl of something steaming. Emma waited nearby, patiently holding a basin. When the bone witch saw Jen, she jumped to her feet, and her bone cloak animated with a clatter, lifting the limp girl and setting her down gently on the stones.

"She was transformed," Alice said, "and something hurt her badly. There was no wound when she changed back, but . . ."

Magda sucked her teeth. "I don't know much about Readers and their magic," she said. "But I'll do what I can. Emma, go and get fresh water."

The servant girl obeyed silently. Michael sat at Jen's side as the bone witch bent to her task. Alice put a hand on his shoulder for a moment and tried to think of something comforting, but the words stuck in her throat. He rubbed his eyes with the back of his hand, then looked up at her, expression serious but composed.

"I'll stay with her," he said. "You make sure the others are all right."

Not knowing what else to do, Alice nodded and turned away. Flicker came with her, and eventually she said, "I didn't expect to find you here."

Last they'd talked, Flicker had been headed back to his own world, to try and convince his tribe to help in the struggle against the old Readers. He gave an embarrassed shrug.

"I can only spend so long arguing with Pyros before I go crazy. I wanted to see you and talk strategy, but when I got here—" He waved a hand. "Coryptus looked like he needed help keeping order."

"Thank you," Alice said.

"What happened?"

Voice low, Alice explained, "The old Readers sent creatures to attack us. Ending can keep watch on the library portals, so they sent them flying through the real world and took us by surprise. It was . . . bad. Not everyone made it."

Flicker's hair, always sensitive to his emotional state, darkened until it was as dull as burned-out embers.

"I didn't expect them come at us this way," Alice went on. "Maybe we should have kept everyone in the library after all. But there were attacks almost every day, and—"

"I'm sure you did what you could." Flicker looked at the creatures around them, who were casting surreptitious glances in their direction. "You always do, I should know that better than anyone."

"But it's not *enough*." Alice lowered her voice to a whisper. "These are people who trusted me to defend them, and now they're *dead*. Jen could die any minute, for all I know. Soranna's hurt, just because she tried to warn me, and . . . and . . ."

"Alice," Flicker said, glancing around again. "I understand. But . . ."

*But not here, he means. Don't talk about it in front of the others. Not where they might see that I don't know what I'm doing, and get scared.* She wanted to scream. *No matter what I do, it's* never *enough.* She swallowed, blinked away tears, and clenched her jaw so hard, it ached.

"Sister Alice!" This was Dex, approaching with Isaac supported on one arm. *Another casualty.* At least he seemed conscious now. "I'm glad to see you're uninjured. Brother Isaac is recovering, but I'm sorry to have had to abandon the battle at such a crucial moment."

"The library creatures are going back outside to look for anyone who got hurt," Isaac said, raising his head. "We need to organize them, and make sure—" He paused, looking at her. "Alice? Are you all right?"

Alice's teeth were clenched too tight to speak. Her hands balled into trembling fists.

"Sister Jen was injured," Dex said. "I'm sure Sister Alice is upset."

"I'm sorry," Isaac said. "But we need to figure out what we're doing next."

We *need to figure it out. Meaning* Alice *needs to figure it out.* She forced her mouth open and gasped for breath. *What if Alice doesn't know? Then what?*

"Organize the creatures, look for wounded," she said, very quietly. She felt like if she spoke any louder, she would scream. "Get Flicker to help you."

Isaac nodded. "Do you think it would be best to—"

"Figure it out!" Alice snapped, turning away before he could see the tears rising to her eyes again.

Isaac started to say something more, but Alice was already stalking into a nearby aisle. She reached out for the fabric of the labyrinth and tugged a pathway into place, a connection between *here* and *there.* Another step, and she was gone.

## CHAPTER FIVE

# ENDING'S CHOICE

ALICE WALKED THROUGH THE library at random for a while, the dust of the floor coating her bare feet. Then she sat, cross-legged, with her back to one of the shelves. She closed her eyes and waited. As always, it didn't take long.

"Hello, Alice." Ending's voice was a low, soft rumble, nearly a purr.

Alice opened her eyes. The angle of the light had changed, and directly opposite her was a patch of deep shadow. In that darkness, two great yellow eyes gleamed bright. A jet-black tail extended out into the light, swishing gently back and forth and raising tiny waves of dust.

"You heard," Alice said.

It wasn't a question. Ending was a labyrinthine, a maze-demon. The twisted, folded space that encompassed the library was ultimately her creation, and she knew everything that happened within it.

"I did," Ending said. "If anyone can help Jen, Magda can. She is a skilled healer."

"She shouldn't *need* help," Alice said. "She shouldn't have gotten hurt in the first place. If I'd thought about the old Readers coming at us overland, we could have set lookouts, had more warning. Everyone could have been safe by the time those things arrived." She squeezed her eyes shut. "Jen's hurt and other people are dead because I can't *think*. Because I don't know what I'm doing."

"A great many more would be dead if you weren't here," Ending said. "Perhaps everyone in the library, and me along with them."

"You don't under-
stand." Alice's eyes
stung with the tears
she could no long
restrain. "I saved
them once, and now
they expect me to
*keep* saving them."

"You told them you would," Ending said.

"Because I didn't know what else to do!" Alice said. "Because I thought we'd have more time, that we'd be able to . . . to *do* something. We beat the Ouroborean, and I thought that meant we could beat anything they could throw at us." She took a shuddering breath. "But we have to beat them *every time*. The old Readers don't care how many of their creatures I kill. Sooner or later, every one of us is going to end up like Jen, even if we keep winning. And if we lose, even once, then that's the end. For everybody."

Alice folded her legs and pulled her knees to her chest. There was a moment of silence, and then the soft padding of Ending's footsteps. Alice looked up in surprise. Ending normally preferred to remain in shadow, but now she moved over to Alice's side. She looked like a cat, not quite a house cat but something more akin to a panther, so big that her head was on a level with Alice's. Her fur was soft, inky black, rippling like velvet, but now Alice could see its smooth perfection was flawed. Long scratches ran down Ending's sides, half-healed wounds that had scabbed over.

"You're hurt," Alice said.

"It's nothing," Ending said. "A memento from my

struggle to keep my brothers and sisters away."

That meant the other labyrinthine. Each Reader had one as their servant, to guard their fortress and contain their library. Ending had told her that the magical portal-books *leaked,* allowing whatever was on the other side to slowly trickle into the real world. Putting too many of those books in the same place was a recipe for disaster. Only the labyrinths created by the labyrinthine allowed the Readers to keep their libraries under control.

"I'm sorry," Alice said. "I know this has been hard on you too."

Ending sat down beside her, folding herself into a ball in a way that was so like a house cat that it made Alice smile. Hesitantly, she put a hand on Ending's shoulder, feeling the taut muscle beneath the silky fur. After a moment, Alice leaned against the great cat, inhaling her musky smell and feeling the warmth of her massive body.

"I fight because I have no other choice," Ending said. Her deep voice resonated through Alice's skull where they were pressed together, making her teeth buzz. "My siblings will fight until they can banish me, or bind me in a prison. Their Readers will allow nothing less. But you did not have to pick up this burden." Ending's head lay on her paws. "You knew it would be dangerous."

"It's not the danger that bothers me," Alice said. "Not the danger to *me*, anyway. I always knew *I* could get hurt. But all the rest of them keep looking to me for answers, and I just don't know. I do everything I can think of, and I'm still failing them. I promised to keep them safe, and I can't do it."

"You could walk away," Ending said.

"You know I can't. The old Readers would follow me. And I couldn't leave everyone alone." Alice took a deep breath. "There has to be something we can do. Some way we can beat the old Readers, once and for all."

There was a moment of silence. Sitting against Ending as she was, Alice had felt the labyrinthine tense when she said "once and for all." Just for an instant, but she knew what it meant.

"There *is* a way, isn't there," Alice said. "Something you haven't told me."

"It's . . . possible," Ending rumbled.

"Why haven't you said anything?"

"I wasn't sure you could do it. I'm still not sure. And if you fail, you will die for certain, and probably the others as well. There is no middle ground."

Alice shivered.

The last time Ending had talked like this, Alice had ended up in the Palace of Glass, and nearly been pulled inside a mirror. *But I did find what I was looking for* . . .

"Why? What is it I'd have to do?"

"I told you why the labyrinthine serve the Readers," Ending said.

"You said that a long time ago there was a creature that threatened to destroy all labyrinthine," Alice said, trying to recall the conversation. "The Readers bound it, and agreed to keep it prisoner in exchange for the labyrinthine's service."

"Yes. The Readers need us to protect their libraries, but we need them more. My siblings are too frightened to risk rebellion against the Readers, to call this bluff. Releasing the prisoner would mean the end of everything."

"Can we find this prisoner?" Alice said. "Kill it, somehow? That would set you all free. You wouldn't need the Readers anymore."

"To destroy the prisoner is beyond anyone's power, I suspect," Ending said. "But the Great Binding that holds it could be altered. If there were another Reader, if she were powerful enough to take control of the Great Binding, then the labyrinthine could fight back." The big cat hesitated. "It might be possible."

"Me, you mean," Alice said flatly.

Ending's voice was soft. "There is no one else."

Ending had talked about this before. *She said she needed a Reader, but a different kind of Reader.* One she could treat as an equal instead of a master.

"What makes you think I'm strong enough?" Alice said. "I've only just started learning Writing."

"It's not a matter of skill," Ending said. "The required changes are simple to make. But the Great Binding requires a great deal of power. The drain could kill you outright."

Alice remembered when her simple ward had malfunctioned, siphoning away all her energy dangerously fast, as though someone were sucking the blood from her body and replacing it with ice. She shivered involuntarily.

"Even if you survive," Ending continued remorselessly, "the surge could damage you. Leave you feeble-minded, or worse."

There was a long silence. Alice thought about Emma, once a prospective apprentice, whose mind Geryon had erased when she wouldn't obey. She thought about Jen and Soranna, lying injured on the library stones because of her. She thought about the creatures who might never find the friends they were now searching for outside.

"If it doesn't work," Alice said. "If I . . . die. What happens to you?"

"The old Readers will fix the Great Binding before it unravels, if that's what you mean," Ending said. "What it means for me, personally, depends on whether they are feeling merciful." Her lips pulled back from long ivory fangs. "I am not optimistic."

*And god knows what they'd do to everyone else here. But...*

"That's no worse than what we've got coming to us already," Alice said, forcing a brisk tone. "If we lose, I mean. And we *will* lose, in the end. They can hurt us, but we can't hurt them." In her mind's eye, she saw ant-like specks vanishing in a blast of flames. *They're depending on me. I won't fail them again.*

"Alice." There was more emotion in Ending's voice than Alice had heard before. "Do not make this decision lightly. Reaching the Great Binding will be hazardous enough, but taking it on yourself—"

"It's not impossible, is it?" Alice said. "You told me there's a chance."

"There is," Ending growled.

"Then we'll take it." Alice blinked away the last of her tears. "Any chance is better than no chance at all. Tell me the plan."

◆

The rest of the day passed in a blur. Alice returned to the assembled creatures and did what she could to help. Many of them were injured, with more coming in every hour as the search parties outside found those who'd been trapped or badly hurt. More than once, Alice had wished she'd bound some creature with healing powers; instead, she tied bandages, used Spike's strength to fetch and carry, and did her best to keep the more excitable refugees calm.

When Isaac and Dex asked if she was all right, she brushed them off. *Tomorrow. I'll tell them everything tomorrow.*

In the evening, Alice led a small delegation of the more daring creatures back up to the house to see what could be salvaged. Most of the fires had burned themselves out, and the water-sprites helped quench those that remained. The damage was not as bad as Alice had feared. Only a small section of the outer wall had actually collapsed, although the roof was essentially gone and most of the third floor open to the elements. Geryon's suite, on the first floor, was safe behind its wards, along with its cache of magical books. Alice's search party ransacked the bedrooms for undamaged blankets, filled baskets full of food from the kitchen, and went back to the library.

Flicker crafted a small bonfire for his own dinner, which he kept under careful control so as not to endanger the bookshelves. He could shape flames with his bare hands, pull them apart, or mold them like wet clay. Periodically he tugged a chunk loose and popped it into his mouth like candy. Alice found herself wondering what it tasted like.

Eventually, the apprentices settled down to sleep, along with those creatures that were human enough to need rest. Lool, the clockwork spider, and a few others who didn't need sleep volunteered to keep watch. Alice suspected Ending would be a sufficient guardian, but she didn't argue, only laid her blanket on the dusty library floor and collapsed, exhausted. Isaac spread out beside her, and after a moment she felt his fingers hesitantly intertwine with hers. Alice squeezed tight, and didn't let go until she fell asleep.

She expected bad dreams, nightmares of fire and pain, or else the eye from the Palace of Glass that had haunted her most nights. Instead, she found herself floating alone in warm, comforting darkness, with a familiar voice echoing through her mind.

**Alice.**

Like the eye's voice, or Torment's, but not. Another labyrinthine. *The Dragon.* She hadn't heard from it since it had exhausted its power saving her in Esau's fortress. Since then, no matter how hard she pulled, the thread that led to its prison-book refused to respond.

*I'm here,* Alice thought back. *Is this a dream?*

**Of a sort.**

*Have you recovered?* she thought eagerly. *We need your help—*

**I am still too weak, little sister. Speaking to you like this is all I can manage, for now and some time to come. I must sleep.**

*Oh.* Alice floated in the emptiness, thinking. She crossed her arms, or felt like she did, though she couldn't see if she had a body or not. *Why talk to me now, then?*

**I can . . . hear your dreams, sometimes. They give me clues as to what happens in the waking world.** The Dragon's alien voice seemed unutterably weary. **I heard you talking to Ending. She wants you to go to the Great Binding, doesn't she?**

*She doesn't* want *me to,* Alice thought. *I asked her for a way we can strike back at the old Readers.*

**That is how she bends you to her will. Works her**

**way into your confidence, until you think her ideas are your own.** The Dragon paused. **She is dangerous, little sister.**

*You've told me that before.* Alice felt anger rising up inside her. *At least she's doing* something, *even if it might be wrong.*

There was a long silence.

*I'm sorry,* Alice thought. *I know you didn't choose to be stuck in a book.*

**I did, in a way. And there are times . . .** The Dragon heaved a sigh.

*Are you saying I* shouldn't *go to the Great Binding? I have to do* something, *or everyone here is going to die!*

**I told you once that I would let you decide your own path. I can't—**

*That's a bunch of nonsense,* Alice thought hotly. *You pop into my head with some kind of cryptic warning, but what good does that do me? I'm not going to let my friends get hurt if there's anything I can do to stop it. They all* trust *me. I can't let them down.*

Another silence. This one stretched on and on, until Alice was certain the Dragon was gone. Then, so quietly she almost couldn't hear, it said, **Be careful, little sister.**

## Chapter Six
# COUNCIL OF WAR

ALICE AWOKE WITH A crick in her shoulder from where she'd held Isaac's hand all night, and a warm, fuzzy weight on her chest. She blinked and sat up, which caused Ashes to tumble from his perch on her collarbone into her lap. He looked up at her accusingly, a small gray cat with all four paws in the air and his tail swishing dangerously.

"This is the thanks I get?" he said. "I go out of my way to comfort you after a hard day, and you're flipping me upside down as soon as you wake up?"

"Sitting on my chest staring at me isn't comforting, it's creepy," Alice said, grinning. "And I haven't noticed you turning over again."

Ashes kneaded the air with his front paws. "Well. While I'm here, a little belly rub wouldn't go amiss."

Alice shook her head as she scratched the soft fur of his stomach. "There's this thing called *dignity* that some cats have been known to have. You might want to look into it."

"A cat is always dignified, no matter what position he finds himself in," Ashes said. "A half-cat even more so."

Ashes was Alice's oldest friend at the Library. He was the one who'd snuck her inside in the first place, and so in a sense it could be said that all this was his fault, although she suspected Geryon and Ending would have gotten her into the library one way or another anyway. He was Ending's son, and claimed to be half cat, half labyrinthine, though he'd never displayed any particular powers other than a knack for finding his way around his mother's labyrinth and an almost supernatural aversion to water.

After a few moments of scratching, Ashes grabbed Alice's bare arm with all four sets of claws, which was his way of signaling that he'd had enough. Alice yanked her hand back just in time to avoid scratches, and Ashes flipped over, yawned, and stretched before slinking off of her lap.

"Where's Isaac and the others?" Alice said. The makeshift bedrolls around her were empty.

"Some of them went up to the kitchens to get some food for breakfast," Ashes said. "They thought they ought to let you sleep in, given the day you had yesterday."

Breakfast, in fact, sounded awfully good. She reached out for the fabric of space her labyrinthine powers gave her access to, and felt for the tiny vibration that told her where other humans were in the labyrinth. A quick twist opened the way, and she and Ashes turned a corner and found the other apprentices sitting around a tablecloth spread over the dusty floor, overloaded with baskets of pastries and plates full of sausage, tubs of scrambled eggs, and oily potatoes. The invisible spirits that ran Geryon's kitchen believed in breakfast in a grand, greasy style.

In addition to Isaac, Dex, and Michael, Soranna was there, still pale-faced but sitting upright and helping herself to sliced ham. Flicker was also in attendance, looking a bit awkward as he incinerated handfuls of wood shavings from a small bowl for breakfast. All five of them looked up as Alice entered, and Soranna shot to her feet.

"Alice!" Isaac said, getting up a little more slowly. His obvious pain made Alice wince. "How are you feeling?"

"Better," Alice said. "Please, sit. Soranna, are you all right?"

Soranna nodded. "I was worn out, that's all. I'm sorry I couldn't help yesterday."

"You did enough just by warning us." Alice turned to Michael. "How's Jen doing?"

"A little better," the boy said. He'd recovered his glasses, and he adjusted them nervously as he spoke. "Magda said she thinks her life isn't in danger, but she doesn't know how long it'll take her to recover."

Alice let out a sigh of relief. It was unfair to be too pleased, of course. Some of the library creatures *had* died. *Still. Some good news.* She grinned at Michael and took a seat beside Dex, helping herself to a pastry and a glass of milk.

"I've been asking our guests if they know anyone who might be helpful fixing up the house," Isaac said. He watched Alice's expression cautiously, and she remembered her outburst the day before. "There are earth-sprites who can work stone. I'm not sure about the roof, but I thought maybe your tree-sprite could help—"

He stopped as Alice held up a hand. Alice flinched at the worried look on his face.

"I'm sorry I snapped at you," she said. "I know you're helping." She looked around the table. "You're all helping."

"We'll get through this," Isaac said.

"Brother Isaac is right," Dex said. "Sister Jen will recover, and we will persevere."

"But we won't," Alice said. "Get through it, I mean. You had it right yesterday, Isaac. They'll keep coming and coming, and every time, there's a chance that more of us are going to get hurt or worse. Eventually there'll be no one left to fight back."

There was a shocked silence. Michael cleared his throat.

"But what's the alternative?" he said. "You can't be thinking of surrender."

"They'd never accept it," Soranna whispered. "I've heard the way my master talks about you, his plans. Better to die fighting." She swallowed hard. "Much, much better."

"I'm not giving up, and I'm not going to surrender." Alice put her hands on the table, pressing her knuckles against the wood. "Ending and I have a plan. We're going to free the labyrinthine from their service to the Readers."

Another silence. They all seemed stunned.

"Are you certain that is wise, Sister Alice?" Dex said. "The labyrinthine are notorious for their deviousness."

"And their cruelty," Soranna said. "Torment nearly killed us all."

"Without Ending, we would never have gotten this far," Alice said. "I trust her. And we need to take risks if we want to survive. At the very least, if the labyrinthine turn on their masters, the old Readers will have a lot more to worry about than us."

"Not to mention they won't be able to attack us so easily," Isaac said. "But can you really release them? Aren't they bound to the Readers by contract?"

Alice explained, briefly, about the Grand Labyrinth and the Great Binding there, and how the fear of what it contained kept the labyrinthine in line.

"It takes all the Readers to power the binding, and yet you plan to shoulder the burden *yourself*?" Dex said. "Sister Alice—"

"You'll die," Soranna said. "It's too much."

"Ending doesn't think so." Alice didn't mention that even Ending had been uncertain. "The harder part is going to be reaching the binding to make the change."

"Where is it?" Michael said.

"On an island in the South Atlantic," Alice said. Ending had explained the difficulties of the journey in detail. "There's a shortcut that will take us close, but there's no direct portal. And the island is surrounded by the Grand Labyrinth, which all the labyrinthine helped build." She raised one hand and made a fist. "I might be able to help push us through it, but Ending says it won't be as easily controlled as an ordinary labyrinth. There are guardians, too—"

"I would imagine," Dex said. "Guardians and traps and wards to protect the most vital treasure of the Readers." She smiled. "When do we depart?"

Alice let out a breath. Every time she raised the stakes, they stood by her, even if it meant risking their own lives. Looking around the table, she could see this time would be no different. Michael was nodding, Isaac looked thoughtful, and Soranna bore an expression of grim determination.

Flicker said, "I admit I don't know this business of bindings and labyrinthine very well. But if there's a chance to hit back at the old Readers, then I'm not going to miss it."

"You may change your mind when you hear the plan," Alice said. "It involves boats."

A wash of green surged through Flicker's hair, and he shuddered. "I survived the last time, didn't I?"

"We're all with you," Isaac said. "But what about the people here?"

*This is going to be the hard part.* She took a deep breath.

"Someone has to defend them. Ending can help, but . . ." She met his gaze and forced herself not to flinch. "Isaac, I want you to stay behind."

She could see the pain blossom in his eyes, and it tore at her heart. Hastily, she continued, "You're the strongest fighter, after me." Alice looked around the table for confirmation, and no one was willing to dispute it. "And it may not be for more than a few days. When something attacks the library, you have the best chance of dealing with it."

"I get it," Isaac said. "You're right. I just . . ." He shook his head. "I want to help."

"You *will* be helping," Alice said. "Isaac, please. I can't be in two places at once."

"But if something happens to you on the way there," Isaac said, "and I'm not around—"

"Nothing will happen to her, Brother Isaac." Dex threw an arm around his hunched shoulders. "We will all make certain of that."

Soranna nodded fervently. Michael said, "I'll be leaving Jen in your care, then."

"I'll keep her safe," Isaac said. "I'll keep everyone safe." He raised his head, looking from one face to the next, and his gaze finally came to rest on Alice's. "Just . . . come back quickly, all right?"

They spent a few hours in a whirlwind of preparation, filling several large baskets with food from the kitchens and adding some bags of apples and carrots from the storeroom. Alice asked everyone to keep the mission a secret from the library creatures until after they were gone, to keep panic to a minimum. Isaac assured her that with Ending, Magda, and Coryptus to help him, he could keep order.

*Isaac.* Part of Alice wanted to ask him to come along after all. Partly because of the comfort of having his reliable strength at her side, but mostly because of the distant, fragile look she saw in his eyes. *I hurt him.* He'd covered it well, but she'd seen it in his face.

*There's no way out.* Being a leader meant making practical choices in everyone's best interest. *If I took Isaac along to spare his feelings, and people were killed here at the library, then how would I feel?* She gritted her teeth. *I can sort things out with him when I get back.*

If *I get back,* a tiny voice in the back her mind said. *This could be the last thing he ever hears from you.*

*In that case,* Alice thought at herself furiously, *then I'll be dead and not in any position to care about his feelings.* She fought hard to put the whole problem out of her mind and concentrate on the task at hand, and *almost* managed it.

Ending had brought them all to the back of the library, outside a tall cluster of shelves arranged in an octagon. From inside, Alice could hear the rhythmic sound of waves striking the shore, and she could smell the salty tang of the ocean. Now and then, a seagull cawed.

Dex was looking curiously up at the empty bookshelves, while Michael seemed more interested in studying his shoes. Soranna had eyes only for Alice, while Flicker's hair had faded to its dullest red and he flinched with the sound of each wave.

*My team.* It didn't seem like much of a force to assault whatever the Readers had built to safeguard their greatest treasure, but Alice felt a warm swell of pride in her chest. There was no one she'd rather have at her side.

*Except, maybe—*

"All right," she said, quieting her own thoughts. "Let's get started. There's no percentage in hanging about."

## CHAPTER SEVEN
# CYAN

Dex, Soranna, Michael, Flicker, and Alice squeezed between the shelves, each carrying a heavy basket of food. As always, there was a peculiar sensation of shrinking, becoming smaller with each step until what had been ordinary bookshelves towered like mountains. Alice pushed out into the space inside the octagon, which now looked like it was several hundred yards across.

Or possibly wider. They'd come out onto a sandy beach, at the base of a tall, rocky cliff. Ahead, a mild surf crawled up and down, and the ocean stretched out to the horizon. Only wispy clouds in the vague shape of a set of bookshelves suggested the opposite end of the enclosure.

The sand underfoot was brilliantly, blindingly white, and

pleasantly warm to the touch. A little way off was a boulder, which Alice expected held the book that had created this pocket of space. At its base were gathered a small group of people Alice guessed were water-sprites. They looked much like Flicker—short, thin, androgynous—but their hair varied between deep blue and sea green, and floated around their heads as though they were underwater.

"Pick me up, would you?" said a familiar voice. "This sand is murder on my paws."

Alice found Ashes curling around her ankle. She reached down and lifted him to her shoulder, where he settled with the ease of long practice, claws digging into her leather overshirt.

"Come to see us off?" Alice said.

"Mother asked me to be here." Ashes sniffed, and Alice smiled at his haughty tone. The cat cared about people more than he liked anyone to know.

The others had come through behind her by now, and were admiring the view.

"It's beautiful," Soranna said.

"It reminds me of home," Dex said. There was a hitch in her normally cheerful voice. "The Most Favored and I would often visit the sea, to—" She broke off and shook her head.

"Master Einarsson took me and Jen out to sea once,"

Michael said. "But it wasn't like this. Just cold and storms." He sighed. "And Jen fell overboard trying to catch a fish."

"Let's not keep them waiting," Alice said, pointing to the sprites. As the group set off, she fell back until she was alongside Flicker, who was staring out at the water with wide eyes.

"Are you all right?" she said.

"What?" Flicker blinked and looked back at her. "Fine. I'll be fine. I told you, the water wouldn't actually *hurt* me, even if I fell in . . ." He trailed off, looking like he was going to be sick.

"You don't have to force yourself to do this," Alice said. "I'm sure Isaac could use your help."

"She's right," Ashes offered. "Take it from me. Wandering around with Alice is a good way to get soaked." He licked a forepaw. "You don't catch *me* volunteering."

"No." Flicker's face went hard. "If this is our chance to really hurt the old Readers, I'm not going to stay behind just because I might get a little wet." He looked back to the ocean. "I just need to . . . get used to the idea."

The leader of the water-sprites, an older man with hair the near-black of the deep ocean, raised a hand as they approached. There was a creature sitting beside him. It resembled a small dog, or perhaps a fox, with pointed ears, a narrow snout, and a long, bushy tail. Its fur was a brilliant blue-green that put Alice in mind of gemstones.

"Welcome," the water-sprite said, with a sweeping bow. The others behind him followed suit. "We are honored to be of assistance."

"Thank you for your help," Alice said. "I understood you were going to be providing some kind of transportation?"

"This is Cyan," the water-sprite said. He snapped his fingers. The fox-like animal stood up, looking alert. "He will take you and your companions wherever you need to go."

"He will?" Alice said, a bit doubtfully. Cyan stepped closer and *yipped* cheerfully.

"He seems a little small." Ashes jumped from Alice's shoulder to the sand, sniffing in Cyan's direction. "And not very bright."

"Ashes!" Alice said. "Be nice."

Cyan turned in the cat's direction, sniffed hesitantly, then *yipped*. He opened his mouth and a small stream of pure water gushed out, as if he were a water fountain. It splashed all over Ashes, who jumped sideways and hissed, every bit of fur standing on end.

"That means he likes you," said the water-sprite, unperturbed. "He wants to play."

"Play? *Play?!* I'll show you play!" sputtered Ashes,

raising a paw. Cyan *yipped* joyously and spat another stream of water, which the cat hurriedly dodged. He circled around to take cover behind Alice's leg, tail bristling.

"Down, Cyan," the water-sprite said. Cyan sat, and the sprite went on. "I assure you, in the ocean, he'll be more than large enough for your needs."

"If you say so," Alice said. On her last journey, Erdrodr had made a boat out of a ball of ice, so why not a fox? *I wonder if anything can surprise me anymore.* "We'll take good care of him."

"Thank you," the water-sprite said. "It grieves me that we are unable to do more."

He bowed again, and the small group of sprites walked away, back into the ocean.

"Alice." Ending's voice came from the shadow of the boulder. Her eyes glowed from within it, huge as yellow moons. "You are prepared?"

"I think so," Alice said, looking over her shoulder at the other apprentices and Flicker. "As much as we can be, anyway." She looked down. "Ashes! Stop stalking the boat!"

"Look at his tail twitching!" Ashes said. "Smug, I call it. Can you blame me?"

Ending rumbled. "Ashes."

"All right, all *right*," Ashes muttered. "I'll leave the stupid boat alone."

"You will go with Alice," Ending said. "She may need your help."

"I will—*what*?" Ashes' tail went bushy again. "I—what—*why*?"

"I don't think—" Alice began, but Ending cut her off.

"You are Ashes-Drifting-Through-the-Dead-Cities-of-the-World," she said, "and you are, as you are so fond of reminding us, only *half* cat. The other half is my blood, labyrinthine. In the Grand Labyrinth, you may be useful."

"But they're getting there by *boat*," Ashes said.

"Nevertheless."

"Boats go on the *ocean*," he pleaded. "There are waves. *Storms*."

"Ashes." Ending's voice sank to a growl, and the cat flattened himself to the beach in abject terror. He looked so miserable that Alice reached down to pick him up, and he huddled into a tight ball in her arms.

"We brought a tarpaulin," she told him. "For Flicker. You can share it with him. Right?" She looked up at Flicker, who sputtered.

"Of course," he said. "I'm happy to share with . . . whatever sort of animal you are."

"A cat," Alice said.

"A half-cat," Ashes said, voice muffled because he was speaking into Alice's armpit. "More's the pity."

"The Grand Labyrinth," Ending said, calm, as though the whole exchange had gone smoothly, "is broken up by barriers called Veils, places where the maze narrows to a single gateway. The Readers who created them set tests and guardians at each one, and you will need to find a way through." She shook her huge head. "I regret I cannot be more informative than that. They kept any knowledge they could of the defenses from the labyrinthine."

"We'll get through them," Alice said, with more confidence than she felt. She looked over her shoulder again, and Dex gave her an encouraging nod.

"And you remember what you must do, when you reach the Great Binding?"

Alice nodded. She only had to make a small change to the spell, changing the source of its energy to herself, a tiny bit of Writing.

"Then go," Ending said. "And I hope my faith in you has not been misplaced."

"Thank you for your help," Alice said. "Take care of everyone here, if you can." *Isaac.*

Ending nodded. There was a flash of ivory fangs, and

then she vanished. The apprentices were alone on the beach, with Flicker, the miserable Ashes, and Cyan, who was excitedly chasing his own tail.

Alice put Ashes and her basket down, then scrambled up to the top of the boulder. There was a book there, a heavy tome with a bronze cover and curling script titling it *The Azure Sea*. The others handed the baskets up to Alice, one by one. Ashes jumped up on his own, but Dex had to lift Cyan into Alice's arms. The cat sneered at the fox-thing, who looked back at him with wide-eyed glee.

The other apprentices climbed up beside Alice. Michael, second to last and shorter than most of the others, got a hand up from Dex. Soranna was shortest of all, but before Dex could bend over again she swarmed athletically up the rock, as easily as though it were a knotted rope. Michael adjusted his glasses, looking a bit flustered.

"Let's go through together," Alice said. They each took a basket, and Ashes resumed his place on Alice's shoulder while Dex put a hand on Cyan. Alice reached out, flipped open the cover of the book, and read:

*"Another beach spread before them, just as blindingly white as the one they'd left . . ."*

## CHAPTER EIGHT
# THE AZURE SEA

ANOTHER BEACH SPREAD BEFORE them, just as blindingly white as the one they'd left. They were on an island so small, Alice could have run across it in a few minutes. A clutch of scraggly palm trees grew in the center, their trunks ringed by bushels of dead brown leaves like beards. Beyond them was glassy smooth ocean, stretching unbroken to the horizon. The sun was high overhead, and she was already growing warm.

Ashes looked around at the palm trees, the perfect ocean, and the immaculate beach.

"Ugh," he said. "I'm in hell."

At Alice's gentle prod, he jumped down and gingerly

walked across the sands. The others set down their baskets and looked around.

"I admit," Dex said, "that my studies have not included extensive training with a map and compass. No doubt yours have prepared you more thoroughly, Sister Alice?"

"Not really," Alice admitted. "But Ending said that the boat would know the way." She looked down at Cyan. "Go on. Do something."

Cyan *yipped* and sat back expectantly.

"Don't just sit there," Soranna said, glaring at Cyan. "Make yourself useful."

With another *yip*, Cyan chased his tail in a quick circle, then sat down again.

"Must be broken," Ashes said. "So sad, we'll have to go home, no other option."

"Perhaps it's waiting for something?" Dex said.

Michael cleared his throat. "You've never had a dog, Alice?"

Alice shook her head. "My father didn't like them."

"They're not like cats," the boy said. "You give them commands."

"Because they lack all dignity," said Ashes, under his breath.

"May I try?" Michael said.

Alice stepped aside. "Feel free."

Michael looked down at Cyan and adjusted his glasses.

"Cyan," he said in a firm voice. "Boat!"

Cyan *yipped*, spun rapidly in a circle, and ran to the water in a spray of sand. He hurled himself into the modest surf, turned around several more times, then faced them all and *yipped* again.

"Is this supposed to be accomplishing something—" Ashes began.

There was a noise like *foomp*. Cyan's fur puffed outward in all directions, sending a spray of salt water over the apprentices and eliciting a shriek from an outraged Ashes. The air was full of fine blue hairs, settling over everything like snow. As they cleared, Alice could see the little fox-thing had indeed been replaced by a boat, the same blue color as his fur.

She'd been expecting a rowboat, something like they'd ridden on the way to the Palace of Glass. Cyan was much larger and differently shaped, more along the lines of the yachts her father's friends had kept at the marina. He was roughly triangular, with a pointed bow curving back to a squared-off stern, though there was no sign of masts or sails. Cyan's tail, still long and fluffy, whipped excitedly back and forth. From somewhere underwater came a bubbling *yip*.

Dex walked up to Cyan and touched him. Her finger sank in slightly, as though the surface were a firm sponge.

"It's made of . . . hair?" she said, poking it again, then laughed delightedly. "A fur boat!"

"There is no way that can be seaworthy," Ashes said.

"Some breeds of dogs have oily hair that's nearly waterproof," Michael said. "Like a duck's feathers."

"Unless *you* can turn into a boat," Alice said to Ashes, "we haven't got much alternative. Come on."

They loaded the baskets of supplies and then climbed aboard, Flicker taking a running jump to avoid having to get his feet wet. Alice had to admit it was a little strange climbing around on Cyan—*on his back, would it be?*—with the "deck" under her feet slightly soft and spongy. But there was plenty of room, at least, even with their things piled in the center.

She went to the bow and looked down. A pair of eyes, one on either side of the prow, looked up at her, and Cyan gave another water-muffled *yip*. Alice patted his rail, affectionately. *What was it you were supposed to say to dogs?*

"Good boat," she said. "*Good* boat. Now, *sail!*"

Nothing happened. Cyan's eyes looked up at her expectantly.

"Um," Alice said. "Forward! Giddyap! Mush!"

When nothing continued to happen, she sighed and turned around.

"Michael," she said. "A little help?"

The command, unimaginatively, turned out to be "go," which Alice felt like she ought to have guessed. Cyan's tail sped up into a churning whirl, thrashing the water into white foam, and he slowly picked up speed. Before long they were moving at a good clip, the little island receding into the distance behind them. As promised, Cyan seemed to know where he was going, which saved Alice from having to figure out how to steer him. If they'd been on Earth, she'd have said they were heading west, into the setting sun, but by now she knew better than to make assumptions about other worlds.

The Azure Sea was a deep, pure blue, and so flat, it felt more like an enormous pond than the ocean.

As they moved away from the beach, Flicker huddled at the rear, his obsidian spear across his knees, trying not to look at the water all around them. Ashes was curled about beside him. The cat had declared the fire-sprite "the only sensible person here," and once he'd discovered that Flicker's skin was warm to the touch,  Ashes had stuck to him like glue. Dex sat nearby, head tipped back, staring into the endless arch of the sky. Michael leaned over the bow, holding on to his glasses with one hand, muttering to Cyan and getting the occasional *yip* in return. Alice watched him for a moment, then smiled and went to lean against the rail beside Soranna.

Now that Soranna had cleaned up, she looked much as she had when Alice had first seen her, pale and thin as a rake, dressed in rough leather. Her light brown hair was pinned up on the right, but loose on the left, like a curtain hiding part of her face.

She wasn't *exactly* the same, though. The Soranna Alice had first met had cowered at the sight of the other apprentices. She was still quiet, but there was something different in her bearing.

"I never got the chance to thank you," Alice said. "Properly, I mean. If you hadn't come to warn us, the house might have burned down with everyone still inside."

"I'm sure you would have figured something out," Soranna said, in her soft voice.

"It can't have been an easy thing to do."

The girl ducked her head. "My master sent . . . things,

after me." Her hand went to her leg, where she'd been bandaged. "And I had to come some of the way in the real world. By . . . *taxi*." She pronounced the word carefully, as though it were unfamiliar. Alice recalled that unlike Isaac and herself, most of the other apprentices didn't have much experience with the modern world.

"I told you, you were braver than you give yourself credit for," Alice said.

Soranna's eyes fell, but her cheeks went red. "It was nothing. I just . . ." She hesitated.

"Just what?"

"I just tried to imagine what you would do." Soranna's hands tightened. "I'm sorry. I need . . . something to drink."

She moved off. Alice watched her go, bemused, and then saw Dex coming over.

"Did you hear that?" Alice said quietly. When Dex nodded, she went on, "Is she mad at me, do you think?"

Dex laughed. "Quite the opposite. I believe Sister Soranna is quite taken with you."

"What do you mean?"

"What you did in Esau's fortress left a deep impression on her, I think. You are her hero, Sister Alice."

"Hero?" Alice looked at her feet, which left slight dents in Cyan's spongy deck.

"You doubt it?" Dex said.

"I just don't feel like much of a hero," Alice said. "Or much of any kind of leader, to be honest. I keep trying to help, but it never works out right."

"Speaking for those of us who would have died at Torment's hands if not for you," Dex said, "I would say that it sometimes works out very well."

Alice looked sidelong at her. Dex smiled, in her usual sunny way, as though discussing her near-death was something she did every day. "You never give up, Alice. That is the important thing."

The confidence in her eyes did not improve Alice's mood.

Cyan provided fresh water as well, it turned out, through a small fountain in the center of his deck/body. Alice drank several cups' worth, and ate a late lunch of turkey sandwiches and apples, which made her feel a little better. She would have felt better still if Soranna hadn't insisted on fetching the food for her like a servant, but Alice didn't have the heart to tell her not to.

Afterward, she sat down beside Flicker and Ashes, who was stretching luxuriantly in the hot sun of the Azure Sea's world. Flicker was contributing by rubbing his belly.

"Ashes has been explaining to me how important this activity is to his people," Flicker said.

"That's right," Ashes said. "If we don't get to lie in the sun for a nice belly rub at least once a day, we wither away to nothing." His purr was audible even from a distance.

Alice caught Flicker's eye, and the fire-sprite winked. She had to smile.

"I'm glad Flicker has agreed to supply your daily ration, then," she said.

"He's also been telling me a little bit about their history," Flicker went on. "Apparently something called the Pyramids was built just to honor a famous cat?"

"'S right," Ashes murmured sleepily. "An' the big statue thing they've got in the harbor in New York. 'S for cats. Everyone knows cats like to climb up high . . ."

He trailed off, eyes closed, but continued purring. Flicker looked up at Alice.

"What are the Pyramids, anyway?"

"Sort of . . . artificial mountains, I guess?" Alice said. "I've only ever seen pictures."

"And the humans built them without magic?"

"I assume so," Alice said. "Most humans don't even *believe* in magic. I didn't."

"But it's everywhere," Flicker said. "That's like not believing in air."

"Not in the human world." Alice remembered that Flicker had inherited memories of the old days, before the Readers, when creatures from beyond the portals had been free to roam the real world. "The Readers have kept all the magic locked away for centuries."

"Poor humans," Flicker said.

Alice felt like she ought to stick up for her species. "It's not all bad. They—we—have accomplished a lot, even without magic. We can fly, and there's trains and cars and steamships. Telephones."

"What's a telephone?"

"It's like . . . a box that lets you talk to people who are far away."

He glanced at her skeptically, but before he could say anything, there was a *yip* from the front of the boat. Michael shouted, "Portal, ho!"

"What?" Alice shouted back.

"Portal—"

"I understood that part," she said, walking toward the bow. "Why 'ho'?"

"It's just what you say when you see something,"

Michael said. "Like 'land, ho!' Right? Jen and I once read a book about pirates."

Pirates had not featured heavily in Alice's education, so she felt obliged to concede the point. She shaded her eyes with her hand. "Where?"

Michael pointed. Following his finger, she could see a distortion in the air, a shimmering curtain where the light was bent and edged with soap-bubble colors. *A wild portal.* She'd seen one before, in Erdrodr's home. This one, if Ending's directions were correct, would lead them close to the edge of the Grand Labyrinth.

"Can you get us there?" Alice said.

Michael nodded and leaned over the rail. "Cyan's ears stick up, see?" Two large blue ears were indeed protruding from the hull, on either side of the bow. "If you stroke one of them, he'll turn in that direction. But you shouldn't need to; he knows where he's going." His voice rose into the high squeak that people inexplicably used to address infants or dogs. "Don't you, boy? Yes you do!"

The portal was definitely getting larger. It was hard to get a sense of its scale, but Alice thought they'd be through in a few minutes at most. She turned back to the rest of the boat.

"We're coming up on the portal out of the Azure Sea!"

she said. "I'm not sure how things will be on the other side, so everyone might want to hold on to something in case it gets rough." Alice herself had never been on a boat at sea, but she had read stories.

She took a position beside Michael, watching the curtain get closer and closer. It moved, rippling through the air, so it was hard to pinpoint the exact moment they were going to pass through. There was a breath of cold wind, as though she'd opened the door to an icebox, and then—

—an enormous wall of water was poised to crash down on them.

CHAPTER NINE

# EDGE OF THE LABYRINTH

ALICE'S FIRST THOUGHT WAS that they'd come through the portal in the middle of some kind of disaster, like a tidal wave. Or that it was an ambush, perhaps, by some kind of water creature, sent by the old Readers to stop them. Or—

Cyan's bow dug into the wave, sending a wash of foam and spray across the deck. Someone screamed. Alice lost her vision momentarily as freezing, salty water blasted her, ringing in her ears and getting up her nose. She kept her balance only by gripping the spongy rail as hard as she could.

When they were through, she opened her stinging eyes, struggling to peer through the sudden gloom. The sky overhead was dark with clouds, and she couldn't tell if it was day or night. What light there was came from bolts of lightning, which slashed almost continuously from cloud to ocean out to the horizon. By their intermittent glow, she could see another wave rising in front of them already, and another behind that, and another, an endless serrated surface of crests and troughs whipped to a fury by the shrieking wind.

Cyan *yipped* enthusiastically, and his tail churned the water. They started moving, climbing the surface of the wave, and this time made it past the top with only a small spray over the side. Then they were descending again, down into the trench between one wave and the next.

"Everyone"—Alice coughed for a while, until she could breathe again—"everyone all right?"

Someone said "Whee!" which could only be Dex. Michael was still beside her at the rail, holding on to his glasses with one hand and the ship with the other. Alice fought her way rearward, following the rail as the deck pitched back and forth. She saw Soranna gripping several of the wicker baskets of food—the rest of them were gone, swept overboard by the first wave. Behind her, Flicker was curled into a ball, pressed into a corner of the rail with his face against his knees, his hair almost completely dark. For a moment Alice couldn't find Ashes, but then she spotted his frantically lashing tail alongside Flicker's arm; the fire-sprite had curled up around the cat.

"Where are we?" Dex shouted, clinging to the rail on the opposite side. Looking for her was a mistake; the horizon shifted sickeningly with every rise and fall, and Alice's stomach gave a nauseous lurch. She hurriedly dropped her gaze to the deck.

"Somewhere in the South Atlantic, if Ending got things right!" Alice shouted back.

"Are we still going the right way?"

That was what was concerning Alice, too. Cyan's tail was whirling as fast as the fox-boat could manage, but it was impossible to tell if they were being driven backward or sideways by the endless waves and the wind.

"We may have to wait for the storm to die down!" Alice shouted. "It has to pass eventually!"

"No it doesn't!" Soranna put in. "Not if the Readers put it here to defend the Grand Labyrinth!"

That, unfortunately, made a lot of sense. A constant storm would be an excellent way of keeping curious

humans out of the area without tipping them off that something strange was going on. *If we're that close, though, then maybe...*

Alice closed her eyes and reached out for the labyrinth fabric. As she expected, they weren't yet inside, and the space under them was flat and untwisted by labyrinthine magic. But there was an *echo*, a sense that pulled her in one direction. Her eyes snapped open again, and she found herself staring out past the starboard rail.

"We're not getting any closer!" she shouted to Dex, gesturing to where she'd felt the edge of the labyrinth. "It's pushing us away!"

Michael reached down and touched the fox-boat's ears. Cyan *yipped* frantically, almost lost in the storm, and tried to turn, but the next wave came over the rail like another solid wall, submerging the entire surface of the deck. Alice came out of it coughing, the salty taste of the sea burning where water had gone up her nose.

*New plan.* She felt anger rising up inside her. *A bunch of Readers are not going to lose to a little* storm.

"Dex!" she shouted. "I need rope, something nice and thick."

Dex got the idea at once. As Cyan mounted another enormous wave, silvery moon-stuff poured out of Dex's hands, forming into coils of thick cord. Alice waited until they went over the top of the wave, the boat coasting down into the trough, before she edged back along the rail toward Dex. As she went, Alice pulled off her boots, leaving them wedged under the rail.

"You'll need to attach one end of this to Cyan somehow," she said to Dex, who nodded frantically. Her normally frizzy hair hung bedraggled around her neck in long, soaking coils.

Alice grabbed the other end of the rope and bit into it. The moon-stuff felt strange, like liquid metal, and had the tang of copper. Making sure the rest was spooling out behind her, she ran to the rail just as Cyan began laboriously climbing toward the crest of the next wave.

*No time to think about it.* Alice vaulted the rail in a single bound and went over the side.

She was pulling on her threads before she even hit the water, wrapping them tight. There was a moment of shocking cold, and then she was changing. Her body blurred and shifted into the long, powerful shape of the devilfish, an aquatic predator nearly as large as Alice's real body. The moon-stuff rope was now securely trapped between hundreds of tiny, needle-sharp teeth.

It took her a moment to orient herself. Cyan was overhead, a vast dark shape on the surface of the water. What had been cold a moment ago now felt comfortable, and the salt water sluiced over her gills in a rhythm that felt as natural as breathing. She moved with a flick of her powerful tail, pushing herself deeper, steering with her fins.

Below the surface, things were strangely calm. The storm that hammered above with such fury barely penetrated a few feet into the water, and the waves that threatened to swamp Cyan were merely gentle swells. Alice reached out for the labyrinth again, to get her bearings, then pointed herself in the right direction and started to swim.

For a few seconds, it was easy. Then the rope went taut, and all of Cyan's weight was on the other end. Dex had clearly attached the rope securely. Alice felt like her teeth were going to tear from her mouth—it wasn't the best arrangement for towing, but with no hands, it was the best she could do—and her tail whipped at the water without producing much of a result.

Drawing on the power of a second thread while keeping the devilfish securely wrapped around herself wasn't easy. She hadn't practiced calling on her powers in her alternate forms; it was a bit like trying to tie both shoelaces at once, one with each hand. If she let the devilfish thread go now, she would probably drown before she got back to the surface, so she hung on like grim death.

Spike's power surged through her, the dinosaur's considerable strength augmenting the devilfish's own. Alice's fishy heart surged in triumph. The next stroke of her tail felt like the water had turned as light as air. The strain on her teeth grew, but she ignored it, putting all her strength into moving Cyan against the pounding of the waves.

*It's working!* The edge of the labyrinth was getting closer. Alice felt tireless, almost mechanical, her tail pumping like a steam engine. *Just a little more. A little farther!*

The boundary was ahead of them. But as they came forward, it retreated, drawing away from them. Frustrated, Alice reached out for it, *dragging* the edge of the labyrinth closer by sheer force of will. Ordinarily, the fabric of the labyrinth was like infinitely thin silk, twistable and foldable in any direction. *This* labyrinth felt thick and hard, like it was made of car tires, giving only slightly under her mental grip. The boat pushed against it, and the boundary bent inward, refusing to provide an entrance.

*You . . . can't . . . keep me out.* Alice's thoughts felt sluggish, her energy draining rapidly. *Open . . . up!*

She gripped the fabric of the boundary and pulled, as hard as she could. For a moment, she felt a presence, someone else touching the same fabric, and its vibration was familiar. An image flashed through her mind—a single, enormous eye, slitted like a cat's . . .

The boundary gave way. Cyan shot forward, propelled by his tail and Alice's, sending up spray in suddenly calm water.

Like someone shoving on a door and finding it suddenly open, Alice lost her mental balance. Her hold on the fabric and her own threads slipped through her grasp, and she felt her body twist and change. Her fins became hands, slapping uselessly at the water instead of driving her confidently through it. Her clothes returned, waterlogged and weighing her down. Her gills vanished, and Alice suddenly realized she was drowning.

## CHAPTER TEN

# PEBBLES ON THE BEACH

SHE NEVER QUITE LOST consciousness, but it was a near thing. Water pressed at her nose and mouth, and the need to breathe was a clanging, clawing pain in her lungs. Every ounce of strength went into keeping her jaw closed, against her body's frantic instincts. Her hands scrabbled lamely, and her legs kicked, but it wasn't enough to get her to the surface. Alice's vision started to go black at the edges, and she felt herself weakening.

Just when she thought she couldn't bear it any longer, slim arms wrapped around her, and hands lodged under her armpits, pulling her to the surface. She took a convulsive, gasping breath, getting a mouth full of spray along with the sweet fresh air.

"Alice?" Soranna's voice, right in her ear. "I need you to grab the rope. Just hold on."

Dex's moon-stuff rope was right in front of her. Alice locked her hands around it, and found herself hauled upward, over the rail. More hands grabbed her and laid her flat on the deck, breathing hard, water seeping from her soaking clothes.

"Keep back," Dex said. "Let her breathe." Her face came into view. "Sister Alice? Can you hear me?"

*We made it.* Alice tried to speak, coughed, and tried again. "Everyone . . . okay?"

Dex nodded. "Flicker and Ashes are both very wet and unhappy, but they will survive. The rest of us are fine." She shook her head. "I'm afraid most of our supplies went overboard."

"What happened?" Michael said, from out of view. "One second we were climbing another wave, and then . . . this."

"We made it inside the Grand Labyrinth," Alice said. She sat up slowly, so she could see what "this" was.

Cyan was coasting slowly through clear, still water. All around them were little hummocks of rock, barely breaking the surface. Some were large enough to support tufts of grass or small trees, and dozens of white-and-black gulls watched the boat with beady eyes and issued the occasional squawk. Below the surface, Alice could see other shafts of rock, floating curtains of seaweed, and a few darting fish.

Cyan was too big to fit between many of the rocks, restricting them to the larger paths. Navigating would certainly be difficult, which she supposed was only natural. It was a *labyrinth*, after all.

Soranna pulled herself back aboard and sat on the rail, water running off her in torrents. Alice turned to her and gave a shaky smile.

"Thanks," she said. "I had no idea you were such a good swimmer."

"My master insisted I acquire the skill," Soranna said. "He would toss us in the moat in the middle of the night." She shook her head, as though to chase away bad memories. "You *pulled* the boat!"

"Don't remind me." Alice worked her jaw, where an echo of the devilfish's pain still lingered in her teeth. "It's not something I'm eager to repeat."

Soranna brushed her hair back from her eyes. Her expression had taken on that peculiar intensity that made Alice uncomfortable, and Alice realized she'd only cemented her status as a hero in the girl's eyes. She sighed and flopped back to the deck.

"Was *all* the food washed overboard?" she said. "I'm hungry enough to eat some of those gulls."

It turned out that they were not quite reduced to eating gulls. A bag of apples had lodged at the rail, and Soranna had kept hold of a basket full of dried meat, which had not suffered terribly for the immersion. Cyan, *yipping* happily, provided fresh water.

Flicker was still huddled under the tarpaulin, insisting he was fine but not coming out. Ashes, however, had emerged, looking so utterly pathetic that Alice had to stifle a giggle. He glanced up, as though daring her to comment, and shook himself violently.

"I don't care if she *is* my mother and she *is* a labyrinthine," he said. "She is not going to get away with this. Sending me here to this . . . this *disaster*."

"We're alive," Alice said, chewing slightly damp jerky. "That's something."

"There's alive and then there's *alive*," Ashes said. "You naked apes can always take your silly clothes off. What am *I* supposed to do?" He licked his fur and shuddered. "*And* I taste of salt."

"There's plenty of fresh water, if you want to wash off," Alice said.

"I have been washed *quite enough* for one day!"

Grumbling, the cat settled down, licking himself thoroughly and muttering about the taste. Alice tore off some jerky for him, which he gobbled without a word of thanks.

By the time they'd gotten settled, the sun was nearly down, and the apprentices agreed that it wouldn't be wise to begin exploring the Grand Labyrinth in the dark. It didn't feel to Alice like an entire day had passed, but time was always tricky when moving through other worlds, and she was tired enough to sleep for a week. They stripped out of as much of their clothing as modesty allowed, draping it over Cyan's rail to dry. Fortunately, the interior of the labyrinth was much warmer than the outside, even after sunset. Cyan pulled up in the lee of one of the larger islands, and Alice tied Dex's rope around a rock.

The stars came out as the sky darkened, first one by one and then in the thousands. Alice remembered the sky over Flicker's home, spinning fast enough to make her dizzy. Here on Earth, the stars seemed stationary, but she had an echo of the same feeling, the sense that she could fall *up* into the endless black. The Milky Way was a cloudy ribbon of light, stretching from horizon to horizon.

"Alice?" Michael said. He was lying closest to her.

"Mmm?" Alice said.

"I just . . . I don't know if I thanked you. For helping Jen when she got hurt. I watched what happened, but you *did* something about it without hesitation."

"It was what needed to be done," Alice said.

"It was the same just now. I knew we were in trouble, but you—you just *jumped in*." He sighed. "I wish I knew how to do that. I always start thinking about what might go wrong."

"Sometimes I think I ought to be a little more careful," Alice said. *Like when I opened* The Infinite Prison *and let the Ouroborean out.* "But when there's no time, you just have to go with what feels right. I know you can do that. You figured out the right way to handle Cyan quickly enough. And you convinced Jen not to fight me, when we met the first time."

"That was easy." Michael sighed. "I don't like fighting. Jen tells me I'm a coward."

"You're not a coward, I can say that much," Alice said. "We have a lot of power, as Readers. Sometimes doing the right thing means using it to defend people." Alice thought back to her passage through Erdrodr's fortress, the temptation she'd felt to simply smash the ice giants aside. "Sometimes it means *not* fighting, even when we might want to."

"That . . . makes sense," Michael said. "Thank you, Alice."

When he didn't speak again, Alice closed her eyes. *When did I become the one who hands out wise advice? For that matter, where did I get any wise advice?* Some things just seemed . . . obvious. *Maybe that's wisdom, seeing things that are obvious.* She let out a long breath and dropped into exhausted slumber.

Dawn woke her, and she found Flicker huddled over a metal bowl, picking bits from a weak flame and slurping them off his fingers.

"Feeling better?" Alice said.

"A bit." Flicker's voice was grim, with the low crackle of a bonfire in it somewhere. His hair was still mostly dark, though it had regained a little warmth. "That's not an experience I'm eager to repeat."

"I hope we won't have to," Alice said. "Things certainly seem more congenial in here."

He looked up at her, then glanced away. "I heard you saved us. Again."

She shrugged. "I'm the only one who can turn into a fish."

"I . . ." Flicker looked down at his bowl of flames, then shook his head. "Never mind."

Ashes was still asleep, curled in a tight ball beside Flicker, but the other apprentices were getting up. Alice's underclothes were still a bit damp, but the things she'd hung on the rail were mostly dry, though grimy and stiff with salt. She pulled them on, wincing a little at the soreness in her muscles.

"That was refreshing," Dex said, munching on an apple. "But I feel we'd better be about our business, Sister Alice."

Alice nodded. "No telling how long it will take to get through." If it was more than another day or so, they really *would* be eating seagulls. "Dex, get us untied. Michael, you're in charge of steering Cyan. I'll try to keep you pointed in the right direction. Soranna, Flicker, keep watch and shout if anything comes at us, or you notice anything strange. We've got the Veils to look out for, and who knows what else."

"Aye, aye, sir!" said Michael, grinning. Alice assumed this was more pirate talk.

When Michael stroked his ears, Cyan eased out from behind the island and into the wider channel, keeping well away from the rocks on either side. Alice closed her eyes and let the fabric of the labyrinth slip slowly through her mental grasp. As Ending had predicted, she couldn't exert much force on it, but she could at least sense its structure, and gently feel her way ahead to determine the path forward.

Michael steered Cyan in accordance with Alice's vague directions, veering around islands and passing between rock formations and beds of seaweed. Gulls watched them, taking off in squawking flocks when they came too close. Ashes, who had woken up and resumed his place on Alice's shoulder, watched the birds with narrow-eyed interest.

"I wouldn't try it," Alice said. "They're bigger than you are."

"They're all wing," he said dismissively. "Believe me. Large birds are the natural prey of the cat."

"Maybe once they've been roasted and carved," Alice said. Ashes snorted.

"What's that?" Flicker said, pointing over the rail.

They all turned to look. A large, flat island supported three piles of rocks, each about as high as Alice's waist. They looked like cairns, or bits of a tumbled-down stone wall, but they were all unmistakably moving. One rock would slide off the top, then another came down on top of it, and so on, like a continuous avalanche. One particular rounded rock always remained at the center of each pile, and two glassy protrusions on its surface looked disturbingly like eyes. They turned to follow the boat until it passed around another island and out of sight.

"Are they alive?" Soranna said.

Flicker nodded. "In my people's old world there were many rock-creatures. Even rock-sprites, though we haven't had any contact with them in a long time."

"There's another one," Soranna said, and sure enough, a pile of stone watched them with glassy eyes from the shade of a scrappy tree. Now that she knew what to look for, Alice saw them everywhere, ambling around their islands with a rolling gait or simply turning in place to watch the boat go by.

"They don't look big enough to be threatening," she said, after a while. "But I'm happy to leave them alone if they leave me alone."

"A sound plan," Dex said.

An hour or so later, the path came to a dead end. They were hemmed in on both sides by tall, craggy rock formations. Just ahead was an island much larger than the others, big enough that it had a pebbly beach at the foot of a substantial cliff.

"Now what?" Michael said, bringing Cyan to a halt.

Alice prodded the fabric of the Grand Labyrinth. This was definitely the right way to go, she could feel it. All the paths through the labyrinth led to this point.

"I think we get out and walk," Alice said. "This must be the first Veil, and it blocks the way forward."

"So it'll be some kind of test?" Soranna said.

"Or more like a gateway, with guards?" Flicker said.

"We'll find out," Alice said. "Michael, put us on shore."

## CHAPTER ELEVEN

# THE FIRST VEIL

CYAN OBLIGINGLY PULLED ASHORE, allowing everyone to disembark without getting wet. Then the boat collapsed in on itself, shrinking back down to an excited fox-creature. A half-bag of apples and the remaining baskets of supplies were left at their feet.

The sand was much rougher than the Azure Sea beach. Ashes continued to ride Alice's shoulder, looking suspiciously at the gentle surf. Flicker hoisted the sack of apples over his shoulder with a grin, clearly relieved to be back on land. Cyan ran in eager circles around Michael and yipped.

"Shhh," Michael admonished him. "Someone might be waiting for us."

"If there are guards, we won't take them by surprise in any case," Alice said.

"At least the way forward seems obvious," Dex said.

That was true enough. The beach was a semicircle carved out of the base of a sheer cliff. A crack in the rock just wide enough for a person led off the beach and into the island's interior.

"I'll go first," Soranna said, then glanced nervously at Alice for approval. "If there's anything there, I can duck back into the rocks."

"Good idea," Alice said. One of Soranna's creatures allowed her to become briefly intangible and run through solid objects.

Soranna grinned, like a dog given a pat on the head, and moved into the crack. A few minutes later she reappeared and waved the others in.

When she reached the end of the crack, Alice shoved her way out and into a wide, circular space, about the size of a baseball field. The cliff surrounded it on all sides, but another crack in the rock wall was visible directly opposite where they'd come in. In between, the ground was flat and sandy, broken by pillars of weather-worn stone at regular intervals. Soranna waited with her back to one of those pillars, waving frantically.

A larger pile of rocks stood in the center of the circle. At first, Alice thought it was simply a mound of boulders, but the large round stone at its center swiveled, grinding and puffing dust, until two glassy knobs like eyes were visible. The thing drew itself up, boulders scraping and crunching against one another. It was much larger than the little piles they'd glimpsed from the water, easily four times Alice's height, and each of its boulders was bigger than she was.

One of the boulders, at the edge of the pile, began to spin. It moved slowly at first, but picked up speed, until it was a blur of motion. Alice understood what was happening just a moment before the creature let the boulder fall.

"Take cover!" she shouted. The apprentices scrambled toward the pillars.

The spinning boulder hit the ground and shot forward as though it had been blasted out of a cannon. It hit the cliff with an ear-splitting *crunch* and bounded high into the air. Even before it landed, a second boulder shot toward them. This one slammed into the pillar they were taking shelter behind, and Alice felt it shake. Dust sifted down all around them.

"This isn't going to hold long!" Michael said, looking up at the pillar.

"If we split up," Dex said, "we might be able to get around it—"

"That sounds like a great way for somebody to get squashed," Alice said. "Let me handle this."

"Wait, Sister Alice!"

Alice spun out from behind the pillar, feeling Ashes spring from her shoulder. She ran away from the others, and the rock creature rotated to follow her, another boulder spinning faster and faster. Those it had hurled had rejoined the rumbling, crunching pile that was the creature's body. *So we can't run it out of ammunition. But let's try this.*

She wrapped the dinosaur's thread around herself for power, and added the Swarm thread for toughness. Then she skidded to a halt in the open space between two pillars, facing the creature. Its gleaming eyes fixed on her, and it let the boulder fly.

Alice raised her arms and dug in her heels. If she could *stop* the boulder, then it wouldn't return to the creature. She had an image of herself catching it, like a football player. It was only as it came at her, trailing a cloud of flying grit, that she realized the problem with her plan.

It wasn't a matter of strength, it was a matter of mass. The boulder had a great deal more of it than Alice did.

Spike's power didn't help her if she had no way to apply it—she couldn't *push* on the boulder once it had torn her from her footing.

All this went through her mind in the split second before impact. Alice had time to close her eyes.

*This,* she thought, *is going to hurt.*

She was right, though mercifully it didn't hurt for very long.

Alice opened her eyes and saw sunny blue sky, streaked with wisps of shredded clouds. After a moment, Dex's face came into view, her dark, poofy ponytail eclipsing the sun.

"Sister Alice?" she said. "How do you feel?"

"Like something very heavy landed on me," Alice managed.

"Drink this." Dex held out a canteen and poured a stream of water into Alice's mouth. "None of your bones are broken, I think. Your Swarm is quite amazing, and Sister Soranna has applied her healing salve."

One of Soranna's bound creatures could create a thick cream that quickly healed wounds, Alice recalled. They'd used it in Esau's fortress.

"Thanks," Alice croaked. "Is everyone all right?"

Dex nodded. "Sister Soranna drew the creature's attention, while the rest of us retrieved you and retreated. We are back on the beach."

Alice could hear Cyan yipping somewhere nearby. She groaned, propped herself on her elbows, and sat up with a good deal of effort. Soranna, Michael, and Flicker sat nearby, watching her. Ashes padded over and rubbed against her shoulder, and she petted him absentmindedly. Her clothes were scraped and torn, but Dex was right; the Swarm had protected her from more serious injury even after she'd been knocked unconscious by the collision.

"You're sure you're all right?" Soranna said anxiously. "That was quite an impact."

"I think so," Alice said. "My head's a bit fuzzy."

"The boulder lifted you and slammed you against the cliff," Michael said, adjusting his glasses. "I thought we were going to find you smashed flat."

"Sister Alice," Dex said. "You know I have a great deal of respect for you. But there is something I feel I must say."

"Hmm?" Alice looked at her blearily. "What's wrong?"

"Your behavior on this occasion was, not to put too fine a point on it, stupid." Dex frowned. "Please think harder about your safety in the future."

"Thinking about my safety isn't what I'm here for," Alice said. "Remember?"

"Dex is right. There's risks and there's risks," Michael said.

"No need to badger her," Soranna said. "Just because it was a little . . . unwise."

"It was more than that," Dex said insistently. "Sister Alice, please. We are here to *help* you, not to hold you back. You cannot solve every problem on your own."

"I . . ." Alice stopped, looking down at her hands. "I wanted to get it over with before anybody got hurt."

"We all agreed to this journey," Flicker said gently. "We *all* accepted the risk. You don't have to protect us."

"Speak for yourself," Ashes muttered. "*I* didn't agree to anything."

"Flicker's right," Soranna said, ignoring the cat. "You don't have to shoulder everything."

"But I'm supposed to be the leader here, aren't I?" Alice said. "That means keeping everyone safe."

"It means making the best decisions you can," Dex said. "That's not the same thing."

Alice nodded slowly. "I . . . I thought I was best suited to deal with it. I'm the strongest of us, I think."

"Matching strength against strength is not always a good idea," Dex said. "Recall the steel giant in Esau's fortress."

Alice remembered the huge steel hand coming down on top of Soranna, hard enough to crack marble. The girl had turned intangible just in time. She swallowed and nodded again.

"Okay," she said. "So how are we going to get through?"

A quarter of an hour later, her head was pounding. She gulped from the canteen.

"It's too far just to run for it," she said. "Even if Soranna can distract the thing, we have no way of knowing if it will *stay* distracted."

"But we don't have anything that can hurt it," Michael said. "Not if it's solid rock."

"Brother Isaac was able to melt the steel giant's leg," Dex said. She glanced at Flicker, who shook his head sorrowfully.

"I can't make a flame that hot," the fire-sprite said. "And melting rock would be even more challenging than metal."

Alice took a mental inventory of their abilities. Spike wasn't strong enough to crack rocks. Soranna's powers were mostly defensive. Flicker's flame wasn't hot enough. Michael's silver knives couldn't cut solid stone, and neither would Dex's caryatid blades. *What does that leave?*

"Dex," she said, feeling the shadow of an idea worming its way into her mind. "What about your moon-stuff?"

"Shaped into a spear, you mean?" Dex frowned. "I do not think you could throw it hard enough to break rock."

"Not a spear. A thread." Her mind raced ahead. "But . . . a very *thin* thread. Have you ever seen a cheese slicer?"

None of them had, of course. There was a brief digression while Alice explained the need for slicing cheese, and then a somewhat longer one while she explained the concept of cheese for Flicker.

"It's basically a wire, strung between two handles," Alice said. "And you push it into the cheese, and it just cuts through easily because it's so thin."

Michael nodded. "It applies the force of your push over a much smaller area, the same as a knife blade. It's the same reason you can get paper cuts. The only problem would be if the wire wasn't strong enough."

"Right!" Alice said. "But Dex's moon-stuff is practically unbreakable, and you can make it very thin, can't you?"

"I've never tried, but I believe so," Dex said. "But how will we get close enough to cut the rocks with a wire?"

Alice felt her smile returning. "Here's the plan."

## CHAPTER TWELVE
# CHEESE SLICER

SORANNA WENT FIRST, WITH the threads rolled up and slung over her shoulder, while the rest of them watched from the narrow crack in the rock.

The rock-thing spun up a boulder as soon as it saw her, and she ran to the nearest pillar, ducking as a cascade of rock chips flew. She unwrapped the threads Dex had spun and laid one end on the ground. Then she took a deep breath—she couldn't breathe while she was intangible—and ran.

Another boulder slammed out, well-aimed. It passed through Soranna without stopping, hit the cliff face, and bounced high into the air. That seemed to take the rock-creature aback for a moment, and as it paused, Soranna rounded the second pillar, leaving a silver line of moon-stuff lying on the ground behind her. She let out her breath with a whoosh and gasped for air, crouching low as another boulder hit the pillar. With her lungs full again, Soranna ran back to the pillar where she'd begun, a boulder narrowly missing her as she went.

Now the net was in position, but it was still lying on the ground. Alice signaled to Flicker and Dex, and just after the next boulder hit the wall, they both ran, Dex to the pillar where Soranna waited, Flicker to the far end of the threads. Alice held her breath, but they'd timed it well, and they reached cover before another boulder arrived.

Dex fused the ends of the moon-stuff into a single piece, and she and Flicker started climbing the pillars, tugging the bundle of threads behind them. When they were four or five yards off the ground, they let the bundle unroll, so an entire mesh of fine threads hung between the two pillars. They were as thin as cobweb, floating gauzy and frail-looking in the breeze.

Dex looked across at Flicker and waved, and the fire-sprite stopped climbing. When Dex touched the threads again, they contracted, pulling the whole thing taut. Flicker hopped down from his perch on the pillar, Dex following soon after.

The trap was set. Alice stepped out from the crack in the rock, keeping her eyes on the boulder-thing. The others had all volunteered for this job—bait, essentially—but she'd insisted on doing it. She wasn't sure this would work, and if it failed, she wanted to be the one to suffer the consequences. *After all, I've been hit by this thing once already, and I'm still alive.* None of the others could say that.

That wasn't to say she was looking *forward* to it, of course. She wrapped the Swarm thread as tight as she could without transforming herself, hardening her skin, and took a position near the cliff, with the net directly between herself and the rock-thing. It saw her at once, blank white eyes rotating in her direction, and a boulder began to spin, faster and faster. Alice forced herself to breathe deep, planted her feet, and waited.

The boulder hit the ground and shot forward, turning its spin into forward momentum. It came at her in a series of bounding leaps, low to the ground. In the time it took to blink, it passed between the two pillars that anchored the net, and—

Alice let out an excited whoop as rocks landed all around her. *It works!*

The boulder had simply *come apart* in midair. It went through the net without slowing down, and all the force of its motion was concentrated on the hair-thin strands of Dex's unbreakable moon-stuff. Like the sharpest blades imaginable, they sliced through solid rock as if it were thick mist. A single hurtling rock was transformed into a loose collection of debris, chopped into odd shapes like dough under a cookie cutter. Pieces bounced wildly in every direction, a spray of small stones that pelted the ground all around Alice and caromed off the wall behind her.

Rock dust filled the air. No sooner had it cleared than Alice saw a second boulder coming at her. It met the same fate as the first, disintegrating in midair as it collided with the nearly invisible strands. A few fragments hit Alice, bouncing harmlessly off her Swarm-hardened skin. As a third boulder came in and hit the net, she started laughing out loud. She had no idea if it was possible to taunt a pile of rocks, but she certainly didn't want it to stop.

It obliged her, hurling stone after stone from its diminishing stockpile. A pile of broken fragments built up around Alice, and she climbed up to keep it from covering her feet. Dex, crouching behind one of the anchor pillars, gave her a cheery wave, and Alice waved back, grinning like a loon, even as another boulder exploded.

When the last boulder had splintered and crashed to the ground, the rock-creature's head simply sat watching her, apparently impotent to do any more than glare.

Dex stuck her head out from behind the pillar and waved cautiously in the rock-creature's direction. It shifted to look at her, but made no other move. Dex touched the net with one finger, and in an instant the silvery moon-stuff dissolved into nothing.

"It worked!" Michael came out from the crack in the rock, with Ashes riding on his shoulder and Cyan prancing joyfully at his heel. They picked their way over the field of debris and met up with the others, who'd gathered near the center of the clear space.

"It worked," Alice agreed. She glanced at the silent, staring rock creature.

"Let's get moving. That thing gives me the creeps."

There were general nods of agreement. They filed past the rocky head, which rotated to watch them go. Another crack led through the cliffs on the side opposite from where they'd come in. They squeezed through, in single file, and found themselves on another pebble beach, facing a landscape of small islands and distant, circling gulls not very different from the one they'd left behind.

"I suppose it was too much to hope that we'd be done with boats." Ashes sighed.

"Okay, Cyan," Michael said. "Go! Boat!"

Cyan yipped and jumped gleefully into the water, expanding rapidly into his furry boat form. Ashes eyed him with distaste.

"My opinion of canines is *not* rising on this journey."

"He may be more vulpine than canine," Michael said. "And *I* like him. Ow!" he added as Ashes swatted him on the side of the head and jumped down.

"I apologize for Ashes," Alice said to Michael. "He's a cat, and—" She paused, and decided that seemed like a complete description. "He's a cat."

"He forgets I've seen him beg Jen for belly rubs," Michael said. "I know he's soft at heart."

He wandered over toward Cyan. Dex came over to clap Alice on the shoulder.

"My apologies if I was harsh earlier," she said.

"No apology necessary," Alice said. "And thank you. You were right, I *was* being stupid. If it happens again, please tell me."

"A service I'm happy to provide," Dex said. "Sometimes we all need a reminder that there are many ways to approach a problem."

"And that I'm not alone," Alice said. "I can't do this by myself."

"And you don't have to," Dex said. She grinned. "Though I must say, the Grand Labyrinth is proving friendlier than I anticipated."

"*This* is friendlier? We nearly drowned and I was squashed by a boulder!" Alice paused and reminded herself that this was a girl who had once had her arm bitten off by a crocodile and apparently taken it in stride. "Let's just hope it stays that way."

## Chapter Thirteen
# A FEAST

Several hours later, Alice was beginning to regret that remark.

The attacks had started almost as soon as they'd left the island of the first Veil. The sea began to froth with small jumping fish, whose wide-open mouths were thick with needle-like teeth. Dex and Michael had cut them out of the air with swords and flying knives, while Alice batted aside those that got through and Flicker skewered them with his spear.

No sooner had they passed through the school and out the other side than huge hairy spiders, floating on rafts of viscous white bubbles, had paddled in their direction. This time Alice took the lead, plunging into the water as the devilfish and shredding the creatures one after another while the other apprentices fought at the rail, like old-fashioned sailors repelling boarders.

The latest assailant had been an enormous crab, its legs arching out of the water and folding down over Cyan's sides to pluck at his passengers with huge claws. Alice had fought with a sword made of moon-stuff and Spike's prodigious strength, and she and Dex had cut the multi-legged thing to pieces. It reminded Alice of their progress through Esau's labyrinth, the constant assault by hostile creatures too dumb to realize they were outmatched.

With a final slash, she severed the last of the claws, and it landed with a *thud* on the deck. Her muscles burned. Even with Spike's strength, there was a limit to her endurance, and she knew she was coming up on it. But the sea, for the moment, seemed clear.

"Everyone okay?" Alice said.

Dex, still encased in silver caryatid armor, gave a nod. Michael and Soranna stood back to back at the bow, splashed liberally with crab goop. Flicker crouched in the center of the boat, a spear in his hands.

"Where's Ashes?" Alice said.

The cat poked his head out from under an overturned basket. "Are they gone?"

"I think we left them behind," Michael said. He patted Cyan's rail fondly. "*Good* boat." Cyan made a sound like *brrriiiii.*

"Can you find us somewhere we can pull up?" Alice said. "I think we all need a rest."

Michael nodded and began stroking Cyan's ears. Dex let her caryatid armor fade away and stretched, grinning broadly.

"On the plus side," she said, "our food problem is solved!"

"Solved?" Alice said, frowning. "How?"

Alice had to admit that it *smelled* delicious. Michael remained skeptical.

"Crabs are basically water spiders, aren't they?" he said. "You're eating *spider.*"

"I've eaten spiders," Soranna said. "They're crunchy. Not as good as crickets."

That turned Alice's stomach a little. Soranna had grown up on another world, where her master kept humans in a primitive state. It wasn't something she talked about much, and the others were content not to ask.

"I'm going to try it," Alice said, leaning forward. "How bad can it be?"

They'd made a fire pit in the center of Cyan's deck, a thin slab of moon-stuff to protect the boat piled with the rest of the baskets and some dry grass they'd found on a nearby island. Flicker had started the blaze, which now burned merrily. Dex had collected several of the enormous crab limbs that had fallen into the boat, cut them into smaller segments, and propped them above the flames. When she declared them done, they cracked the scorched shells open to reveal juicy, pinkish meat.

"The Most Favored and I ate crab regularly," Dex said, picking apart the steaming meat with her fingers and popping morsels into her mouth. "She enjoyed all the fruits of the sea, but crab was her favorite."

Soranna hadn't taken any convincing. Now Alice pulled a sliver off, blew on it until it was cool, and took a tentative bite. Her eyes widened.

"It's good!"

"It'd be better with some seasoning," Dex said. "And butter, of course. But an improvement over nothing at all."

Michael, watching the others eat with such evident enjoyment, eventually sighed and gave in, still muttering about spiders. Once she was full, Alice tore off some strips for Ashes, who also raised no protests.

"Are you all right?" she said to the cat while he ate. "We've had our hands full, and I haven't been able to look after you."

Ashes swallowed and licked his lips. "I'm a half-cat," he said, "and I can take care of myself."

"Of course you can." She scratched him behind the ear, and he pushed his head against her hand. "I'm sorry your mother made you come with us."

"I suppose I would have wanted to come along anyway," Ashes muttered. "Someone has to make sure you stay out of trouble. I only wish . . ."

"Wish what?"

"Nothing." He bolted another strip of crab. "I wish that this were *over*, and we were home safe. I have a bad feeling, Alice."

"You're not the only one."

Ashes lowered his voice. "Has the Dragon told you anything more?"

"Not since he warned me not to trust Ending."

"I'm sure my mother knows what she's doing," Ashes said, not sounding sure at all. "It would be nice if she would tell *me* a little more, of course."

"Do you feel anyone manipulating this labyrinth against us?"

"I don't think so," the cat said, yawning. "As far as I can tell, it's just awful all by itself." He walked around in a circle once, and curled up against Alice's side. "Fire-boy wants to talk to you."

Alice looked up to see Flicker coming over. A piece of their cook fire danced on his palm, his fingers shaping and molding it like clay. He bit off a chunk, swallowed, and rolled the rest into a ball.

"How are you holding up?" she said as he sat down next to her.

"All right," Flicker said. "It's just . . ." He sighed.

"Just?" Alice prompted.

"I can't help but think you would have been better off if I'd stayed behind. I'm not strong enough." He stared moodily into the fire. "I should have known better, but I let my anger blind me to the obvious. I'm not a Reader, and I can't keep up."

Alice blew out a long breath. She was tempted to just tell him he was wrong, but Flicker deserved better than that. It wasn't as if she hadn't wondered the same thing— not that he was a burden, just whether he was only going to get hurt. *But it's not that simple.*

"I'm glad you came," Alice said. "That attitude is every- thing we're fighting *against*, I think. The idea that it's only the Readers who matter, and everyone else is just pawns on the game board. We've seen where that ends."

"Very noble." Flicker gave a weak smile. "It doesn't change the fact that the Readers are more powerful than anybody else. You can do things that it scares me to think about."

"But the others have had to rescue me twice already," Alice said. "No one is powerful enough to do everything themselves, not even the old Readers. They have servants. I'd rather have friends."

Flicker nodded, though he didn't look truly convinced. Alice sat in silence a moment longer, then gently dislodged Ashes and got to her feet.

"Time to move on," she said, feeling out along the fabric of the Grand Labyrinth. She was getting better at interpreting its unique geometry, and she thought she sensed another barrier stretched ahead of them. "I think another Veil is close."

## CHAPTER FOURTEEN
# HALOGELKIN

CYAN PULLED UP ONTO another beach, shrinking back into his fox form after everyone piled out and running in circles with excited *yips*. The island was smaller than the last Veil, but with high cliffs blocking any view of what lay beyond it. A broad, sandy path led into the interior, tufted here and there with clumps of wild grass.

"Will it be another guardian, do you think?" Dex said. "Or some kind of test?"

"A test sounds less dangerous," Flicker said.

"Unless it means the island is full of traps," Michael said. "Pits and spinning blades and collapsing rocks and so on."

"Everyone keep an eye out for spinning blades," Alice said. "Or anything else."

Ashes scrambled up onto Alice's shoulder, his tail shifting against her back. She scratched him absently behind the ear as they started forward, her mental grip hovering over her threads. Dex walked beside her, followed by Michael and Soranna, with Cyan trotting behind. Flicker brought up the rear.

The path curved around a rock wall and opened out into a large circular space, a sandy arena half ringed by cliff face. Set into the stone was a door, a huge iron thing easily twice Alice's height, with massive hinges and an enormous keyhole. It was flecked with rust, as though it had stood untouched for decades.

"A door?" Michael said. "That's the Veil?"

"Maybe we have to pick the lock," Alice said.

"I could step through it," Soranna volunteered, "and see what's on the other side."

"Aye, ye could," said a voice, "but what ye'd see might not be th' same as what'd be there if ye opened the thing, ye see? It's the labyrinth, it changes things around all tricksy-like. And it doesn't care for those that try t' cheat."

A swirl of dust fountained upward in front of the door, clearing to reveal a stocky man of roughly Alice's height. His clothes were old-fashioned and shot through with silver and gold thread, so he glittered as he moved, an effect enhanced by rings on his fingers and bracelets on both wrists. His lanky brown hair was tied into a fantastic multi-strand braid that incorporated several gold hoops and bands. Even his eyes gleamed gold, not the yellow of a cat's but the smooth, buttery shine of precious metal.

"As for pickin' th' lock," he went on, in his strange accent—it sounded like a mix of Irish and German— "there be no need for that. I'll open th' door for ye, fair 'n' square, if ye can best me."

"You're going to fight us?" Alice said, tensing.

"A fighter, eh?" He grinned and raised his fists in a classic pugilist's pose. "Nah, that be a bit uncivilized. 'Tis more of a . . . contest. Wits, ye see?"

Michael stepped forward, adjusting his glasses. "What kind of contest? Can we choose?"

"Ever since the geas was laid on me, I been challengin' whoever comes by here. Not many, truth be told, but the contest is a tradition, and ye can't mess with tradition. Here it is, plain an' simple. If ye can touch me, with yer hands or feet or anything ye can throw, then ye wins and I'll open up the door, honest truth. If an hour passes, and ye can't lay a finger on me, then the center of the labyrinth remains forever closed."

He waved a hand, and a tall hourglass materialized on a rock ledge overhead, sand already streaming out of the top bulb.

"Just touch you?" Soranna looked at Alice and winked, then went on, "That doesn't really seem like a fair contest. It can't be all that—"

She lunged forward in mid-word, hand outstretched, to tap the small man on the forehead.

"—hard!" she shouted triumphantly. But her hand passed through her quarry as though he wasn't there. A moment later, he shimmered and vanished, and there was movement all around them. A dozen copies of him, each identical down to the gleaming golden boots, appeared wearing identical grins.

"The girl has the right spirit!" the closest one crowed. "But it'll take more than quick hands to grab ol' Halogelkin!"

"That's not fair!" Alice shouted. "How can we touch you if you're not solid?"

"Oh, there's flesh an' blood in the mix," one of the duplicates said, and then another added, "But a fair dose of dust an' magic, too! Which is which, now, that's the trick, isn't it?"

As one, the twelve Halogelkins let out a laugh that was

close to a cackle. Then they all started to run, jump, spin, and twirl as though they'd gone mad.

"Get him!" Alice shouted.

Pandemonium erupted. Each apprentice ran after the closest duplicate, skidding and stumbling in the sand. Flicker lunged for one of them, missing by inches, while Dex tripped as she tried to fake one out. She thought she got a hand on Halogelkin's boot, but he merely looked down with a mocking smile before dissolving into mist. Soranna was turning in circles as two duplicates raced around and around her. Cyan, who apparently thought this was all great fun, ran madly at Michael's heels with enthusiastic *yips*. Even Ashes had jumped down from Alice's shoulder and was stalking one of the duplicates, rear end wiggling as he lined up for a pounce. Before he could spring, though, his prey dashed right toward him, and the cat leaped into the air with a startled hiss.

Alice herself managed to corner one of the Halogel-kins against the cliff face, match him feint for feint as he tried to dodge away. She was certain, from his cagey movements, that this was the real one, but when she finally lunged for him, her arm passed through his body like it was made of smoke.

"Ah, 'twas a good try, though!" said another duplicate, passing behind her. "Have ye ever thought ye might be a ballplayer? I think ye've got a talent!"

*Let's see if he laughs* this *off*, Alice thought with a savage grin. She pulled the Swarm thread tight around herself, and her body dissolved into a pile of bouncing black swarmers. As they righted themselves on the sand, she split them into teams, seven or eight heading for each of the duplicates. The teams spread out, surrounding the Halogelkins. Dex shouted in delight, and the apprentices moved to complete the circles.

"Oi!" Halogelkin shouted. "That's a good trick!"

One of his duplicates leaped over a line of swarmers and scampered away. Another tried to do the same, but not fast enough to avoid Michael's outstretched hand. The image blurred and vanished.

Alice's head was already splitting from the effort of moving so many swarmers at once, but it was working. Between the others, the swarmers, and the walls of the cliff, Halogelkin was running out of room.

"O' course, splitting yourself into a hundred parts might be thought by some to be unfair," Halogelkin said. "But I've always been a generous sort. Ye won't mind, then, if I do the same?"

One of the duplicates jumped up onto the cliff face, hanging from a rock by one hand. The air around him shimmered, and suddenly copies of Halogelkin were pouring down, dozens at once, overlapping one another in a mad scramble of gleaming gold and braided hair. They dodged around the apprentices, laughing in eerie synchronicity. Alice lunged at them with the swarmers, but all the images she touched vanished, leaving scores more. Michael hurled silver knives into the crowd, popping the Halogelkins like soap bubbles, but they merely pointed at him and laughed harder.

A few minutes later, Alice had returned to human shape, and she and the others were huddled in the center of the island, surrounded by a capering, cackling horde of Halogelkins. Cyan was the only member of the group who seemed completely undaunted, still running from one duplicate to the next, *yipping* and pouncing. All the apprentices were panting for breath, their faces streaked with sweat. Alice's head hurt like someone was driving nails in behind her eyes from trying to focus on too many things at once.

"This . . . is not . . . going to work," she gasped out.

"Is he cheating?" Soranna said darkly. "What if there isn't a real one?"

"I'm sure there is," Michael said. "I think I spotted him a couple of times. But he keeps splitting off new duplicates, so I can't keep track of him."

"While this game is better than fighting for our lives," Dex said, "time is against us. The sand is halfway through the glass. If our elusive friend is to be believed, when it is gone, our quest will be a failure."

"Give me a couple of dozen cats, and I'd clear him out," Ashes said. "The problem is that none of *you* can do a proper pounce." Cyan *yipped* at him, and Ashes shot back, "You don't count!"

"If there was a tree here, I'd be able to grab him," Alice said. She hadn't had time to prepare any of her magic acorns, unfortunately. "Isaac could put him to sleep. But—"

"I have an idea," Flicker said.

The apprentices all looked at him. He'd been quiet thus far, chasing after Halogelkin with grim determination but no more success than any of the others.

"I'm certainly open to suggestions," Alice said.

"Twice now," Flicker said hesitantly, "Dex has made nets out of moon-stuff."

"I don't think that will help here," Dex said.

"I know. But it made me think. There has to be *some*

difference between the real Halogelkin and the duplicates."

"The duplicates aren't solid," Michael said.

"Exactly." Flicker ventured a smile. "How about this . . ."

With twenty minutes left of their hour, Alice and the others broke from their huddle. They'd been gathered around a patch of tough, dry grass growing up out of the sand. Now each of them carried a twist of it, and Flicker touched the tip of each, one by one. These impromptu tapers caught fire, and the apprentices fanned out, touching them to the clumps of dry, half-dead grass scattered all over the island. Soon several small flames were blazing.

The hordes of Halogelkins stopped their circling and watched curiously.

"Well, this is new," one of them said. "But if ye're hopin' to burn me out, I'm afraid ye'll be disappointed!"

"I've got gold in my shoes!" another duplicate said, jumping into one of the fires to demonstrate. The flames didn't even tremble. "It'd keep my toes cool in a furnace!"

"Ignore him," Alice whispered to Flicker, when most of the grass was lit and burning. "Stick to the plan."

Flicker nodded. He went to the closest blaze, grabbing

handfuls of it. The fire became near solid in his hands and he squeezed it into a fine line of flame and laid it on the ground. It sat there, burning without a source, and Flicker spooled more of it out like a rope. He reached the next tuft of burning grass, leaving a solid line of fire. Once there, he grabbed another handful of flames and began again, linking the burning grass to the next fire.

"I don't mean t' alarm ye, but yer time's running out," Halogelkin said, through one of the duplicates close to Alice. "Are ye sure ye want to just stand and watch?"

Alice gave him a shrug with exaggerated nonchalance, but she did look at the hourglass. There were at most ten or fifteen minutes left. *Hurry, Flicker.*

Flicker was moving as fast as he could, laying lines of fire. The island began to resemble a web of flame, smoke curling upward in sheets from the unnaturally regular constructions Flicker had built. They weren't much of a barrier, though. Even without the Swarm protecting her, Alice could easily leap from one side to the other.

"I'll keep working," Flicker said. "Alice, go!"

She nodded, and reached for the Swarm thread again. Once more her body dissolved into a pile of swarmers, and they fanned out in all directions. Tough as they were, the little creatures could run through the fires with no more than a passing discomfort. Alice distributed them evenly around the island, a few in between each of Flicker's lines of flame. Halogelkin's duplicates edged away from them.

Michael stood poised, a dozen silvery knives hovering around his head. Flicker was still laying new tracks, crossing and recrossing the ones he'd already laid, dividing the space into smaller and smaller pieces.

*Here we go.* Alice could feel the headache building again already, but she set all the swarmers into sudden motion, each lunging for whichever of the Halogelkins was closest. Some of them caught the duplicates, which vanished noiselessly as the swarmers' beaks touched them. The rest of the Halogelkins sprang into motion, running around the island in a mad frenzy.

*Watch,* Alice mentally urged her friends, her swarmers running back and forth. They chased after the duplicates that came their way, but were careful never to cross the streams of fire. *Watch carefully . . .*

"Brother Michael, there!" Dex shouted, pointing.

The nearest swarmer turned to look. One of the lines of flame had shifted, and the curls of smoke above it were disturbed. All around, Halogelkin's duplicates continued their cavorting, but they didn't cause the fires to waver with the wind of their passage or the smoke to ripple as they moved through it.

Michael's knives flashed out. One, two, three of the duplicates vanished as a knife touched them, and another ducked under the slashing blades. That Halogelkin shimmered and split into five more copies, all running in different directions. But when they crossed the lines of flame, only one of them left a trail of smoke behind him.

"That one!" Soranna said. "Hit him, Michael!"

More knives zipped across the island. Halogelkin ducked and spun, the blades missing him by inches. Dexterous as he was, though, he didn't notice Alice moving several swarmers into his path until it was almost too late. He drew up short in a spray of sand, backpedaling rapidly, and Michael threw three more knives at him, leaving him nowhere to dodge.

Halogelkin's hand came up, viper-fast, and he caught one of the blades between two fingers a few inches from his face. The duplicates stopped moving, all at once, and turned to look at him.

"Well," Halogelkin said, and tossed the blade in the air, end over end. It vanished at the top of its arc. "I believe I would call that a fair touch."

Abruptly, all the duplicates burst into cheers. They slowly faded from sight, but their voices remained, filling the island with the sound of a jubilant crowd. Alice collected herself and turned back into a girl, wincing at the spike of pain in her temple.

"A contest is a contest," Halogelkin went on. "And no man or sprite can call me a cheat. Ye got me fair and square." He grinned and waved a hand, and the huge black door swung open on noiseless hinges. "Ye may venture on yer way."

Dex let out a whoop of delight, and Michael grinned broadly. Even Soranna lost her usual grim aspect. Flicker came over to Alice, hair flaming a brilliant yellow. Impulsively, Alice wrapped him in a hug. In the background, Cyan *yipped* in triumph.

"I don' suppose I could dissuade ye from going on?" Halogelkin said. "Ye seem like nice enough sorts. It's a shame, what'll happen to ye."

"What do you mean, what will happen to us?" Alice said.

"I'm bound not t' reveal the secrets of the labyrinth. But them as laid my geas were not the kindest of folk. Ye'll be better off if ye turn back, I warn ye."

"We know the old Readers are nasty," Soranna said.

"We'll be careful," Michael added.

"But we need to get to the center," Alice said. "Thank you for the warning. And thank you for playing fair."

Halogelkin gave a broad smile and a wink. He bent over, one arm in front of him in an exaggerated bow, and then vanished, the ghostly cheering of his duplicates slowly fading away.

"An excellent plan," Dex said to Flicker. "I admit I found myself at a loss."

"Very clever," Michael said, pushing up his glasses. "Well done."

"Yes," Alice said. "Well done. We couldn't have done it without you." She met Flicker's pupil-less gaze, and raised an eyebrow. He smiled, and gave a little shrug, but the bright colors of his hair gave away his pride.

"Hey! Get away from me, you little brute!" Ashes climbed Alice's back, claws digging into her shirt, and took up his usual position on her shoulder. Cyan chased around her legs, exuberantly spitting a thin stream of water. "Heavens save me from things with more enthusiasm than brains."

"There's nothing wrong with a bit of enthusiasm," Alice said. "We won, didn't we?"

"We did." Ashes licked a paw. "In no small part thanks

to my own contribution. But we are running out of day-light."

"He's right," Dex said, looking at the sun. "Should we spend the night here?"

Alice frowned, feeling for the fabric of the labyrinth. "I think the center is close. We should try and make it before dark. The sooner we get there, the sooner we can get back."

"You've got my support," Ashes said. "The less time we spend in this place, the better."

"As long as we don't have to fight our way through every crab and sea-slug in the ocean this time," Michael said.

## CHAPTER FIFTEEN
# A CHOICE

THEY LEFT HALOGELKIN AND followed a short tunnel through the rocks to another beach, Ashes riding on Alice, and Cyan at their heels. It was eerily silent. There were no squawking gulls here, and even the lapping of the waves on the shore seemed subdued, almost subliminal. The quiet magnified any sound the apprentices made, so that every kicked pebble sounded like a rock clattering across a museum floor. They waited without speaking while Cyan got into the water and fluffed back up into a boat, and then climbed aboard.

The water was startlingly clear, Alice noticed. She could see the bottom, even as they moved away from the beach and it grew deeper. Nothing moved, no darting fish or swaying seaweed. It looked like a scene in an aquarium before any fish had been added, utterly sterile. The steady swish of Cyan's tail, almost inaudible before, now filled the world.

"You said it's not far, Sister Alice?" Dex said, in a whisper.

"Not far." Alice could feel another Veil already.

"Good." Dex looked around and hugged herself. "I do not like this place."

The others seemed to agree. Soranna had been carrying the bag with the last of the apples, and she wordlessly shared them out, along with some cold crab meat that Alice had saved. Ashes gobbled up a little bit of the latter, then pressed himself close against Alice's side, staring out at the water. The tip of his tail swished back and forth.

After another hour, the sun was nearing the horizon, and the light was shading into orange and red. Ahead of them, a sheer cliff rose from the water, with only a narrow landing at the bottom for Cyan to pull up against. Stone steps had been carved into the rock, angling upward.

They disembarked. Even Cyan seemed to be affected by the strange quiet, shrinking back to his fox form and following Michael without so much as a *yip*. Alice led the way up the steps, the setting sun just peeking over the side of the cliffs and throwing their long shadows against the wall. As they climbed, something came into view at the top, a glossy black obelisk that shone with reflected light. When they were close enough, Alice saw that there were words inscribed there.

SUBMIT TO JUDGMENT.

"Judgment?" Michael said. "Of what?"

"Let me go first," Alice said, wrapping herself in the Swarm thread. She picked Ashes off her shoulder and placed him gently on the steps. Dex caught her eye, and Alice gave a slight smile. "I'll call for help if I need it, don't worry. Be ready for anything."

The others nodded. Alice stepped forward, climbing the remaining stairs to stand before the monolith. It was taller than she was, so she had to crane her head back to see the top.

"Well?" she said. "I'm here." She leaned to the side— they were nearly at the top of the cliff, so it should be easy enough to scramble around the black stone if she had to—

"You are the one to be judged?" The voice rang out, deep and sepulchral. "You speak for all?"

Alice looked over her shoulder. Dex, at the head of the group, nodded encouragingly.

"Very well."

The world flickered around her, and disappeared.

After a moment of vertigo, Alice found herself in a vast, empty room. The floor beneath her was black marble, shot through with a brilliant crimson like a trail of fresh blood under the glossy surface.

Directly in front of her was a hovering shape, an outline of tattered black cloth. It looked like a hooded cloak stretched over a human form, but nobody was visible, only the flowing, ragged end of the cloak as it whipped in an intangible wind. Something about it was *off*, the shoulders too broad and the empty sleeves too long for a man, giving it an almost ape-like appearance. In the depths of the cowl, two red lights glowed, their gleam hinting at eye sockets and a bony face that wasn't *quite* a human skull.

Alice swallowed, and reminded herself that she'd faced down stranger creatures than this. She straightened up and looked it in the glowing eyes.

"Where am I?" she said. "And who are you? And where are the others?"

**"So many questions."** The voice issued from somewhere inside the hood, deep and booming. It sounded flat and bored. **"I am bound by ancient contract to**

test your resolve, your willingness to sacrifice. I have brought you here, to this temporary space, for that purpose. If you wish, you may call me Reaper." One empty sleeve gestured. "As for your companions, they are right behind you."

Alice spun on her heel. A row of eight-sided crystals hung in midair, one sharp point a foot above the ground. Inside the nearest one was Dex, arms raised, hanging limp as though she were dangling from her wrists. Her head lolled to one side, and her open eyes were gray and sightless. She was perfectly still. Beside her, another crystal held Soranna, similarly immobile. Then Michael, glasses slipped down his nose to dangle from his ears, and Flicker, his burning hair as dead and gray as coal. At the very end, a tiny crystal held Ashes, curled into a tight ball.

"Let them go." Alice spun, fury and fear rising inside her. She grabbed for her threads. "Let them go *now*."

"Put your tiresome magic aside," Reaper said. "It will not avail you."

"I said—"

"I heard you."

Alice closed the distance between them in a few strides, Spike's power already filling her limbs. She grabbed for the edge of Reaper's cloak, ready to pull and tear. With

no warning, he was simply gone, as though he had never been. When she turned, she found him hovering beside the row of crystals.

**"You are the victim of a fundamental misunder-standing,"** Reaper said. **"This is not a real place. It exists because I will it. Here my power is absolute. If I wish you to be hurt, you will feel pain."**

Alice doubled over. It felt as though something had uncoiled inside her limbs, barbed wire pressing outward from her bones and tearing her flesh apart. She wanted to scream, but her jaw was locked tight.

Reaper floated closer. **"If I wish you to die, you will die."**

The pain vanished. Alice tried to draw breath, but it wouldn't come, as though her throat had fused solid. She brought her hands to her neck, fingers tightening into claws, but there was nothing there, no noose to pull free. She tried to move toward Reaper, to strike him, but after a single step she fell to her knees, her vision fading to gray.

**"I trust I have made myself understood."**

Her throat loosened, and she drew in air in a convulsive gasp. Tears filled her eyes, and for long moments all she could do was breathe.

"Can we proceed?" Reaper said, his voice as bored as a train conductor announcing stops.

"My friends," Alice said, her voice wheezy. "What have you done to them?"

"I have . . . stopped them. Temporarily."

"Bring them back."

"You are in no position to make demands of me," Reaper said. "But I will, if you pass the test."

"What test?" Alice looked up, then climbed shakily to her feet. "What do I have to do?"

"You must give up what you hold dearest." Reaper turned in the air to face the line of crystals. "Simply choose one of them. You and the rest may proceed to the center of the labyrinth."

"And the one I choose—"

"Will be lost. Forever."

Alice stood stock-still, heart pounding, her chest still aching. Reaper floated along the line of crystals.

"Not such a difficult test. No monster to fight, no puzzle to solve. No tricks. Just a choice." He rotated in place, red eyes glowing under his hood. "Are you ready?"

"I won't do it."

"Then you fail. You will never reach the center of the labyrinth."

"We'll find another way!"

"There is no other way." The hood shifted as Reaper cocked his head. "You should be grateful. You all knew, before you came here, that some of you might not survive. Rather than leaving who perishes up to the luck of battle, you can decide for yourself. And they need never know, of course."

"What makes you think you know anything about us?"

"Foolish. I can see into your mind as easily as you Read one of your prison-books. Choose."

"No."

"The cat, perhaps." Reaper drifted behind Ashes' crystal prison. "He is a lesser creature. And his blood is labyrinthine. Twisted and deceitful by nature."

The awful part was that those *were* Alice's thoughts, the nasty voice at the back of her mind she couldn't quite silence. She spoke aloud to drown them out.

"Ashes is my oldest friend," Alice said, facing him across the row of crystals. "He's helped me more times than I can remember."

"He mocks you. He carps and complains."

"He stayed to warn us about the Ouroborean, when he might have tried to escape."

Reaper shrugged his huge shoulders and drifted on. **"The fire-sprite, then. Not human, not even of your world. Why should you care about his fate?"**

"Flicker had every reason to hate me, when I went to his world," Alice said. "But he helped me even so, because he'd made a bargain. And when he found out why I was really there, he managed to look past his hatred. He's doing everything he can for his people."

Reaper gave a deep, irritable sigh, like the whisper of dank air from a freshly opened tomb. He stopped behind Michael. **"The boy? A recent acquaintance."**

"When the apprentices came to kill me, *he* listened to reason." Alice shook her head. "And Jen is waiting for him."

**"This girl."** The black shape moved to Soranna. **"She would sacrifice herself for you, if you asked. I can see it in her mind. Surely, if she is willing . . ."**

It was true, of course. If Soranna were able to speak, she would have agreed, Alice knew it. *But that doesn't make it right.*

"She's just . . . confused. She spent her whole life as

part of something twisted and evil, and she's still breaking out of that. But she *is* breaking out of it. I watched it happen, in Esau's fortress." Alice swallowed. "You can't say it's okay for her to die just because she thinks that I'm something I'm not."

**"Then this one,"** Reaper said, reaching the end of the row. Dex hung quiet and lifeless in her crystal, so unlike her usual, energetic self. **"The eldest. The most responsible. It is only fitting. And you know she would agree to give her life for any of the others."**

"I know she would," Alice said quietly. "That's the sort of person she is. But that doesn't mean she should have to. Dex is . . ." A sly voice, at the back of her mind. *She would insist, wouldn't she? If it meant saving everyone. She would smile, and say . . .* Alice shook her head again, at a loss for words. "I won't."

**"You must."**

"I *won't*!" Alice shouted. "How many times do I have to tell you?"

**"Then you will abandon your quest? Condemn all your friends and those who depend on you, because you could not make a sacrifice when it was required?"**

"I won't do that either."

Alice wrapped herself in Spike's thread again. Then she swung her fist like a sledgehammer at Dex's crystal. Tiny cracks webbed outward from the point of impact. She hit it again, sparks of pain shooting through her knuckles.

"I'm going to get them out of here." *Smack.* "And then I'm going to deal with *you*." *Smack.* The cracks expanded only slightly. "And then we are all." *Smack.* "Going." *Smack.* "Home."

**"Foolish. As though you have that option."**

"There is always an option!" Alice shouted.

**"Is there?"**

Suddenly Alice's feet felt as if they'd been glued to the floor. She looked down and was horrified to see that her boots had changed into black marble. As she watched, the blackness moved upward, past her ankles and up her legs, turning her flesh into cold, dead stone.

She turned back to Dex and renewed her efforts, slamming her fists against her crystal as hard as she could. Pain shot through her arm with each impact, and she felt something pop inside her hand with a stab of agony.

**"Sometimes there is no other way,"** Reaper said. **"Sometimes the enemy is too strong."**

"Never." Alice pounded the crystal again. One of the

cracks was almost two inches long. She tried pushing her fingernails into the gap. By now the marble had reached her thighs.

"Sometimes," Reaper said, **"you must give in. Give up. Stop fighting."**

"I won't." Alice drew back her throbbing fist. "I can't."

**"Then you will die. And your hopes with you."**

"I can't do that either."

She brought her right arm around in one final punch, a wild haymaker that landed with a *crunch* she was fairly certain was her own bones. The crack stretched out, another half an inch, but that was all.

The numbing marble passed her waist, freezing her hips, and raced up her torso. When the cold invaded her lungs, she felt her frantically beating heart go still as it changed to dead stone.

A moment of panic gripped her—the faintest doubt shooting through her mind like the crack spreading through the crystal. *If I die here, then the rest of them will never get out of the Grand Labyrinth. If I could ask them, wouldn't they agree that it's better—*

*If I had to choose one of them, then maybe—*

*No!* Her mind recoiled from the prospect. *No, no, no! Never.*

**"Choose."**

"I won't."

Alice brought her hand around, one more time. It wavered, halfway there, and froze into black marble. The transformation raced up her neck, freezing her throat. Even the pain was gone, replaced with dull, numb emptiness.

**"Choose."**

She could no longer speak. But her lips shaped the word *no*.

Darkness raced in from the corners of Alice's vision, her eyes freezing into the blank, empty eyes of a statue. As the light faded away, she heard Reaper's distant voice, and for the first time there was something more than vague disinterest there. Irritation, perhaps, mixed with respect.

**"I suppose,"** he said, **"you pass."**

Everything went black.

"Sister Alice?" Dex said. "What's wrong?"

Alice looked around, eyes wide. She stood at the top of the stairs, just where she had been before Reaper claimed her, but the black slab was gone, and the path to the top of the cliff stretched in front of her. She turned back, and found Dex and the others all free from their crystals, and all staring.

"The obelisk just . . . disappeared," Michael said. "Did you see anything?"

*It was all . . . a dream?*

*No.* Reaper's voice came from the back of her mind. *I was called to judge, and I have enacted my will.*

*And if I had chosen?*

**Then you would have lived with the consequences.**

"Sister Alice?" Dex stepped closer. "Are you in distress?"

Alice wrapped her arms around Dex, pressed her face to her shoulder, and sobbed.

## CHAPTER SIXTEEN

# THE CENTER OF THE LABYRINTH

Y OU'RE SURE YOU DON'T want to talk about it?" Dex said, sometime later.

They'd climbed to the top of the cliff and sat down on a gentle, sandy slope. Alice sat beside Dex, hunched over, arms wrapped around her knees. The others kept a respectful distance, except for Ashes, who was pressed against her side. She'd worked her fingers into his fur, gripping tightly, but he eschewed his usual complaints.

"I don't." When she closed her eyes, she saw Reaper's red gaze staring back at her. Every beat of her heart reminded her of how she'd felt when it had stopped. "I . . . can't."

*You didn't give in,* she told herself. *You* didn't. But there had been a moment where she'd felt close. She'd wondered, just for a moment, if Reaper was right. If the sacrifice *was* worth it, if the ends *did* justify the means. *Was I just lucky that I'm too stubborn to quit fighting?* Her hand was uninjured, but tingled with remembered pain.

"We can rest here for as long as you need," Dex said, her arm around Alice's shoulders.

"We can't." Alice looked up. The setting sun had touched the horizon, and its light was blood-red. "I'm not sure a month would be enough. But we're nearly there. It's nearly over."

"Sister Alice . . ."

Alice gently dislodged Ashes, who mumbled a sleepy complaint, and stood up.

"Let's do what we came here to do," she said.

The center of the island was a rocky plateau, atop cliffs towering over the surrounding seas and providing a commanding view of the rock-choked seas they'd come through. As Alice and the others hiked up the trail toward the top, the light drained from the sky and the first stars were visible on the eastern horizon.

A ring of boulders, weathered and rounded with age, crowned the very top of the plateau. Alice expected to see a portal book on top of each one, like in the cavern of "front doors" she'd used to reach Esau's fortress, but instead there were only a few lines of spiky characters hacked directly into the rock. She could feel the magic in them, but it was locked away.

Beyond, in the center of the ring, was a standing stone twice Alice's height, with one side worked into a roughly flat surface. The marks of the ancient chisels were still visible, crude and irregular. More writing spidered across it, the unfamiliar letters arranged in ways Alice didn't understand. Nevertheless, the whole thing pulsed with *meaning*, the inherent pull of magic to the mind of a Reader. She could see beyond the surface to the spider-web of connections underneath.

"This is it," she said. "The Great Binding."

She could trace the contours of it in her mind. Power pulsed through threads that ran off in every direction, stretching off into the unfathomable distance. Those were the connections to the old Readers that kept the binding in operation. Another set of threads went *down*, into the island, spreading out and weaving a tight net with something obscured at the center. *The prisoner.*

Alice had never seen a ward so complex or so tightly woven. *This was made by all the old Readers, working together.* Ending had said it was the first and last time that they'd cooperated like that.

Whatever the prisoner was, it was enormous, vast in both size and power. The binding kept it quiescent. But even so, it slept lightly, its mind pushing constantly at the walls of its confinement. Alice let her own mind skate over the edge of the binding, feeling the regular waves of the old Readers' power pushing the prisoner back, like the steady beating of a heart. She reached out, hesitantly, to touch the edge.

An image appeared in her vision. A single huge eye, silver and cat-slitted. A voice.

**Alice.**

*You?* Alice blinked. *But . . .*

"Alice!" Michael said.

She opened her eyes.

Standing directly across from her was a tall, dark-skinned man, with a tight-cropped frizz of gray hair and a beak-like nose. Alice remembered him from her visions in the Palace of Glass, playing chess with Geryon. *He's one of them. An old Reader.* At his side, standing almost to his shoulder, was a four-legged creature Alice almost didn't recognize. It was a goat, but nothing like the scrawny things she'd seen in farmyards. This one was powerfully muscled and jet-black, with long, curving horns ending in wicked spikes and weird, horizontal pupils like holes in its glowing yellow eyes. *Labyrinthine.*

There was a flash of light in front of one of the other boulders. When it cleared, a woman was standing there, tall and imperious, draped in a flowing white robe. Perched on her shoulder was a night-black bird the size of an eagle. Dex let out a gasp.

"Most Favored . . ." she whispered, gripping Alice's arm.

More flashes. One by one, the old Readers appeared. Most of them were men, and most looked as ancient as they truly were. But one appeared as a young man, blond and handsome as a god; another was a child of eight, wide-eyed and androgynous. One was hugely fat, so large, he barely seemed human, his face almost lost in the rolls and folds of his flesh. At the sight of him, Alice saw Soranna wilt, staring at the ground, her hands shaking.

*All the old Readers, together. Fighting even one of them would be impossible. We don't have a chance.*

And each of the Readers had brought a labyrinthine,

gargantuan animals of every description, all black as onyx. There was a spider and a rat the size of a dog, an ebony snake and towering, black-furred bear. One old man, so thin as to be almost skeletal, had a centipede wound around and around him like a cloak.

"How?" Alice said. "They—"

"They have a back door." Ending's voice, a deep, sibilant purr behind Alice. Alice turned to find the huge cat stalking forward, starlight rippling on her fur. "It requires all the old Readers to agree to open it, and it's been centuries since they agreed on anything."

"Millennia," said Dex's master conversationally. "It's a historic occasion."

"How did you get here?" Alice said quietly to Ending.

"This is a labyrinth," Ending said. "With Ashes here to use as an anchor, I can push my way through. When I felt my brothers and sisters arriving . . ."

Ashes climbed up Alice's back and perched on her shoulder, his claws gripping tighter than usual. She stood stock-still, trying to think. The power flowing off the old Readers was palpable, giving the air a hot, greasy feel. Any one of them would be more than a match for the apprentices.

"Alice Creighton." The old man she'd seen with Geryon

spoke, his voice deep and booming. "Do you understand what you tried to do? To alter the Great Binding? You risk *everything*."

"I understand," Alice said. "You've enslaved the labyrinthine, just like you enslave every other creature that falls within your reach. I'm putting an end to it."

"Stupid girl," Soranna's master said. "You have no idea what the consequences would be."

"You did not know the world before the binding," one of the others said. "Magic running wild, humanity at the mercy of creatures from other worlds."

"Don't tell me this is about protecting *humanity*," Alice said. "None of you cares one bit about the people in the real world. This is about power, just as it always has been. You're afraid of losing a little bit of power." She took a deep breath. "But where has power ever gotten you? Locked in your fortresses, afraid to step outside in case one of your colleagues attacks you?"

"I have lived for three thousand years," said the childlike Reader, voice high and piping. "I have not done so by being incautious."

"Or *kind*," another Reader rumbled. "You are young. These emotions pass away, with enough experience. Live a few hundred years and you'll understand."

"Not that you're going to get the chance," said Soranna's master sourly.

"Enough," said the man who'd first spoken. "You will tell us what has become of Geryon, and what happened to the Ouroborean."

"Geryon is trapped where he can't hurt anyone," Alice said, chin raised defiantly. "And I destroyed the Ouroborean myself."

"Lies," one of the Readers spat.

"Let me take her," said another. "We'll soon have answers."

"Take me, then." Alice gripped her threads tight, power thrumming through them. "Come on!"

Something moved in the corner of her vision. She turned just slightly, not willing to take her eyes off the old Readers, and saw Dex had stepped up beside her, silver caryatid armor shimmering into being. Her hands held long silver swords. On the other side, Michael came forward as well, hovering knives appearing around his head.

"We're all going to die, you know," Alice said, in a low voice.

"We know," Soranna said from behind her. "I'll guard your back."

Flicker joined them, holding out a hand to Dex. She

conjured a moon-stuff spear to replace the one he'd lost, and he hefted it thoughtfully.

"So," he said, voice crackling like a campfire. "Which one do we hit first?"

"A pity," Dex's master said. "She was a truly promising apprentice."

"The labyrinthine has corrupted them," another Reader said. "They are deceitful creatures."

*"They are indeed,"* Ending said, stepping forward.

She growled, and the sound got louder and louder, until it seemed to fill the world, a low, urgent throb like a motorcycle engine. After a moment, she was joined by other labyrinthine. A rising hiss from the snake, a low, menacing *caw* from the crow and a screech from the eagle, an ominous clicking from the centipede. The labyrinthine turned to face their masters, as one, with claws or fangs or horns raised. Several of the Readers retreated a step, and Alice felt the air grow thick with power as they summoned their defenses.

"What is this?" the childlike Reader said. "Have you gone *mad*?"

"Do you really think you can stand against us?" Soranna's master said. Arcs of energy like tiny bolts of lightning already crackled down her arms.

"In the world outside," Ending said, "we could not. But this is a labyrinth. The *Grand* Labyrinth. **And we are *labyrinthine!*"** Her voice grew louder with each word, until it hurt Alice's ears. "HERE *WE* HAVE THE POWER."

"Unless we release the Great Binding," said the Reader who'd first spoken. His goat stood in front of him, head lowered to present his horns, but the man looked at Ending. "You know what will happen when the prisoner is freed. Is that what you want?"

"Circumstances," Ending said, "have changed." Her lips pulled back, revealing long, ivory teeth. "We don't need you anymore."

A tide of black like living ink spread out from Ending's paws. It split into streams, reaching out to each of the Readers between blinks. Ending was *tearing* the labyrinth, not connecting *here* with *there* but opening a path to *nowhere*, a void outside of space itself. The darkness wasn't even black; it was simply nothing, an absence, a hole in the world.

Power lanced and crackled from the Readers, bound creatures invoked and wards triggering. Lightning, fire, ice, and pure force lashed out, but all too late. The void was on them, at their feet, and they were drawn into it with terrifying speed, sucked down as though yanked from below. A few screams and curses were cut off abruptly.

Then the old Readers were just *gone,* as though they had never been. It had all happened so fast, Alice didn't know how to react.

"Wh . . ." Dex's voice was trembling. "What did you do to them?"

"As Alice so elegantly put it," Ending said, "I sent them somewhere they won't be able to hurt anyone. The void outside of space and time."

"Can they get out?" Alice said.

"Not unless we open the way." Ending sounded very pleased with herself. "All their power is useless there. There is no *time,* so nothing can happen. The perfect prison."

"Then . . . we won?" Michael said, as usual getting right to the heart of things.

"Not yet," Ending said. "Alice must assume control of the Great Binding before it unravels."

All of the labyrinthine had turned to regard her, a circle of black animals with glowing eyes. Alice let her threads slip from her mental grasp and looked at Ending. "Now?"

"Please," Ending said.

"Was this . . ." She took a deep breath. "Was this your plan all along?"

Ending nodded. "I am sorry I could not tell you. To even mention it aloud risked everything. I will explain, but please—the binding. If it comes undone, all of this has been for nothing."

"If I'm strong enough," Alice said.

"You are," Ending said. "I believe in you."

"You can do it, Sister Alice," Dex said. "The auguries have always been in your favor."

"Of course she can do it," Soranna said.

"Put an end to this," Flicker said.

Only Michael looked uncertain, glancing from Alice to Ending and back again. His lips moved, as though he were trying to figure something out.

"Ashes," Ending said. "Come here and let Alice work."

"Good luck," Ashes said quietly. He jumped from Alice's shoulder and padded to stand beside his mother.

Alice took a deep breath and walked toward the standing stone, aware of the intense glowing eyes of the labyrinthine on her back. Their stares felt predatory, somehow, and she had to remind herself it was only natural. *Their whole future depends on this. They put their trust in me.* That was steadying, oddly. For better or worse, people kept putting their trust in her, and the only thing to do was try not to let them down.

When she touched the stone, she could feel the binding shudder. The threads that had led to the old Readers were cut off, and without the constant flow of power the whole structure was slowly coming to pieces. The prisoner, far below, shivered and shifted in its sleep.

Working slowly, careful not to damage anything, Alice gathered the drifting ends of the cut threads. Ending had explained to her what to do, but in truth it was so easy, she could have figured it out on her own. The Great Binding itself was so complex, she couldn't hope to reproduce it, but changing the power source wasn't difficult at all. She braided the threads together, into a single thick rope, and drew it toward her.

Then, with one decisive movement, she closed the connection, accepting the threads deep inside her being. With her next heartbeat, she felt power flowing out of her like a warm wave. It happened again, and again, regular pulses of energy passing along the threads to keep the Great Binding intact. In the real world, she fell to her knees, one hand still touching the standing stone. She felt the prisoner quiet again, settling once more into slumber. As the binding stabilized, the drain on her energy grew less, though she still felt weak and feverish. Nevertheless, when she opened her eyes, she felt a rising sense of triumph.

*I did it.* The binding was whole and secure, the prisoner trapped. *And I'm still alive.* Ending had said the drain on her power might be enough to kill her, but after the first jolt she hardly felt it at all. *I beat them.* We *beat them.*

She got to her feet, a little shakily, and turned around with a grin. "It worked. It's done."

Dex gave a whoop. "It's done!"

"It's *done.*" Ending turned to face her siblings. "I *told* you she was strong enough."

The labyrinthine were all talking at once, a chatter of animal voices. Michael stepped toward Alice, adjusting his glasses.

"Now what?" he said.

"Now we have a new world to build," Alice said. "Where Readers don't have to enslave others to gain their power. I'm hoping Ending can take us straight home, instead of having to sail all the way back. And then, I'm going to sleep for a week."

"I told Cyan to wait by the steps," Michael said. "I'll have to go and get him." He lowered his voice. "But I meant what now for *them.* Do you trust them?"

"They owe us their freedom," Alice said, looking around. Several of the labyrinthine—the goat, the eagle, and the centipede—had come closer.

"We do," the centipede said, in a ratcheting, clicking voice. "For the first time in two millennia, we are free."

"We can live as we please," the eagle said.

"Our labyrinths can spread," the goat said. "Until they cover the whole of the world."

"And every other living being is within our grasp," clicked the centipede. "Ours to rule."

"No," Alice said. "You don't get it. We will work *together*. It's no good tearing down the Readers only to put yourselves in their place."

The eagle cocked its head, as though it didn't understand.

*They've lived two thousand years as slaves*, Alice thought. *Be patient.* "Ending can explain it. Readers and magical creatures will live as partners."

"Is that what you told her?" the goat said, looking over Alice's shoulder.

"I did," Ending rumbled. "I must apologize for my siblings, Alice. They are a little . . . uncivilized."

"We'll have to teach them," Alice said. "I know."

"Your faith is touching," Ending said dryly. "But I don't expect they'll learn easily."

"I think we can do it." Alice smiled, but her grin faded as Ending stared at her in silence, lip curled to reveal her fangs, tail twitching. "Can't we?"

"You've done better than I could ever have hoped," Ending said. "And I can't thank you enough. But I must admit, I too am feeling a bit *uncivilized.*"

"You—" Alice looked around. "You can't mean you agree with them."

"I find that I do. We labyrinthine were *meant* for this. We will reshape the world to our liking. If the cursed Readers hadn't interfered, we would have done it long ago."

It felt as though the floor were crumbling beneath her. *The Dragon told me not to trust her.* But Ending was the only one who had helped her when she needed it most. She remembered Ending comforting her in the library, the warm, musty smell of her and the softness of her fur. *She can't mean it. Not after all this time.*

"What about being partners? Readers and magical creatures together?"

"I'm afraid I lied about that," Ending rumbled. "We labyrinthine are deceitful creatures."

"But—" There was a pain in Alice's chest, as though the words had been a physical blow. She glanced at the standing stone. "I can't let you. You know I can't. I control the Great Binding now, and—"

"Ah. There we have the crux of the problem." Ending's lip curled back farther. "My siblings and I would like to be *done* with Readers. For good. Which means that this is good-bye, Alice. Once again, my thanks for playing your part to perfection."

Time seemed to slow down. Alice lunged for the stone, trying to touch it, even for a moment, and rend the binding to pieces. But faster than she could move, faster than thought, blackness poured out from Ending and surrounded her. Over the labyrinthine's shoulder, she could see similar pools of darkness forming at the feet of Flicker and the other apprentices.

"Alice!" Ashes screamed, a high, desperate yowl.

Then the world was a blur as Alice was sucked downward, falling into endless darkness.

# PART TWO

## Chapter Seventeen
# THE VOID

Aʟʟ ᴀʀᴏᴜɴᴅ ʜᴇʀ, ᴛʜᴇʀᴇ was nothing.

Except it wasn't *even* nothing. *Nothing* implies emptiness, and *emptiness* implies a space that has the possibility of fullness, too. This was less than nothing, no space, no emptiness, no possibilities. The universe had contracted to the size of a pinhead, and Alice filled it completely. She was the only thing that existed, or could exist.

She wasn't sure if she had a body or not. She couldn't move, couldn't see or hear, couldn't feel anything. All she had was her thoughts, whirling around and around like a snake devouring its own tail, faster and faster.

"*Our labyrinths can spread . . .*"

"*The labyrinthine lie as naturally as breathing . . .*"

"*I'm afraid I lied about that . . .*"

"*She is dangerous, little sister . . .*"

"*You can't trust Ending. You can't trust any of them . . .*"

*It's a horrible thing,* thought the tiny, still piece of herself in the center of the growing maelstrom, *to feel yourself going mad.*

Her father's face, frowning in disappointment. *But maybe it's what I deserve.*

**"Alice."**

It took her a moment to realize that the voice hadn't come from within herself. To remember that it was *possible* for something to be outside herself.

"Who . . ." She couldn't speak, only think. But it was enough. An image swam into her mind.

An eye, silver and enormous.

"Where am I?" Alice said.

**"Nowhere."** The voice was deep, but Alice thought it was female. **"You are in the void beyond space."**

"Where are you?"

**"Locked away. In the ward you call the Great Binding."**

"You're the prisoner."

**"Yes."**

"Then how can you speak to me?"

**"I am asleep, which means I can dream. In dreams, I**

can sometimes slip my bonds, for a short time."

"Ending said something about time. About a perfect prison for the old Readers."

**"Yes. They are in the void, as you are, but not. For them, time has stopped. But Ending could not deny you time, because she needs you to power the Great Binding."**

"What about the others? My friends?"

**"They are with the old Readers. For them not an instant has passed since they were cast into the void."**

"And . . ." Alice hesitated. She wanted desperately for the voice to keep speaking to her. She was a lifeline, a fragile hold to keep Alice's mind from fracturing in its self-generated whirlpool. She didn't want to say anything to make her leave. *But . . .* "Who are you?"

**"I am the Labyrinthine."**

"You're one of the labyrinthine?" That made no sense. "Then why are they so afraid of you?"

**"Not 'one of.' I *am* the Labyrinthine. The source of them, the creator of them."** The voice paused. **"You may call me the First."**

"The First?" Alice said. "You're their . . . mother?"

**"Yes."**

"How? What happened to you?"

"I came to your world long ago," the First said. "It is very . . . different from my own. More physical. More *real*. I gloried in it. I had known nothing like the life that inhabited your world, and I strove to understand it. I took the creatures that inhabited your world, and I combined them with a piece of my own essence, to observe the results.

"I meant no harm. I was curious."

"You created the labyrinthine."

"Yes. At first I did not understand anything. Day and night, life and death, all of it meant nothing to me. Your world was a puzzle box that I tried to unravel. At times I fear I did . . . a great deal of damage. But, slowly, I learned. About joy, and life, but also about pain, and loss. To understand that other creatures— humans, life made of something as plain and coarse as *matter*, so different from myself—could *feel* as I did, and even feel things that I had never imagined . . ." The First trailed off. "It was not an easy thing for me to comprehend."

"But you did learn?" Alice said.

"I did. And when I did, I saw what my children had become, and I realized the harm I had done. They had my intelligence, some fraction of my power, but they also had all the hunger and ambition of your world. They used the folded space you call a 'labyrinth' to dominate and destroy, to rule over humans for their own amusement.

"I could see that I had been nothing but a curse on this beautiful place I had found, no matter that it had only been through ignorance. I decided the time had come to return home. I would leave, and I would bring my children with me. They would bring something of this world into my home, and with it, who knows what we might have created?

"But they did not wish to leave."

"They turned on you," Alice said, feeling a sympathetic pain. "All of them?"

"Not all. But enough. They collected the greatest wizards of your world, and offered them a bargain; their services in exchange for imprisoning me forever. In my ignorance, I was easily trapped. Those of my children who dissented were bound up in prison-books.

"But my children, who believed themselves so clever, underestimated the humans. With the labyrinthine helping them keep their libraries under control, the wizards' power grew at a frightening rate. They became the Readers, and they have dominated the world ever since."

"But they're gone now," Alice said. "Ending trapped them."

**"She has. And now Ending and her siblings are free to do as they have always wished, to make the world into their plaything. Two millennia of slavery has not made them kinder."**

"I should never have trusted her." Alice felt like she might have cried, if she'd still had eyes. "I should never have trusted *any* of them. First Geryon, then Ending. And now my friends are . . ."

She felt like she should be sobbing, gasping for breath, but she had no lungs, either. Nothing but thought, alone in the darkness.

**"You cannot blame yourself. Ending set this scheme in motion long before you were born. She has infinite patience. That is what makes her the most dangerous of all."**

"Why are you telling me this?" Alice said. "What's the good of it now?" *What's the good of anything?*

She couldn't move, even if there had been anywhere *to* move. She couldn't feel her threads, or the fabric of space.

"If you could escape from here," the First said, "what would you do?"

"Stop them," Alice said at once. "And rescue my friends."

"The only way to stop my children is to free me," the First said. "And that means the end of the age of Readers *and* the end of labyrinths. It means the return of the old times, the wild times, before I even came here, when magic was a natural part of your world."

"That's why I came here in the first place," Alice said. "The Readers have gone on too long as it is. They've twisted the world, and it needs a chance to recover."

"No matter what it means for you? You are, after all, a Reader."

"I didn't ask to be," Alice said. "I'll manage." If she'd had a heart, it would have been beating fast. "*Is* there a way out?"

"Yes. As I said, Ending's prison for you is incomplete. She must allow the flow of time in order to use your power, and that means there is a crack, however miniscule. I can force it wider and get you out."

"You helped me once before," Alice said. "In the Palace of Glass."

"I did. In dreams, I have only a fraction of my power, but sometimes a fraction is enough."

"Once I'm out, what do I need to do?"

"**Return to the Great Binding and destroy it. But it will not be easy to reach. I cannot be certain where you will return to in the real world, and the old Readers' portal will not open for you. You must find another way to the center of the Grand Labyrinth.**"

"I'll find a way." Alice hesitated. "It's me that powers the binding now, isn't it? What would happen if I just . . . died?"

It was a horrible thought, but she had to ask. *If dying means saving the world and all my friends . . .*

"**The binding would take too long to unravel. Ending would have time to find another solution, even if it meant bringing back the old Readers to make a new agreement. She will do *anything* to prevent my release. The Great Binding must be destroyed, once and for all.**"

"All right." Alice couldn't help but feel a tiny bit of relief. *Now, instead of jumping off a bridge, I just need to get past a magical labyrinth into the best-protected place in the world.* "And my friends?"

"**Once I am free, I can retrieve your friends from the void. They will not even know anything has happened.**"

That, at least, was a comfort. But something nagged at her. She *wanted* to believe the First. The feeling that came into her mind along with her was warm, gentle, and kind. It reminded her of her father. *But first Geryon, then Ending...*

"How do I know," she said slowly, "that any of this is true? That this isn't just a trick to get me to let you out?"

There was a long silence.

**"I can offer no proof," the First said. "But once you are free, I cannot command you. You can believe me, or not, and that is as it should be. You are a Reader, and your decisions are your own. If you wish, you can leave this world and its problems far behind."**

The First's words reminded Alice of something the Dragon had said to her, in Esau's fortress, what seemed like a hundred years ago: *"You deserve the opportunity to make your own choices, to walk your own path. Indeed, I believe you will do so, regardless of what Ending, Geryon, or anyone else intends. You must do what you believe to be right."*

*"What if I can't tell for certain?"* she had asked the Dragon.

*The Dragon had sounded as though it was smiling.* *"Which of us can?"*

She took a deep, shaky breath. "All right," she told the First. "Send me back."

**"Be ready for anything."**

"Well," Alice said, stretching her nonexistent limbs. "I'm as ready as I'll ever be."

## Chapter Eighteen

# FLOTSAM AND JETSAM

THE FIRST'S WARNING OUGHT to have been sufficient. Most of the Earth's surface was ocean, after all, especially in the general vicinity of the Grand Labyrinth. But Alice had still been shocked when she'd slid out of the void and immediately plunged into choppy, freezing-cold water.

Fortunately, she'd had the presence of mind to yank hard on the devilfish thread. The transformation had left her well-suited to her new environment, and for a long time she'd gloried in the feeling of *having* a body again, even if it was a fish's. She'd chased down and devoured a few smaller fish, swallowing them raw and bloody, and marveled at how they tasted like the finest meal she'd ever eaten.

At night, she'd surfaced and changed back to a girl to study the stars. She began swimming west, on the theory that if she was somewhere in the Atlantic, this might eventually take her back to the United States. The length of the journey didn't seem to matter much. As the devil-fish, she could rest in the water, find what she needed to eat, and swim until she was tired; nothing else really counted.

On the second night, she'd spotted a ship by its lights, and gotten close enough to identify the American flag at the mast. She followed it, using Spike's strength to power through the water faster than any normal fish would have been able to. To her surprise, it was only another day before land came into sight, bumps on the horizon that slowly grew into beaches and trees. She'd left the ship behind, searching for a place she could come ashore without anyone seeing, and settled on a deserted strip of sand.

Most of the houses visible from the beach were boarded up and dark. A long, empty street lined with

driveways that led only to empty lots spoke of plans that had gone catastrophically awry. Faded signs proclaimed it to be the property of the Ocean Vista community, and strictly prohibited trespassing, but the drifts of cigarette butts and empty bottles suggested the rules were largely ignored. Alice held up a hand, staring at her fingers as though she'd forgotten what they were for.

She hadn't been human for more than a few minutes at a time in days, and had been in the void for an eternity before that. It was some time, therefore, before she got her legs in working order, gathered them under her, and climbed unsteadily to her feet. The rocks were sharp and painful with no shoes, and she pulled on the Swarm thread in what had become an automatic reflex. Thus protected, she walked up the beach, avoiding the debris and slipping through one of the many places where the fence had been cut away. Beyond were rows of identical houses, the empty lots standing out like missing teeth in a smile.

She'd had time to plan as she swam through the endless, comforting ocean. The first part of the plan had worked; this certainly *looked* like the United States. The second part entailed getting back to Pittsburgh, which presented a few obstacles. She had no idea where she was, other than the vague notion that she was somewhere on the eastern seaboard. She had no money, identification, or anything else that might be useful. She had nothing, in fact, except the ruined clothes she was wearing and the threads coiling at the back of her mind. And she hadn't traveled through the human world, the *real* world, in a long time.

It was odd to think about trains and automobiles, the need to buy tickets and check schedules. Even before her father had died, she hadn't traveled much on her own, and the prospect of being lost in another state with no one to help her would once have been terrifying. Now it felt like a minor irritant, a problem but not a really serious one.

*I suppose it's all a matter of perspective.* Of course, in the old days, she reflected, she could have gone to the police and told them what had happened, and they'd probably have taken her home. Telling her story to any authorities *now* would only land her in a mental asylum.

*First things first. Find out where I am.*

It was late evening, the sun already down and the sky rapidly purpling to the color of a bruise. Most of the houses on the street were dark, but at the end of the first row, she saw one whose windows shone with the steady glow of electric light. Alice headed for it, drawn like a moth to the flame. She rang the doorbell, which was a modern electric chime. *Electricity.* She'd almost forgotten about it, living in Geryon's gloomy old mansion, where magic powered everything.

"Hello," Alice said as the door opened. She had practiced this speech in her mind on the way here. "Do you have a newspaper you can spare? Yesterday's would be fine."

"Good Lord." The woman who'd opened the door had short, bobbed hair and spoke with a Southern accent. She was older than Alice's father, with thick, horn-rimmed spectacles and a skeptical expression. "What're you doing out at this hour?"

"I'm just . . ." Alice's mind went blank. She had genuinely forgotten that in the human world, a girl her age might not be allowed to wander about whenever she wished, and she had no idea what would be plausible. "Lost?" she finished, hopefully. "And if I had a newspaper, I could find where I'm supposed to be."

"And are you going to *walk* there?" The woman peered closer. "You haven't even got any shoes!"

"I . . . left them. To dry." Alice raised her arms. "I fell in the water, you see."

"I see." The woman sucked her lower lip. "Well. You'd better come in."

"You're not going to call the police, are you?" Alice said as the woman escorted her into a tidy kitchen. The walls were covered in floral print wallpaper, and there were pictures hanging everywhere, mostly amateur watercolors, with a few photographs mixed in.

"Couldn't if I wanted to," the woman said. "We're not on the phone here. They never built the lines." She gestured to the battered wooden table and chairs. "Sit, sit. You want something hot to drink? Hot cocoa?"

Alice hadn't realized until that moment how much she missed hot cocoa. "Yes, thank you. That would be wonderful."

"If you *want* to go to the police, I can take you into town when the bus comes," the woman said. "But I got a feeling that's not what you want."

"No," Alice said.

"What's your name? Mine's Nancy."

"Alice," said Alice. "Alice Creighton." Last names seemed to be a thing of the human world, too, like cars and radios. It had been ages since she'd used hers.

"Alice is a nice name," Nancy said, busying herself with a saucepan. "You're not from around here, I take it?"

"Honestly, I don't even really know where here is," Alice said.

Nancy named a town, and Alice shook her head. She named another, larger town, and when Alice didn't know that one, either, she rolled her eyes and said, "Florida. Have you heard of Florida?"

"I've heard of Florida," Alice said. She had a vague image of palm-lined beaches and crocodiles.

"That's where we are. Down near the end." Nancy poured hot milk from the saucepan into a mug, and spooned in chocolate syrup. She set it in front of Alice. "Give that a stir and let it cool off. So how do you come to not know what *state* you're in?"

"I was on a boat," Alice said, improvising. "A ship, I mean. I . . . stowed away. Then somebody found me and I had to jump overboard and swim for shore."

"Where were you headed?" Nancy said suspiciously.

"North. I'm looking for my family."

"Family." Nancy's face softened. "That's important, in times like this."

She turned away, looking out the kitchen window for a while. Alice blew on the cocoa and, cautiously, took a sip. It was thick and sweet, and brought back memories that felt like they were from another world. Mrs. Juniper, her old tutor, had always made her cocoa as a reward for a job well done. Alice wondered where she was now, and what had happened to her father's old house, and if there was another little girl now living in her room.

"Here," Nancy said, interrupting her thoughts. "You wanted a newspaper, right? This is yesterday's."

It was a cheap one, the ink already smearing. Alice's first concern was the date. It said April 25, so today was April 26. She'd gotten out of the habit of tracking the calendar closely, but that meant it had been at least a month since she and the others had set out in search of the Grand Labyrinth.

The headlines told the usual stories, celebrities and politics and local color. A famous baby had been kidnapped, apparently, and a ransom might or might not have been demanded. Hindenburg, the president of Germany, was having a public feud with someone named Hitler. The American presidential election had already begun.

Above them all, though, was a large headline in slightly frantic type: "MASS INSANITY CONTINUES, EMERGENCY CONFERENCE CONVENED IN D.C." The subheads read: "New York, Pittsburgh, Seattle Affected; Thousands Flee Cities; Reports of Panic in London, Athens, Rome; Scientists Suspect Airborne Fungus—Ergot Poisoning; President Hoover Urges Calm."

Alice read. In a few cities, residents had begun seeing inexplicable things—streets where no streets should be, or tunnels that led to the wrong places. Creatures no naturalist had ever catalogued, strange lights and sounds. People had gotten lost in their own neighborhoods, their own *houses*, found in tears hours later and describing endless staircases or roads that looped back on themselves whichever direction they ran. An increasing number weren't found at all.

The best that ordinary human science could do, in the face of this, was a diagnosis of "mass insanity," some kind of infectious airborne contagion causing the people in the affected areas to go temporarily mad.

*The labyrinths are spreading.* Alice hadn't imagined it would happen so fast. Her gut twisted as she followed the story, reading about teams of investigators finding nothing out of the ordinary in places where the residents had run screaming. *The labyrinthine are toying with them.* The authorities would never imagine that it wasn't a natural phenomenon they were dealing with, but something magical under the control of a malicious intelligence.

She wondered how long it would take before the scientists and politicians would admit what seemed utterly insane—that the world they lived in, the world of laws and normality, was a paper-thin film over something deeper and darker. *And even if they admitted it, what could they do? Send in the police? The army?* Machine guns and tanks would be useless against something that could shift space itself, could let you wander forever in a maze made of familiar landmarks.

Alice had never really thought about how vulnerable the real world, *her* world, was. The old Readers could have ruled the world, but—as Geryon had once explained to her—why bother? Besides, culling potential apprentices and scraps of magic from the world was easier if humans knew nothing about it. *But the labyrinthine don't care about any of that.* To them, the world was simply a toy, to be played with and broken as they pleased.

"MASS INSANITY," the headline screamed. She wondered if that was better or worse than the truth.

*I have to stop them.* It wasn't only her friends' lives at stake.

She realized she'd been sitting quietly for a very long time. She took another sip of cocoa, and found it tepid. Nancy, leaning against the kitchen counter, regarded her quietly.

"It's all they talk about on the radio, the last week or

so," Nancy said when Alice looked up. She nodded at the paper. "You think your family's caught up in all that?"

Alice nodded.

"Well. I don't blame you for wanting to go to them." She looked at one of the photographs on the wall. There was a boy in it, Alice noted, not much older than she was, standing beside a much younger Nancy. "But you look dreadful. Stay here tonight. We'll find you something to wear, and in the morning we'll talk to someone about getting you on a train."

Nancy let Alice have a bath. Though the water was only lukewarm, stripping out of her soaking leathers and scrubbing the salt and grime from her skin was still an unutterable pleasure. Afterward, they rummaged through a trunk of old clothes and found a boy's shirt and trousers that fit well enough that they wouldn't actually fall off. Nancy heated up pea soup for dinner, with slivers of ham. She talked constantly, perhaps so that Alice wouldn't have to—about the weather, the bank failures, the letters her son sent home from where he was trying to make it in the west, and how he didn't write often enough. When she got onto the latest cinema stars, Alice could only smile and nod.

She excused herself early and went to her bed, which was a ratty old thing wedged into the corner of what was clearly a boy's room, with pictures of pretty girls and baseball stars pinned to the walls. Alice surprised herself by falling into a deep, dreamless sleep almost at once.

She awoke before dawn, to a silent house.

There was a window beside her bed, and she forced it open, slowly, so it wouldn't squeak. It looked out into the overgrown backyard, and the drop was only a couple of feet. Alice looked down at her new clothes with a feeling of guilt, but she couldn't bring herself to try and get back into the outfit ruined by seawater and sun.

In the yard, she paused for a moment, taking hold of her threads, and grinned. Then she vanished, with a chorus of *quirk*s and the patter of hundreds of tiny feet. When Nancy finally woke, she'd find the house over-shadowed by an enormous tree, whose long, low-hanging branches bore enough huge, juicy apples to fill a barrel.

## Chapter Nineteen
# ON THE ROAD AGAIN

It was easiest, Alice found, to travel as the Swarm.

People didn't see her, for the most part, or if they did, they didn't react badly. A swarmer, moving fast, was easy to mistake for a rat or a squirrel. Alice guessed that running around as a dinosaur was likely to attract unwanted attention.

A train would have been faster, but sooner or later, she was bound to run into some well-meaning authority figure who was less sympathetic than Nancy to a girl traveling on her own, and that would lead to complications. It wasn't that Alice was *worried* about the police, exactly, but she didn't want to be forced into a situation where she had to hurt someone to get away.

She didn't have a map, but she figured she didn't need one, at least at first. All she needed to do was head north, and that was easy enough, following the coast or the stars at night. The swarmers were fast and practically tireless, and in their many-bodied form, Alice felt as though she could run forever. Miles fell away under her tiny, skittering feet, roads and fields and suburban backyards.

There was a certain peacefulness, a *clarity* to the journey that was refreshing. At the end of it, there'd be questions to answer and decisions to be made, but for the moment all she needed to do was run and keep running. She squirmed under fences, or tore a hole through them with Spike's strength. When she came to a river, she changed into the devilfish and swam it. When a forest blocked her path, she took on the tree-sprite's form and the vegetation parted in front of her.

The tree-sprite provided her food, too, when she made her infrequent stops to rest. All she had to do was touch a tree, and it would grow fruit for her. The diet was a little monotonous, but that was somehow fitting. The days blended together, running, resting, pausing for food, and running again.

In spite of the peace, there was one thing that preyed on her mind. *Isaac.* The First had promised that the friends who'd been with her were safe, locked away out-side time and space with the old Readers. *But what hap-pened to Isaac, and Jen, and the other refugees?* Had the labyrinthine tossed *all* the apprentices into the void? Alice couldn't decide whether to hope for that or not. She ached to see Isaac again and know that he was all right, but if he'd been imprisoned, then at least nothing worse had happened to him.

Either way, there was nothing to do but push on. Here and there, she caught sight of the newspaper headlines. The front pages were nothing but the "Madness Crisis" now. Manhattan Island had been enveloped by a fog so thick, it obscured the skyscrapers. In Seattle, enormous multi-finned creatures had been seen swimming in Lake Washington. In Rome, ancient suits of armor were reportedly floating through the streets and assembling into legions. Officials repeated the lines they'd been given, that it was all hallucinations caused by fungus or dangerous gas, but the papers paid less and less attention. Preachers were talking about the Book of Revelation and proclaiming the end of the world.

When she entered Maryland, Alice veered west. In the rugged, wild forests of the Appalachian Mountains, she found she could transform into the tree-sprite and let the branches carry her from one tree to the next, moving much faster than even the Swarm could run. It was practically like flying.

In the flat land on the other side of the mountains, she moved more cautiously. In West Virginia she picked a small town at random and walked into the general store. The proprietor, an old black man with short gray hair and a face like tooled leather, might have been surprised by the solitary girl in ill-fitting boys' clothing and no shoes, but he gravely accepted the fat apples she offered him as a gift and agreed to let her inspect a map. Alice plotted a course that would intercept the Monongahela River, which flowed in lazy curves all the way north to Pittsburgh, where it joined the Allegheny to become the Ohio. Somewhere on the north side of those rivers was the Library, Geryon's estate.

That night, she halted in a grove of trees by the riverbank, a comfortable distance from the nearest human habitation. The lights of isolated farmsteads glowed in the distance, but there was no one to see her but a few horses. The black tide of swarmers gathered together and flowed into a girl, and Alice stretched her arms and yawned.

She'd grabbed sleep when she felt like she needed it along her journey, though she didn't seem to need as much as she did when she was a girl. *Maybe swarmers don't sleep.* Whatever the reason, a few hours at a time seemed sufficient. She settled down against the trunk of a tree. A moment later, as she reached to the tree-sprite thread, it shaped itself around her, bark going comfortably smooth. A thick carpet of moss grew up to be her pillow.

She'd never done this before, spent so much time in the outside world while using her powers. It felt strange, but also oddly freeing. *I can do whatever I want.* The thought was a little scary, to be honest. She was beholden to no one. No human authority could stop her, not for long. She could go anywhere, one tiny step at a time.

*Unless the labyrinths cover the world, and there's nowhere left to go.*

She released all her threads except for one. The black one, the Dragon's thread, led back to the book she and Isaac had gotten trapped in so many months before. Pulling on it got her nowhere. The Dragon had never responded to her control, or even her pleas, except when she'd nearly died in the depths of Esau's fortress. It hadn't spoken to her since its brief warning, before she'd left for the Grand Labyrinth. Nevertheless, Alice liked to hold the thread.

"I should have listened to you," she said with a sigh. "Though you have to admit you could have been a little clearer. But I still don't know what else I could have done. I wish . . ." She shook her head, not sure what to say.

Staring up at the stars, she could feel a faint tension in the thread. Someone else was touching it, and there was only one person that could be. Isaac was out there, somewhere. *He's alive.* Alice let that thought fill her mind as she fell asleep.

The factory towns around Pittsburgh proper were mostly empty, with police barricades blocking off many areas. Cars clogged the road, abandoned when traffic grew too dense. Houses and shops were locked up, and streetlights were dark. The great steel mills stood quiet, chimneys that normally belched smoke around the clock gone cold.

Alice could feel the fabric of Ending's labyrinth now. It was patchy, at first, like the edge of a sweater that's slowly unraveling. Only this was the reverse—the sweater was *growing*, new threads weaving themselves into place as the twisted space of the labyrinth spread.

After crossing the river on a railway bridge, Alice

shifted back to a girl. Here the labyrinth was solid and complete, the fabric as firm as it had ever been in the library. If she'd wanted to, Alice could have taken it in hand, connected *here* to *there,* and stepped through to her own bedroom in an instant.

But that would alert Ending to her presence, without a doubt. She could feel the great cat's presence, distant but attentive, sensitive to any disturbance in the fabric like a spider squatting in the midst of her web.

Most of the population had evacuated, but Ending was clearly unwilling to let all her new toys escape her. Alice could feel other people, faint pressures in the fabric of the labyrinth. For the most part, they were still, doubtless hiding from a world that had apparently gone mad.

*Do I try to find them?* She was torn. *What can I do?* If she exerted her powers to help the trapped civilians, Ending would catch her sooner rather than later.

She was still chewing on the problem when she heard a decidedly human scream.

Before she was consciously aware of it, she'd started to run. She skidded around a signpost on bare feet and saw a short street, lined with three-story brick buildings. A girl around her own age was running toward her, dressed in a white cotton dress and a long fur coat that was far too large for her. Behind her was what looked like the contents of a garbage dump come to life, a four-legged creature bigger than a car, its body made up of broken machinery, shattered bottles, automobile parts, and scraps of radio, mixed with shreds of torn newspaper that fluttered on its skin like fur.

"Get down!" Alice yelled to the girl, wrapping herself tight in Spike's thread. She was in motion as the transformation took her, two legs changing into four. She felt herself grow into the shape of the dinosaur, not much larger than a pony but immensely dense and strong, with four long, sharp horns protruding from a bony crest around her head. She lowered those horns as she charged, aiming for the broken refrigerator adorned with jagged scraps of steel that served the trash-monster as a skull.

It came on to meet her, and they collided with a scream of grinding metal. Spike was much heavier than he looked, and the unexpected impact knocked the trash-monster sprawling, while Alice, her body well-adapted to just that type of impact, was barely fazed. She didn't give the thing time to recover. Letting Spike's thread slip just far enough to change back into a girl, she grabbed the Swarm as well, hardening her skin. She reached into the thing's refrigerator mouth and pried it apart, the joints howling piteously as she forced them the wrong direction. Its teeth scraped at her, tearing her baggy clothes but having no effect on her magic-toughened body, and before it got a foot up to scrape her away, the hinges gave way entirely. Alice ripped the refrigerator door free and tossed it aside, then jumped down as the trash-creature collapsed, bits and pieces falling off as it decomposed into its component junk.

She landed with easy grace and turned away from the ongoing *crunch*es and *ping*s of the monster's metallic demise, to find the girl staring up at her from where she lay in the street, openmouthed and wide-eyed. Alice raised her hands in what she hoped was a non-threatening manner.

"It's all right," she said. "You're safe now. If you stick close to me, I'll get you—"

She went no further, because the girl screamed again, scrambled to her feet, and ran. Alice instinctively looked over her shoulder, then came to a belated realization. *It's me, isn't it?*

*I can't blame her. If, before I knew about magic, I'd seen a girl turn into a* dinosaur *and back, I'd have been . . . well, probably fascinated. But I'd know I* ought *to be terrified, anyway.*

She'd had a dream, once, that she'd changed into the Dragon and hadn't been able to change back. The people of the city had surrounded her, throwing stones and calling her a monster. *Is that what I am to humans now?*

She hadn't chased after the girl. There were hundreds of people still in the city, and there wasn't time to help them all. *If I can get back to the First and undo the binding, I can save everyone.* But guilt still gnawed at her as she ran.

She didn't know exactly where the Library was—the first time she'd come there, Mr. Black had driven her in his ancient Model T, and every other time she'd left, it had been by portal—but she could feel the center of the labyrinth, where the fabric was densest, and she went in that direction. Before long she passed beyond the suburbs and into the dark forests that surrounded the estate. The trees swayed as they carried her from one branch to the next, Alice riding a rolling wave of vegetation as she shaded her eyes against the sun and looked for the broken roof of the place she'd called home.

## CHAPTER TWENTY
# REUNION

S HE'D BEEN PLANNING TO avoid the library entirely, hoping not to attract Ending's attention, but as soon as Alice got close to the house, she was forced to change her plans. She could feel someone human through the fabric of the labyrinth, deep in the manifold aisles of endless bookshelves, and there were only a few people it might be.

The library's doors stood open, as they were never supposed to. Inside, the once-orderly shelves looked as though they'd been hit by a hurricane. Many had toppled, like endless rows of dominoes, and books lay in drifts on the floor.

The front of the library looked *wild*, like the back of it

always had. It was still changing, little by little—even as she watched; a distant shelf toppled with a groan and a crash. Dust puffed into the air like smoke rising from an explosion, sparkling in the light.

Nothing alive was in evidence, no magical creatures, not even any of the ubiquitous library cats. Alice felt along the fabric of the labyrinth, carefully, and detected no sign of Ending's presence or attention. She started toward the distant hint of human presence, threading her way through the now-twisted aisles.

Time was hard to reckon, but she guessed it was nearly an hour before she came to a half-tumbled circle with nothing in it at all. It was the spot, she realized, where the Ouroborean had once chased her. It had originally been a jungle, but now there was only a half-circle of shelves and a cluster of dry, dead trees and crunchy, desiccated fallen leaves.

Something was huddled in there. A lumpy shape, a faded gray-blue, that made Alice's heartbeat quicken. She ran over, bare feet *crunch-crunch-crunching* in the leaves.

"Isaac!" she said.

He raised his head blearily. He'd been curled up under his ancient, battered trench coat, and his glazed eyes still looked half-asleep. He blinked. "A . . . *Alice?*"

He barely had time to raise his arms before she was on top of him, wrapping him in a fierce hug. He smelled of sweat and dust, and his clothes were filthy, here and there crusted with dried blood. When he smiled, his teeth stood out a brilliant white in his grubby face.

"Oh, thank all the powers," Isaac said. He pulled away long enough to look at her for a moment, then hugged her again, even tighter. His voice was a murmur at the nape of her neck, thick with emotion. "I thought you were dead."

"I'm okay." With a start, she realized his shoulders were shaking. "It's all right, Isaac. I'm okay. I . . ." She blinked back tears. "I was scared for you, too."

"It's been weeks," he said.

"I know," Alice said. "It's a long story."

A quarter of an hour later, they were sitting opposite each other beneath a dead tree, and Alice had told at least part of what had happened to her. Once she'd started talking, Isaac had pulled away from her, and now he sat carefully apart as though embarrassed by his emotional moment. He had several canteens full of water, and Alice drank greedily from one as he thought about what she'd told him.

"So," he asked eventually, "the others are . . ."

"Alive," Alice said, wiping her mouth with the back of her hand. "But trapped. They're better off than I was. They don't *know* they're trapped, and they won't until we get them out again."

"I suppose that's something to be thankful for."

"What about Jen and the others here?"

Isaac looked at the ground. "After Ending came back and we knew things had gone badly, I started helping people escape into the books. A lot of them ended up on Flicker's world; Pyros said he would get the ice giants to help take care of them. That's where I left Jen. She hadn't woken up yet, but Magda said she was getting better. Emma went with her, too."

"What are *you* still doing here?"

"Some of the people who were taking shelter got scattered. I've been trying to track them down and get them through a friendly portal. And..." He paused, then looked up at her. "I hoped you might come back. I knew it was stupid, but if you were going to come back to *anywhere*, it was going to be here."

"Isaac..." Alice's heart flip-flopped like a landed fish, and she swallowed. "How did you know things had gone badly?"

"Ah." Isaac cleared his throat. "You'd better come out."

For a moment, nothing happened. Then, silently, a small gray cat padded out from beneath a dry, cracked log.

"Ashes!" Alice said.

"Look." The cat's voice was barely a whisper. "If you're going to tear me in half, just do it, all right? I won't stop you. I just—"

Alice, who had been bending over to scoop him up, froze. "Ashes, what are you *talking* about? Why would I ever do that?"

"I *helped* her, didn't I?" He hung his head miserably. "You heard what she said. I was only there because my presence was like an anchor that helped her get to the island. And it turns out I've been helping her prepare you for this all along. I was the one who brought you into this library in the first place!" His ears lay flat. "If you want to hate me, I can't blame you."

"Oh, Ashes," Alice said, for a moment struggling to find her voice.

"Ending brought him back here afterward. He told me some of what happened," Isaac said. "That you and the others were . . . gone. And he gave me enough warning that we were able to get most of the injured and children to safety."

"You didn't know what Ending was up to, Ashes. Not really," Alice said. She was certain of this. Ending would never have shared her plan with one of her children. "You just wanted to help me." She bent over, so they were face-to-face. "You have nothing to apologize for."

He blinked, yellow eyes on hers. Then, tentatively, he leaned forward, and his tiny pink tongue licked the end of Alice's nose. Alice laughed and snatched him up, feeling him start to purr even as he began complaining.

"You're filthy," he said. "Ugh. What have you been *doing*?"

"Running," Alice said. "And swimming, and sleeping in ditches."

"Well, you smell like it, anyway."

"I was going to ask," Alice said to Isaac, "how you were managing in the labyrinth without me."

Isaac nodded at Ashes. "He's been leading me, for the most part."

"Isn't that dangerous?" Alice looked down at Ashes. "If Ending finds out . . ."

"I thought you would have wanted me to," Ashes said grumpily. "Besides, Ending isn't paying as close attention as she used to. She and her siblings are already fighting over the boundaries, where the labyrinths are going to meet. They're dividing up the world between them."

"Ending's labyrinth is really growing?" Isaac said.

"It's already reached the city," Alice said grimly. "I passed through on my way here. Most of the people have run away. They think everyone's gone mad."

"I don't blame them," Isaac said. "How could they be prepared for this?"

"Can they do it?" Alice asked Ashes. "Cover the entire world?"

Ashes nodded, ears flattening again. "The more powerful they are, the bigger their labyrinth gets. The bigger it gets, the more powerful they become. It was only the Readers that kept them in check."

There was a long pause.

"So what do we do?" Isaac said, into the silence.

"We have to stop them," Alice said.

"I knew you would say that," Isaac said, resigned. "We *could* run away into a book, go live with Pyros—" He caught her eye. "No. I suppose not."

"I did this," Alice said. "I set them free. This is my responsibility."

"You couldn't have known—"

Alice cut him off. "It doesn't matter. It's not about guilt, it's about solutions. Like after I trapped Geryon. I don't know if it was the right thing to do, but I *do* know I need to clean up the mess I've made."

"All right," Isaac said. "How do we do it?"

"When I was in the void"—the thought still made her shiver—"I spoke to the prisoner. The creature that's imprisoned under the Great Binding. She calls herself the First. If we let her out, she says she can banish the labyrinthine forever."

Isaac's eyes narrowed. "You believe it? Something that both the Readers and the labyrinthine wanted locked up?"

"I believe it *because* they want it locked up. Ending waited for *centuries* to spring her trap, because she had to be sure of maintaining the Great Binding. The First is the one thing that really scares her. And . . ." She had a hard time putting the feeling into words, the strange familiarity, even kindness she felt from the First. "Yes. I believe it. And I certainly can't think of any other options."

"So we let the First out, and hope for the best."

Alice nodded. "Right. To do that we need to get back to the island at the center of the Grand Labyrinth, so I can get my hands on the binding."

"Get *back*?" Ashes said, and gave a yowling groan. "*Please* don't tell me we're going on another boat trip."

"It wouldn't work," Alice said. "With the labyrinthine against us, we'd never get through the Grand Labyrinth that way."

"It seems like we're stuck, then," Isaac said with a frown.

"I think there might be another way to get there. Call it a hunch," Alice said. "But there's only one person I can think of who might know what it is."

## CHAPTER TWENTY-ONE
# RETURN TO THE INFINITE PRISON

T HE SUN WAS SETTING, throwing long shadows from every rock and tree. The lawn looked like pictures Alice had seen from the Great War. The grass was ripped up in long furrows from the eye beams of the sunhawks, punctuated by broad craters where they'd focused their attention. Recent rain had churned the exposed earth to mud, which squelched wetly between her toes.

"Are you sure you want to come with us?" Alice said to Ashes, who had resumed his usual place on her shoulder. "If Ending catches you, she'll . . ." She trailed off, not sure what Ending would do, but certain it would not be pleasant.

"I'm sure," Ashes said. "You might need my help, after all."

"We will," Alice said.

The labyrinth had spread here, too, engulfing the house itself. The back door led into the kitchen, as usual, but one of the kitchen's doors led to the third floor, and another opened onto a city street Alice didn't recognize. She peeked into what had been the storeroom stairwell and found it led to an aisle of toppled bookshelves.

"Stay close," she told Isaac. "This is going to be a little tricky."

Once again, she wished she could simply grab hold of the fabric of the labyrinth and twist it to her will. But Ending, even if she was distracted, could feel that kind of interference. Instead, Alice gently ran her mental grip along the fabric, searching for a path that went where she wanted. She led the way out the door that went to the third floor, then along a corridor that shifted with every twist and turn they took. Isaac kept his hand on her arm, and she eventually slipped her hand into his, their interlaced fingers giving her a warm feeling.

"Wait," she said, pausing in front of a doorway.

"It's through here?" Isaac said.

"No, but it's my old room." The room on the other side

was, anyway, even if the doorway was one that had originally led to a broom closet. "There's some things I might need."

She opened the door. Her room was a mess, with daylight visible through a distant hole in the roof. Subsequent wind and rain had left Alice's familiar bed and desk damp and smelling of mold. Her nose wrinkled.

"You never showed me your room," Isaac said, stepping in behind her. "There's not much here."

"I never needed much," she said.

A few books on the desk were bloated with damp. She nudged open her trunk with one toe and rummaged. She had some spare clothes and underthings, and an old set of boots she could still just about squeeze into. There was an old pack, too, and she threw everything inside, along with some other spares—canteen, knife, a roll of linen bandages. *I wish I had time to make more acorns.*

"Are these your rabbits?" Isaac gave the stuffed animals on the windowsill a poke. They were waterlogged, too, and had slumped into a bedraggled, almost resentful posture. "They're . . . cute."

"They're from my old house," Alice said. She looked at them for a moment, then shook her head. "They were just about the only things they let me bring."

"Sorry." Isaac patted one of them on the head. It squelched. "Do you want to bring them along?"

Something about that made her smile, the way he made the offer even knowing it was patently ridiculous. "They can stay and keep watch," she said. "I don't think I'm ever coming back here."

They picked their way through some of the more damaged parts of the house, and eventually reached what had been Geryon's suite, where all signs of the sunhawks' attack stopped. The wards he'd set around these rooms would keep them standing, Alice was certain, even if the rest of the house had burned to the ground.

A short corridor inside led to several doors. One went to Geryon's bedroom, another to the study where she'd trapped him. At the end of the hall was the practice room, where she'd first learned to grasp the threads of magic and summon the Swarm. And off to one side was a heavy, solid-looking door that led to the vault.

Alice opened it carefully, preparing to step through into someplace else entirely, but the vault was just as she remembered it, a set of chests in a wide variety of sizes and shapes on shelves set into one wall. And a low table against the other wall where Alice herself had placed a pair of books, a heavy tome and a thin volume bound in red, which now contained the two halves of a spell. The larger book was labeled *The Infinite Prison*.

"Are you going to need my help?" Isaac said, looking nervously at the book.

Alice shook her head. "I don't think so. I've done this before. I can talk to him, but he can't do anything to me."

"What if he won't tell you anything?"

"He will. He knows I'm his only chance at ever getting out of there."

Isaac frowned. "Are you *planning* to let him out?"

Alice didn't reply. She looked at Ashes, who sighed and jumped down from her shoulder to the table. Then she took a deep breath and laid one finger on the book's cover.

Instantly, the world around her was replaced with velvety darkness. In front of her, and all around her as well, was Geryon—an army of him, mirrored endlessly into the infinite distance, all identical and moving as one. He looked just as she remembered, his clothes scuffed and shabby, his face all sagging jowls and fantastic sideburns. But his eyes had changed. They went wide at the sight of her, and there was a desperation in them she'd never seen before.

"Alice!" He stepped forward, and an infinity of reflections stepped with him. "You're back. Are you—"

He paused, and mastered himself with obvious effort. Alice thought about her time in the void, and felt a touch of sympathy. This place was not much better, as eternal prisons went, although at least Geryon still had a body. She was impressed at how quickly he reconstructed his haughty, imperious demeanor, with only a trace of fear visible at the edges.

"What are you doing here?" he said, affecting a bored tone. "Have you repented of your disastrous plan?"

"I need your help," Alice admitted.

"Of course you do, you foolish girl. You were in over your head the moment you arrived here." He extended a hand. "Let me out. We can discuss things."

Alice wondered if she'd ever been naive enough to take *that* at face value. "Tell me what I need to know, and I'll consider it."

"Don't be stupid. This whole mess can still be rectified, you know. What's happened out there? Have the others—"

"It's not your concern right now," Alice snapped. If she was being honest with herself, she didn't want to discuss the situation with Geryon in part because she wasn't eager to admit he'd been right. *I should never have trusted Ending.* "Are you going to answer my question or not?"

His mouth worked silently for a moment, sideburns twitching. Finally he said, gruffly, "What is this question?"

"I need to get to the island that holds the Great Binding," Alice said. "I can't go in through the Grand Labyrinth."

"The Readers' portal there requires a collective agreement to activate—"

"I can't get that either." Alice leaned forward. "But there must be another way. Why put the binding on a desolate island in the first place, unless it was because there was a portal nearby?" *I hope, I hope. There* has *to be a way.*

Geryon's eyes narrowed. "Why? What could you need there?"

"As I said, it's not your concern."

"It's my concern if it means you're going to destroy the world!" Geryon said. "The Great Binding is not to be trifled with. The prisoner—"

"Are you going to tell me," Alice grated, "or not? I don't have time to argue with you."

"Assuming I know something, why should I tell you?"

"If you tell me," Alice said, "I'll let you out."

There was a long pause. Geryon tried to keep his expression calm, but his hands were trembling.

"You're lying," he said.

"I'm not."

"Why should I trust you?"

Alice shrugged. "What have you got to lose?"

There was another moment of resistance, and then Geryon's shoulders slumped. He looked, suddenly, very old indeed.

"You're right," he said. "There's a natural portal. But it may not be of much use."

"Where is it?"

"In Greece." He closed his eyes. "In the hills north of Athens, there's a cave. Look for a mountain with three tall, narrow peaks, and head to the west of its base. You'll be able to sense it when you get close." He shook his head. "The humans once thought the cave led into the afterlife. After the Grand Labyrinth was constructed, we placed a guardian there to prevent anyone from wandering in."

"I feel like I know that story," Alice said. "And on the other side?"

"There's a natural portal to the island. But no one has used it in thousands of years. Things may be very different."

"I'll manage," Alice said. "Thank you."

"Let me out." He'd dropped the mask entirely now. When he opened his eyes, they were full of naked hunger. "Please. You don't know what it's like."

"I do," Alice said quietly. "And I will, I promise." She hesitated, and then added, "Eventually."

Geryon's scream of rage and pain, abruptly cut off, still echoed in her ears when she blinked and returned to the real world. She took a half step backward, and Isaac put a hand on her shoulder.

"Everything all right?" he said.

She nodded. "I have what we need."

"What did you tell Geryon?" Ashes said from the table.

"The truth," she said. "I'm going to let him out of there, as soon as I can figure out how to do it safely. No one should be imprisoned forever, even him."

"So where are we going next?" Isaac said.

"Greece, I think. But we have a stop to make first."

## CHAPTER TWENTY-TWO
# VELNEBS SOME WITH ENCOUNTER ODD AN

Can I say that I don't like this idea?" Isaac said as Alice walked to the other side of the vault. "My master's labyrinthine was never friendly to me, even before. If Decay finds us there—"

"I don't feel very good about it either," Ashes muttered. "Not that anyone listens to me."

"He'll probably try to kill us," Alice said. She picked a thin book off the shelf and brought it back to the table. "But we're going to need the Dragon's help when we get to the Grand Labyrinth."

"Neither of us has ever been able to summon the Dragon," Isaac said. Alice felt tension along the Dragon's thread they shared as Isaac's mental grip touched it. "It takes too much power."

"I may be able to do something about that," Alice said. "But I need the Dragon book to do it." She shook her head. "Hopefully Decay will be as busy as Ending is, feuding with the others. If not we'll . . . think of something."

"Just like we'll figure out a way to get halfway around the world?" Ashes said.

"One thing at a time," Alice said. "First we retrieve the Dragon."

"For a reason you won't explain," Isaac said.

"Not yet, anyway," Alice said. "Not until I'm sure that I'm right." At the sight of his expression, she smiled. "You were the one who stole the book in the first place."

"I suppose I was." He sighed. "All right. Let's go."

Isaac took her hand again, and Ashes jumped up on her shoulder. Alice flipped the book on the table in front of them, read the words as they swirled into comprehensibility, and found herself standing in utter darkness. She took hold of the devilfish thread and pulled it around her, so that her hands began to glow an eerie green, lighting the room.

They were in the "cave of front doors," with connections to every Reader's fortress. She and Isaac were standing in front of a large boulder, part of a circle of similar rocks that ran all the way around a large cavern. Each boulder bore either the name of a Reader or a scratched-out mess where one had been, long ago.

So much had started here. This was where she'd first met Dex, Ellen, and Garret, and coaxed the timid Soranna out of the darkness, before venturing into Esau's fortress together. Now Ellen and Garret were dead, and Soranna and Dex were locked away outside of space itself. *Isaac and I are the only ones left of that original group.* Alice took a deep breath. *I will get them out.*

"Stay here a moment," Alice said, depositing Ashes on the floor.

"What? Why?" Isaac said.

"So I can put on clean clothes," Alice said patiently. "I didn't want to risk changing in a place where Ending might turn up at any moment." Here, at least, they were far from any labyrinth.

"Oh." Isaac scratched his cheek and looked away, embarrassed. "I'll just wait here, then?"

"Just a minute."

Alice went around the back of the boulder, pulled off

the now-ragged things Nancy had given her, and changed back into the outfit she'd retrieved from her room. It was a little small, but it felt good to be wearing something clean again, even if she herself still needed a bath. *Swimming as the devilfish doesn't seem to clean me off much.* Her hair hung in stringy, uneven clumps, and she ran her fingers through it and sighed before tying it back out of the way.

"Okay," she said, coming back around the boulder. A hint of a blush was visible in Isaac's face, even by devilfish light, but she ignored it. "Have you used the portal to your master's fortress before? Do you know where it leads?"

He nodded. "It's a small room at the end of a long passage toward the main stairs."

"It *was*," Ashes pointed out, scrambling back up to Alice's shoulder. "The whole place will be covered in Decay's labyrinth by now."

"This is going to be tricky," Alice said. "You'll have to describe where we want to go, and I'll try to find it. Do you know where the Dragon's book is kept?"

"I think so. There's a room near Anaxomander's study where I was never allowed. I don't even know how to open the door."

"We'll—"

"Figure it out?" said Ashes and Isaac together, sharing a smile.

"Exactly," Alice said. "You're getting the hang of this."

The small, square book on the boulder labeled *Anaxomander* pulled them in, and Alice found herself blinking in sudden light. They were still underground, but the walls were shot through with veins of multifaceted crystal that glowed from within, a soft white light that refracted into a rainbow of colors. The air was frigid, and Alice's breath puffed into white clouds of steam.

"Brr," Ashes said, huddling closer to Alice's neck. "This is not a good place for cats."

"Where are we?" Alice said. "In the world, I mean."

"Greenland," Isaac said. "We're underneath a glacier. It's like a river of ice."

Alice reached out and touched one of the glowing crystal veins. It *was* ice, cold enough that she snatched her hand back at once. "No wonder it's freezing in here."

Isaac pulled his huge, battered coat around himself a little tighter. "You get used to it."

"This place looked a lot warmer when I saw you in the bath," Alice muttered.

"There's a hot spring," Isaac said, then frowned. "When were you watching me in the *bath*?"

"Never mind," Alice said. She could feel the labyrinth spreading through here, not yet as strong as Ending's but growing rapidly. "Lead the way. I'll tell you if I feel anything change."

Isaac nodded. He led them to a huge, gloomy spiral staircase, winding away in both directions around a central pillar made entirely of mirror-smooth ice.

"Down leads to the master—I mean, to Anaxomander's rooms, and mine," Isaac said quietly. "Up leads to the library."

"Down it is, then," Alice said, then froze. The fabric of the labyrinth gave an unmistakable vibration. "Something's coming!"

"Decay?" Isaac said. "Has he found us already?"

"I don't *think* so." Alice furrowed her brow. "It feels smaller, not like a labyrinthine. There's three of them, coming down the stairs."

"Velnebs," Isaac said. "Let me try to talk to them."

"Who?"

"Servants, sort of." He turned to face the stairs to the library, then looked over his shoulder. "They can be a little . . . odd."

"At this point, I don't even know what counts as odd," Alice said quietly.

The creature that came around the curve of the stairway was almost humanoid, with four limbs and a head in roughly the right places, but it gave the impression of having been assembled wrong. Arms and legs both ended in wide, grasping hands with long, slender fingers, which it used to cling to the ceiling and skitter along it with the agility of a spider. It wore a ragged linen tunic and belt, through which the arch of its spine was clearly visible, but its head appeared to be on backward, grinning down at Alice right side up even though the rest of the creature was upside down. And the grin was disturbing, too wide, showing big flat teeth like a row of tombstones between a ragged mustache and a bristly beard.

Two more of the things came behind the first, also clinging to the ceiling, another with a beard and one female with long, thin hair that hung in a wispy cloud around her upside-down face. When Isaac waved at them, they came to a halt, almost directly above him.

"Alarm door the of aware made was one this," the leader said. "Returning be would Isaac Master realize not did ones these."

Alice blinked.

"Did I miss something?" Ashes said.

"They can get a little mixed up when their heads are back to front," Isaac whispered. He raised his voice. "It's, uh, good to be home. Is everything all right?"

"Alarmed most been have ones these," the velneb said. "Wishes ones' these to responds longer no it and, library the beyond expanding is space-twist the."

"He says the labyrinth is expanding, and it's turned against them," Isaac said.

"You can understand them?" Alice said.

"You get used to it," he said again.

"Do you think they'll help us?" Alice said quietly. "If they think you're still working for Anaxomander . . ."

"I think so," Isaac said. He raised his voice. "Can you come down here, please? I'm getting a crick in my neck looking up at you."

"Isaac Master, course of," the velneb said.

Alice had been expecting it to creep down the wall, but it simply released its grip on the stone and dropped. Something strange happened to its limbs as it fell, the bones and joints shifting in a way that made her stomach turn, so that when it hit the ground with all four hands splayed, it was roughly the right way up. Its *head*, however, was still reversed, hair hanging in strings from its scalp and beard pointing at the ceiling.

"Um," Isaac said, and put his hands in front of his face, making a twisting motion.

"Apologies my." The velneb's head revolved slowly clockwise with a series of gristly *pops* and *cracks* that made Alice wince. When it had turned through a hundred and eighty degrees, it gave them its tombstone grin again. "Is that better, Master Isaac?"

"Much."

"Wish I could do that," Ashes said, in Alice's ear. "It'd be handy for grooming."

"Do you know when Master Anaxomander will be returning?" the velneb said. "He must be informed that the library has gone awry."

"I think he'll be back . . . soon," Isaac said, glancing sidelong at Alice. "But he's sent me to look into things while he's away. I've got some business to take care of downstairs, and then we're going to need a portal to . . ."

"Greece," Alice prompted. "Near Athens."

"Right," Isaac said. "Greece."

The female velneb looked down at them suspiciously. "Master our serve doesn't she and, Reader a she's," she said. "Another of apprentice the be must she."

"She's with me," Isaac said hastily. "We're on assignment together."

The velneb in front of them bowed its head. "These ones would be glad to serve, Master Isaac. This one knows just the book. But getting to it with the library in chaos may be difficult."

"Ashes," Alice hissed. "Can you go with them? Guide them through the labyrinth?"

"Me?" The cat sounded shocked.

"The sooner the book is ready, the sooner we can get out of here," she said.

"A fair point," Ashes said, staring at the velneb, who gazed back grinning and wide-eyed. "You won't take too long, will you?"

## CHAPTER TWENTY-THREE
# THE DOMAIN OF DECAY

AFTER REPEATED ASSURANCES THAT they'd be as quick as possible, Alice and Isaac left Ashes clinging to the back of a velneb as it scrambled back up the wall and spidered along the ceiling toward the library. Isaac and Alice went in the opposite direction, down the dished stone steps, into the lower levels of Anaxomander's fortress. The labyrinth was weaker here, but Alice kept a grip on the fabric nonetheless, watching for unexpected detours.

"You grew up here?" she said, looking around as they descended. It certainly seemed like a gloomy place, the washed-out glow from the ice making everything look as pale as milk.

He nodded. "It must seem strange to you, when you grew up with humans."

"Everything seems a little strange to me," Alice said.

"It wasn't bad, though," Isaac said. "I never thought it was, anyway, while Evander was here. Master—Anaxomander, I mean, took us out through the books pretty regularly, to other worlds and even to spend time among the humans. We might have to live in the real world one day, he told us."

His voice had a hitch in it, and she could understand why. Evander had been his foster brother, a fellow apprentice, until Anaxomander had cold-bloodedly traded him to Esau as though he were nothing but livestock. Isaac had later watched him die at the hands of Torment, Esau's rogue labyrinthine, after being driven mad.

"Sorry," Alice said quietly. "I didn't think."

"It's all right. I don't want to have to avoid talking about him, just because of what happened at the end." He took a deep breath. "That would be like losing him all over again." He looked around. "We used to race up and down this staircase, you know. Once I used the iceling to make a slide, but he said that was cheating."

He stopped in front of a carved stone arch larger and more impressive than the rest. It looked ancient, the blocks rounded and uneven, like something out of the ruins of a lost civilization.

"Anaxomander told me once that he never built this part of the fortress," Isaac said, looking up at it. "Something else lived here, something very old."

"Older than him?" Something about the space and the chill made Alice feel like whispering, as though she were in a church.

"Older than humans, he said." Isaac shuddered. "I used to dream about it coming back and finding us here."

Alice stepped forward, breath puffing ahead of her. Isaac followed.

"So what are we looking for?" she said.

Isaac pointed. "That door leads to his study. Just beyond it."

Alice didn't see anything that looked like a door, just a sheet of ice rippling from ceiling to floor, as though a waterfall had frozen in mid-torrent.

"You're sure?" Alice said. "It doesn't look like there's a way to open it."

"I've seen him coming out," Isaac said, putting his

hand against the cold surface. "It just sort of bends aside for him."

"Can you melt it with the salamander?"

"Probably, but it would take forever. Look how thick it is."

"What about the iceling? It lets you control ice, doesn't it?"

"Snow, really."

"Ice is just a lot of snow packed together really tight," Alice reasoned. "Give it a try."

Isaac nodded slowly. Alice felt power humming through him as he took hold of his thread, a kind of shiver in the air all around them. He glared at the wall of ice, eyes narrowed.

"Not working?" Alice said.

"There's . . . *something* there," Isaac said. "I can't quite get a grip on it."

"Maybe—"

"Give me a minute." He gritted his teeth. "I can do this. I've just got to—push a little—"

There was a noise like *whuff*, and everything went white. Alice took a step backward in panic, instinctively reaching for the Swarm thread. The air was full of stinging, blinding crystals. "Isaac? Are you okay?

Isaac was laughing, she realized. The whiteness was snow, which had blasted outward from the wall of ice to fill the corridor with a miniature blizzard, and was now cascading down all around them.

"Sorry," he said. "That caught me by surprise. I could feel it giving, and when I pushed, it just . . . went. Hang on."

He turned away and made a gesture with his hands, as though parting a curtain. The drifting snow leaped out of the way, swirling past them, revealing a doorway and a darkened room beyond.

"Perfect!" Alice said with a grin. "You're amazing."

Isaac flushed again, rubbing the back of his head. "I . . . uh . . . thanks."

He looked like he wanted to say something more, but Alice was already stepping into the room, calling the devil-fish's glow to her hands. It looked a bit like Geryon's vault, though instead of being locked in chests, some of the books were trapped in blocks of ice. Others were simply piled to one side, including a familiar volume bound in weathered snakeskin. Its cover read *The Dragon.*

"You were right!" she said, snatching it up and toppling the pile in her haste. A thrill went through her when she touched it, the Dragon thread in her mind vibrating in sympathy. "Thank you, Isaac. I know I haven't explained everything."

"I trust you, Alice," he said from the doorway. "You've always been right so far."

A dry hiss of a voice spoke up from behind him.

"That," it said, "remains to be seen."

Isaac spun around, but something long and pitch-black was already crawling across him. Alice remembered the centipede in the Great Labyrinth, each glossy black segment of its body bigger than her head, a pair of pincers at one end that would easily have fit around her waist. Its legs moved in eerie unison, ripples of motion passing down the length of its body, making soft *click-click-click* sounds. It wound its way up Isaac's leg and across his chest, huge head pausing at his throat, while the rest of its length trailed off into the corridor. Isaac had gone very still.

"If I bite this boy, Miss Creighton, he will die, very quickly and in a great deal of pain." A pair of long fangs hovered above Isaac's neck. "Believe me, the results are not pleasant to look on. If you value his life, I would not do anything rash."

Alice realized she'd raised her hands and grabbed her

threads, automatically. She met Isaac's gaze, and found him wide-eyed, but not panicked. *That's something.* She lowered her hands and let out a breath.

"Decay, is it?" she said.

"Indeed." The centipede shifted its body with a chorus of clicks. "I must admit I was skeptical of this project, but you have proven to be everything Ending claimed you would be."

"Let him go," Alice said. "I'm the one you want."

"I think he will be useful to ensure your good behavior. Clearly Ending's prison was not sufficient, but it's not a mistake we plan to make again." Decay shifted again. "She sends her regards, by the way. She informed me that she'd belatedly discovered the two of you passed through her domain, and that you might be paying me a visit."

"You sound almost like you trust her." Alice forced a smirk. "I would have thought you'd know better after so long."

"Very clever, Miss Creighton. Divide and conquer, is it? But we know that game better than anyone." Decay's multifaceted eyes shone with dozens of pinprick glows in the light of Alice's hands. "The labyrinthine are *finished* working with the Readers."

"You might be," Alice said. "There are others—"

"This is tiresome. Come along, or the boy will suffer."

"All right!" Alice held up her hands. "You can't begrudge me the attempt. It's *just* like the time I had to fight that giant wasp."

To Decay, this probably made no sense. To Isaac, she hoped, it would be a message. *Just like when we fought the giant wasps.* At which time she'd hurled him high into the air, after he'd transformed into . . .

She saw from his eyes that he'd got it. She felt the power flow, and then his body was dissolving, flesh disintegrating into drifting snow as he transformed into the iceling.

Decay was fast, but not fast enough. His fangs clamped down harmlessly into the soft snow of Isaac's new body, smoky, greenish poison spurting uselessly. At the same time, Alice charged, pulling on Spike's thread for strength. Her punch was unscientific but delivered with enthusiasm, slamming the black centipede across the corridor.

"Go, Isaac!" she shouted. "Back to the library!"

"But—"

"I'm right behind you!"

Isaac whirled down the corridor like the snow devil he currently was. Before Alice could follow, Decay had recovered, his coiled body filling the doorway. She went at him again, one fist raised, the Dragon book tucked under her arm. This time, he dodged her blow, and darted forward to wrap himself around her. The sensation of his legs pricking all over her skin made her want to scream. But she'd expected this, too—as he coiled tighter, she wrapped herself in the Swarm thread, pulling on it until her body fell apart into a pile of black, furry swarmers. These bounced and rolled all over the corridor, slipping through Decay's writhing grip as he crashed unceremoniously to the ground. As he thrashed to right himself, Alice got moving, tiny legs a blur as she sped down the corridor.

## Chapter Twenty-four
# HUNTED

THE SWARMERS FLOWED TOGETHER as soon as they passed through the ancient doorway, turning back into a girl with a book under her arm. Isaac was already coalescing out of the storm of snow he'd become. She caught him by the arm, still running, stray flakes landing all around her.

"Are you okay—" he began.

"Later!" she panted. "Run!"

They ran, sticking tight to the central, icy pillar as they rounded the spiral staircase. Isaac was puffing beside her, already short on breath, and she was fighting a stitch in her side. She could call on Spike for strength, but that wouldn't make it any easier to breathe. The stairs were steep, like running up the side of a mountain.

A clattering, clicking sound came from below them, getting louder quickly. Alice felt a tug at the fabric of the labyrinth, weak as it was here. She fought back, pressing down, making it impossible for Decay to shift himself ahead of them. There was a hiss of rage, and the clatter redoubled.

"We're . . . not . . . going to make it," Isaac gasped out.

"I've got . . . an idea," Alice said. "Get on my back!"

"What?"

Keeping her hold on the labyrinth while manipulating her threads wasn't easy, but she'd had a lot of practice recently splitting her attention. She grabbed Spike's thread, not just for strength but wrapping it around herself as tight as it would go, until she felt her body start to change. She fell to all fours as her limbs thickened, her body expanding into the dinosaur's heavy-boned frame. Spike's endurance matched his strength, and he could run for days, although his plate-like feet were not a perfect match for the stairs.

"Back. Right!" Isaac grabbed hold of a spiny plate and vaulted aboard. As Spike, Alice barely felt his weight.

She redoubled her speed, charging up the steps as fast

as she dared. The biggest problem was turning—Spike didn't corner well at the best of times, and keeping a tight spiral as she ascended was harder than it looked.

"He's still coming!" Isaac shouted, looking behind them. "Getting closer! And, um, I think he's getting *bigger,* too."

Alice risked a glance as they turned. What had been an enormous centipede was now truly monstrous, the size of a charging bull, its mandibles extending in front like lances. It ascended the steps like the slope wasn't even there, legs rising and falling with swift, unerring precision. Fangs the size of butcher knives still dripped greenish poison.

"We need you alive, Miss Creighton," Decay's voice hissed, still cold and collected. "But don't think that doesn't mean I can't hurt you. I am not the only poisonous creature under the ice. You will scream, I promise you that."

"Alice!" Isaac shouted. "We have to go faster!"

Alice tried to shout back, but all her dinosaur body could manage was a screeching honk. She was having increasing difficulty keeping Decay from twisting the labyrinth around them. This was his home ground, and her powers were secondhand—she was amazed she'd

matched him for this long. The earth underfoot rumbled as they passed, and she screech-honked again. *Do something!*

As he had below, Isaac seemed to catch her meaning at once. She felt his power gathering again, stronger than before, and she heard him gasp with the pain of pulling so much at once. Decay, monstrously oversized, came closer and closer, his mandibles only feet from Alice's hindquarters. In desperation, she prepared to turn and fight—*if I can at least knock him backward*—

Something rumbled overhead, and there was an explosion of snow from the ceiling. It was followed by another, then another, the veins of ice that ran through the rock blasting down into powder as they passed. Snow was suddenly everywhere, falling around Alice in gentle flakes, coating Decay's armor plates a dusty gray. The centipede was still coming, and Alice screech-honked one more time. Do something *better!*

The first rock hit the ground behind them with a clatter.

The ancient rock was honeycombed and glued together with ice. As Isaac blew that ice into snow, the stones began to shift, and then to tumble. Alice found some last reserve of strength, and surged away from Decay just as a jagged boulder the size of a bus dropped from the stairway onto the centipede. More rocks followed, large and small, a thunderous cacophony that drowned out all other sound and filled the stairway behind her with a flying mix of dust and snow. Decay screeched, his still-free head whipping back and forth, but he was pinned in place, and the rocks were still coming down. Alice lost sight of him as the gray-white cloud billowed upward.

She felt Isaac slump with exhaustion. The door to the library was coming up, just ahead—they couldn't have run much farther in any case. Alice slowed to a halt, skidding on steps slippery with flying snow, and hastily shifted back to a girl. She caught Isaac under the arms before he could collapse. His eyes were open, but he was panting for breath, and his legs felt unsteady.

"That was brilliant!" she said, shouting over the continuing noise of falling stone.

"I remembered . . . what we did . . . against the Dragon," Isaac said. "Ice . . . and rocks. Here we already had the ice." He swallowed hard. "Probably too much to hope that it killed him."

"He's still there." Alice could feel Decay, momentarily stunned and trapped, but still touching the fabric of the labyrinth. "Can you walk? We need to get out of here."

He nodded, and she released him. Isaac took a tentative step, wobbling like a baby deer, and then another with more strength behind it. Alice grabbed the fabric of the labyrinth, twisting a passage from *here* to *there* that would lead right to Ashes. The air beyond the doorway went hazy and shimmering.

*You won't escape.* Decay's voice rang in her mind, through the fabric. She felt his grip slam against hers, strength against strength, blocking her way. *Not that way. This is my domain. Whatever powers you've stolen, you are still merely a Reader. You are no match for one of us.*

"Isaac." Alice stopped walking. Isaac halted, a few steps ahead, and looked back.

"Are you all right?" he asked.

She didn't feel all right. Her teeth were clenched and her eyes were closed, all her mental energy focused on the passage. Even speaking was an effort.

"Take my hand," she said. "When I say, pull me through the doorway."

"Why—" He stopped, and there was a moment of silence. She felt his hand against hers. "All right. Say the word."

*You are nothing!* Decay raged. *Your time—the time of all the Readers—is past. This is our time, and our labyrinths will cover the world. You are—*

*I know what I am,* Alice told him.

She bore down on the fabric, as hard as she could. It was like tug-of-war, or arm-wrestling, a contest of raw power without finesse. She'd never tried this before, against Torment or Ending or any of the others, never believed that her borrowed strength could be a match for one of the demons of the labyrinth. But inch by inch, she forced Decay out of her path, her whole body quivering with the effort.

*Not possible,* he said. *This is not possible!*

She felt the connection snap into place. "Now, Isaac!"

Isaac pulled her to the doorway. Her legs moved, automatically, following him in a stumbling run. All her attention was on the other world, the world of twisted space, fighting now to press back Decay's increasingly desperate assault. She felt the fabric shift around her as they passed through.

"I was beginning to wonder what happened to you," Ashes said.

Alice let go of the fabric and staggered, leaning heavily on Isaac's grip. He squeezed her hand tight.

"Alice?" the cat said.

She opened her eyes.

They stood in a hexagonal room carved from stone, its

walls shaped into rough shelves, packed with disorderly stacks of books. Doorways led to identical hexagons with more doorways, stretching on and on. *It's a beehive!*

A half-dozen velnebs clung to the shelves, or hung upside down from the craggy ceiling with their weird heads reversed. Ashes was in the center of the room, next to a large green book.

"I'm okay," Alice said. "But we have to get out of here. Decay is coming."

"Decay?" one of the velnebs said. "But he serves the master. Why would he attack you?"

"He's rebelled," Isaac said quickly. "Turned against our master. We're going to escape until he gets back. You all should do the same, if you can."

Alice hadn't thought about that. She could easily imagine Decay turning his fury on the velnebs.

"Rebelled!" The word went around the room. "Rebelled!"

"Do you have somewhere you can hide?"

The nearest velneb nodded. One of the ones on the ceiling said, "Creatures-book the of some by favors owed are ones these. Returns master the until worlds their in us shelter will they."

"Good," Isaac said. "Go as soon as you can."

Alice could feel Decay's grip, scrabbling through the fabric. "Come on." She reached for Ashes, and he scrambled up to her shoulder. Isaac still had her other hand.

"Did you get the Dragon?" the cat said.

Alice patted the book under her arm. "I did. That's the right portal?"

"If you trust these things." Ashes glanced suspiciously at the upside-down creatures.

Alice reached for the green volume next to Ashes, then looked up at the velnebs.

"Thank you for your help."

"Welcome you're," they chorused.

*We will find you,* Decay whispered in the back of her mind. *And when we do—*

Alice opened the book, and read, "She found herself on a rocky hilltop, under a darkening sky . . ."

## CHAPTER TWENTY-FIVE
# THE WORLD COME UNDONE

SHE FOUND HERSELF ON a rocky hilltop, under a darkening sky. The green book sat atop a short stone pillar.

"Are we in the right place?" Ashes said from her shoulder. "Those velnebs didn't make much sense half the time."

"I have no idea," Alice said. She looked over her shoulder. The hills rose into mountains behind her, she could tell that much by their outlines against the sky, but she couldn't see enough to tell if any of them had three narrow peaks. "I think we need to wait for daylight."

"That sounds good to me," Isaac said. "I don't think I could walk another step."

"Do you think you could manage a few more?" Alice said. "I'd like to get away from the portal-book and find some shelter." She didn't think anyone could follow them here, but she was far from certain about the extent of the labyrinthine's powers.

Isaac gave a weary nod. "While we still have some light, then."

They walked down the slope of the hill and across the next valley. A little way on, Alice saw a stand of trees, ragged little things all huddled together as if for warmth. A tug on the tree-sprite's thread made them bend out of the way, creating a cozy pocket for the three of them. A further touch, and a few dead, dry branches dropped free, while live branches bowed toward them bearing heavy, juicy fruits.

"That comes in handy," Isaac murmured. He gathered the deadwood, and lit it with a spark from his salamander. It soon grew into a cheery little fire, the warmth dispelling the bone-deep cold of the ice caverns.

"More often than you'd think," Alice agreed. She munched on one of the fruits. "I need to figure out how to do something besides not-quite-apples, though. I've tried experimenting, but it always comes out disgusting."

"Apples are fine with me."

Isaac took a bite of his own, and leaned back. There was just enough room for the three of them in the little shelter, and when she lay back Isaac's shoulder pressed against hers. He felt warm, even through his coat. They were silent for a while, finishing the apples and throwing the cores into the fire. Ashes snuggled up against Alice's other side, and began a low purr.

"Can I ask you something?" Alice said.

"What is it?" Isaac shifted against her.

"Do you ever think about how things could have been different?" Alice said. "If you'd done things differently?"

"Sometimes," he said. "But it's an easy way to drive yourself mad."

"I wanted to find out what happened to my father," Alice said. "I wanted revenge. And that's brought us . . . all this."

"You can't blame yourself," Isaac said. "You didn't know."

"Maybe I should have." Alice sighed. "I think back and try to figure out where I could have taken a different path."

"Some of those paths might have ended up with you dead," Isaac said. "Or still working for Geryon, not knowing what he did to you. You might never have met me, or we might have been enemies."

Something hurt in Alice's chest, a sweet, sharp pain. She swallowed.

"I'm glad I met you," she said, very quietly.

Isaac pressed himself a little closer. Alice felt her heart thumping. There was so much she wanted to say, a lifetime's worth. Except—

She cleared her throat after a long silence.

"There's something I should tell you," Alice said. "Something I've figured out. I hope . . . I mean, I'm not sure . . ." She swallowed. "Isaac?"

More silence. Then a soft snore.

"He wore himself out," Ashes said. "What did you do to him?"

"He saved me, I saved him," Alice said. "The usual, really. What else are friends for?"

"If you ask me," the cat said, "friends ought to keep you out of situations where you need saving."

"That too." *But all I ever do is drag everyone in after me.* "Do *you* ever have any regrets?"

"Of course not." Ashes yawned. "I'm a cat."

Alice smiled softly, settled back between her friends, and closed her eyes.

In the morning, after they'd eaten a hasty breakfast of more almost-apples, Alice climbed to the top of the hill to get a good look at the mountains. She was immensely relieved to see that there was indeed one with three tall, narrow peaks, just as Geryon had described.

They started walking in that direction, Alice leading the way. She couldn't travel as the Swarm—it was too easy to lose track of landmarks from three inches off the ground—and in any event Isaac wouldn't have been able to keep up. So they skirted the edges of the hills and fought through clumps of tiresome nettles, until about midday when she spotted a dirt road going in roughly the right direction. After that, they made much better progress.

In the mid-afternoon, they crested a small rise, and Alice stopped short. There was a car in the road ahead, an old one, the body speckled with rust. A man sat on the hood, while a child played in the weeds at the side of the road. Alice looked back at Isaac.

"What's wrong?" he said.

"There's someone there." They hadn't seen any people since they'd arrived, aside from lights in the distance. Alice didn't know the local geography at all, but she'd gotten the impression they were well back in the hinter-lands. "They look like they're waiting for something."

"They could be taking a rest," Isaac said, frowning.

"Or it could be a trap," Ashes said. "Plenty of creatures can look human from a distance."

"How many of them have cars?" Alice said. She shook her head. "Come on. Isaac, if they're human and they're going to be trouble, just put them to sleep."

"Humans," Ashes muttered darkly.

The man was dressed in a thin coat, a vest, and a gray slouch hat, and he had a rifle slung over his shoulder. The child was a little girl, five or six, in a blue dress that had seen better days. The man saw them coming, but evidently he didn't think they were a threat, because he made no move for his weapon.

"Hello!" he said, when they came closer. "Can you understand me? You look like foreigners."

Alice knew he couldn't be speaking English, but she understood him perfectly. For the first time this felt odd to her. She'd grown used to universal comprehension among all manner of magical creatures, from different worlds and cultures, but she hadn't had much occasion to speak to foreign *humans*. If she concentrated, she could tell that the man was speaking another language—Greek, she assumed—but the words arrived in her mind with the same effortless comprehension as her native language.

"I understand," she said, and as he nodded she wondered what she sounded like to him. *Do I have an accent?* "Are you all right?"

"The car needs oil." He thumped the hood. "Or so my son says. He's walking to the nearest village to get some." His eyes narrowed. "You haven't come from the city, have you?"

Alice shook her head cautiously. The man looked her up and down, and sighed. He had snow-white hair poking out from around his cap, and his face was as wrinkled and tanned as old leather.

"It's a hard road," he said, "with no shoes."

Alice had almost forgotten she'd lost her boots again. She shrugged. "I'm used to it."

The old man nodded. He gestured to the little girl, who had left off playing in the dirt with a stick and half hidden herself behind a nearby tree, staring at the strangers suspiciously. "You can come out, Ann. They're only kids. And look, they've got a cat."

The girl remained where she was. Alice wondered what she'd do if they knew that she and Isaac were a lot more dangerous than anyone else he was likely to meet on the road.

"What are you doing out here?" Isaac said.

"Running away," the old man said simply. "Things have gotten bad, in the city."

"Bad how?" Alice asked, though she wasn't sure she wanted to know the answer. "We left quite a while ago."

"At first they said everyone was going crazy. The soldiers and the police tried to establish order, but . . ." He shook his head. "Strange things. If you haven't been there, you'll think I'm crazy, too."

"I won't," Alice said.

"The city was *changing*. Out of the corner of your eye, when you weren't quite looking at it. The ruins, you know? The tourists come to see them. But they started to spread, like they were taking over. Modern buildings turning into old, broken walls, old columns, white statues. Like the ghost of a city, coming back. And there were things hiding out there. I could hear them."

Alice's throat felt thick. This was the same thing that was happening all over the world. *The labyrinths will spread,* Decay had told her. *Your time is over.* He'd meant Readers, but it applied to humanity as well.

"I have seen bad times," the old man said, and she believed it. Every year of them was graven on his face. "Wars, disease, famine. My second son, her father"—he nodded at the child—"died in the Great War. Her mother in the Spanish Influenza epidemic. But even that was something I could understand. This is like a bad dream come to life."

"Where will you go?" she said.

"My brother has a house in the country. I hope to find him there." He grimaced, then shook his head. "I have food, for the three of us, but it is barely enough. I can spare perhaps a little bread—"

"What?" Alice blinked, aware that neither she nor Isaac was carrying obvious supplies. "No! No, it's fine. We have a camp up ahead. Plenty of food."

The old man was silent for a moment. Alice got the sense that he knew she was lying about something, but decided not to press the point.

"If we keep on this road," she said, "can we get close to that mountain?" She pointed to their objective.

The man looked, then nodded. "But there is nothing there. Just woods and rocks. And . . ." He hesitated. "It is a bad place. Superstition, I would have said a month ago. No such thing as monsters. Now, though . . . best to stay away."

"We have friends we need to meet," Alice improvised. "But thank you. And thank you for offering food."

He nodded. "If you change your mind, there would be room for you at my brother's house."

"Thank you." Alice caught Isaac's eye. "We'd better move on while it's still light."

"You wouldn't catch a cat offering up his last mouse when he was starving," Ashes muttered as they passed on.

"Shh," Alice said, but a bit too late. She could hear a piping voice behind them.

"Her cat talked, Grandpa! It talked—"

She and Isaac walked a little faster, until they were out of sight. Alice glared at Ashes, who licked his fur nonchalantly.

"Anyway," she said, "it's a human thing. You probably wouldn't understand."

"He seemed so hopeless," Isaac said.

"They have it worse than we do," Alice said. "At least we know what we're up against. They're just like . . . ants, after somebody's turned the ant farm upside down." She hated the metaphor at once—describing humans as ants was something Geryon would have done. "The world has changed and they don't even know why."

Isaac was silent for a while. "You're right," he said eventually. "That is worse."

## CHAPTER TWENTY-SIX
# THE MOUTH OF HADES

As they approached, Alice could feel the magic protecting the portal, faint but distinct in the non-magical landscape, like a single musical note in a silent room. She followed the feeling, and eventually, they found themselves walking down a narrow gully, paralleling a small, ice-cold stream. Up ahead, the water disappeared into a cluster of enormous boulders.

"That must be the cave," Alice said.

"You said there was a ward protecting it," Isaac said, looking around. "I feel something, but . . ."

"I think that's just to keep normal humans away. It makes them want to ignore this place." She could feel the shape of the spell in the air. "Geryon said there was a guardian, though."

"There's always a guardian," Ashes said. "Readers love nothing more than sticking a horrible monster in front of anything someone else might want."

"I'll keep an eye out for any horrible monsters," Alice said.

Amid the jumble of rocks, there was a narrow passage. They had to squeeze through, one at a time, and the stream water splashed icy cold over Alice's bare feet. Inside, the passage widened into a corridor, and she stamped to get her blood flowing as Isaac wriggled through. She pulled on the devilfish thread, and her hands began to glow, pushing back the dark.

There was more magic in the air here, Alice could feel it. Written somewhere inside were wards to keep the tunnel standing, free of cave-ins and erosion. This place was *old*, like the arch outside Anaxomander's study. From what Geryon had said, it had been here at least since the Readers struck their bargain with the labyrinthine, and probably longer than that. *Thousands of years.*

"There's something on the walls," Isaac said.

Alice raised her hand, and saw that he was right. Some-one had painted figures there, in crude, bold colors, washed out in the devilfish's weird green light. There was a line of them, marching into a cave and down a passage into a swirl of darkness.

"Charming," Ashes said. "Can we move on? I've had enough of caves to last a lifetime."

There was only one path. It sloped gently downward, and Alice felt like it was getting warmer with each step. Stalactites hung from the ceiling, like long fangs, almost brushing her shoulders.

Finally, there was a light ahead, an orange glow like a distant bonfire. It got brighter as they went, so Alice let the devilfish's glow fade. The corridor widened out, becoming a large, round space, with the source of the light at one end.

A wild portal. It looked like a curtain in the air, translucent and constantly in motion. Now and then it would flatten out, offering a glimpse into roaring fire or pitch darkness.

In front of the portal, a huge shape was huddled in on itself. It stirred, and a dog's head rose up. Dark narrow eyes turned toward her. It was big, she realized, bigger even than the giant wolf Torment.

"I think we've found the guardian," Isaac said.

Two more heads rose up, their gazes following the

first. The three necks came together, into a single broad-shouldered body.

Ashes arched his back, hissing, then took off in a gray streak.

"I'd say we have," Alice said.

The three-headed dog leaped to its feet, and the cavern suddenly rang with its enormous, earth-shattering barks. Then the barks abruptly cut off, and the huge thing was advancing toward them. Each head growled, three deep rumbles that combined into a weird tri-tone sound, like an airplane droning overhead. Alice looked at Isaac and shouted, "The Siren! Use the Siren!"

"It's too big—" he started.

"Just do it!"

Isaac nodded, and the ghostly figure of the Siren appeared in front of him, a female figure dressed in long, flowing robes and almost completely transparent. She spread her arms and began to sing as Alice covered her ears, and the effect was immediate. All three heads snapped around, staring at the ethereal creature. The three muzzles began to droop, eyes closing.

"It's working," Isaac said, his voice still tinny. "How did you know?"

"The legend," Alice said. When he looked back at her blankly, she recalled he probably hadn't studied Greek mythology. "A hero named Orpheus goes down into the underworld, and he has to get past a three-headed dog. He puts it to sleep with music. I thought—"

The left head was sound asleep, eyes closed. But the center one suddenly perked up, following the sound of Alice's voice, and began growling again. The right head followed suit.

"That's not good," Isaac said.

"Keep the Siren singing," Alice said. "I think it's working. I'll distract them."

Before he could reply, she ran forward. The huge dog crouched, working itself into a pounce, and her sudden movement caught it off guard. Alice pulled on the Swarm thread and Spike's strength and toughness, and ran straight at the enormous thing. Its jaws opened wide, and she was hit with a blast of warm breath and the smell of rotting meat. She almost choked, and jumped sideways as the huge jaws came down, big enough that it could have swallowed her whole.

"Alice!" Isaac shouted.

"I'm fine!" She dodged to the left, and gave the dog a solid whack on the shin to make sure she held its interest.

The right head was looking seriously drowsy, though the center was still wide-awake. "Keep on it!" She scrambled underneath the beast, and it tried clumsily to follow her.

"Come on, ugly!" Alice said, grinning. *Can't catch me, can you?* She ran straight at it, ducking past its legs and passing directly underneath it again. The dog might not be fast enough to get its jaws around her, but it was smarter than she'd given it credit for, and when she went underneath it, it simply sat down, flopping to the ground with a great *whuff.* Alice was flattened, buried in rolls of warm, hairy skin.

Alice scrambled sideways on her back, pushing folds of skin out of the way, trying to get clear of the dog's bulk. She got her head and arms out from underneath it and took a desperate breath. It had half rolled onto its side now, twisting to get at her. The one head that wasn't asleep came in for a bite, with Alice's legs still trapped. Two huge canine teeth, each as long as a sword, came together almost delicately to pin Alice between them. She put a hand on each one and pushed, throwing all of Spike's strength into keeping the jaws open. All she could see was the inside of the dog's mouth, enormous, yellowing teeth and a flat, red tongue almost as big as she was. A wave of slobber drenched her, and her arms began to tremble with the effort of holding firm.

All at once, the pressure loosened. The dog's enormous head rolled to one side, away from Alice, and she let go of its teeth. Its eyes, heavy-lidded, stared at her for a moment, and then it gave a long canine sigh and fell asleep.

It took Alice a few minutes to get herself out from under the thing, while huge doggy snores echoed around the cavern. Isaac hurried over, Ashes pacing at his heels. When Isaac saw she was all right, he smiled a little teasingly.

"Did the old story say anything about Orpheus getting sat on?" he said.

"Or drooled on?" Ashes said, and shuddered.

Alice rolled her eyes. "Oh, hush. It worked, didn't it?"

Ashes eyed her drool-soaked clothes. "A fate worse than death."

## CHAPTER TWENTY-SEVEN
# THE BONEYARD

I WAS READY TO SPRING into action, of course," Ashes said as they walked over to the portal. "A cat can take on a dog any day, even if it does have three heads."

"Come on," Isaac said. "That thing could have used you for a toothpick."

"It's not about size." The cat sniffed. "It's about strength of mind. Dogs fundamentally don't have it."

"You can fight the next giant dog we find, then," Alice said.

"On second thought," Ashes said, "that sort of thing is probably beneath me."

They stood in front of the wild portal, Ashes once again on Alice's shoulder. Isaac looked nervous.

"I've used one of these before," Alice assured him. "You just walk through it."

"The other side doesn't look very pleasant."

"Geryon did say people used to think it was the underworld," Alice admitted.

"And how are we supposed to find the portal back? It could be miles away, right?"

"My theory is that we'll ask someone," Alice said. "That's what I did when I was looking for the Palace of Glass."

"What if there's no one to ask?" Isaac said.

"Then we'll—"

"Figure something out," Ashes supplied. "Right? Let's go, before our canine friend wakes up."

Alice nodded. She took hold of Isaac's hand again, and they stepped forward. As before, the passage had some of the same feeling of using a portal-book, but instead of being orderly and organized, the power rose and fell around them like a whirlwind. It passed by in an instant, and they were standing on gray, powdery sand.

Ahead of them, stretching as far as the eye could see, was a landscape out of a nightmare. Huge fires burned everywhere, flames the size of buildings leaping up from cracks in the ground and licking into the sky. Above was darkness, no sun or even any stars, so the only light came from the shifting, uneven glow of the fires. Spread across the ashen ground were piles of gigantic bones. Ribs and skulls, leg-bones and vertebrae. The skulls were larger than cars, the rib cages as big as houses. They were all black, streaked with a rusty red at the edges.

Things were moving among the bones, small groups of man-sized creatures. At first Alice had a hard time making them out—they moved strangely, and the flames were often visible *through* them. After a moment, she realized that this was because they were skeletons, their bones the same black as the bones littering the ground, but stuck together in roughly humanoid shapes. What they were doing was less clear. It looked almost like they were *dancing,* a mad, skeletal caper across the blasted landscape in groups of a dozen or more, moving without apparent plan or purpose but somehow staying together.

Ashes cleared his throat.

"Well," he said. "Finding the portal back should be easy. We'll just ask the nearest *dancing skeleton,* shall we?"

For the moment, they decided to find a place to rest.

They picked their way out among the bones, giving a

wide berth to the chasms that spat fire and the nearest bands of skeletons. More cliffs of black rock dotted the landscape, and Alice headed for a sheltered nook where they were unlikely to be seen.

As they walked, she discovered that the rusty red spots on the bones were, in fact, rust. Touching the giant remains revealed that they were made of iron, or something like it, although Alice had no idea if that meant they were actually parts to some enormous machine or left over from a monstrous creature with a metal skeleton. *Or, for that matter, if they were ever covered in flesh at all. The dancing skeletons seem to manage without.* She remembered Flicker's world, with its wheeling sky and no sun, and reminded herself not to make assumptions.

They had to duck under some of the iron bones to reach the cliff face, but with a tangle of broken ribs and half a jawbone shielding them from view, Alice felt reasonably secure. She sat down heavily on the gray sand, and Isaac slumped against the rock with a sigh. Ashes looked dubiously at the ground, then carefully jumped from Alice's shoulder to her lap and settled down.

"It's been a long day," she said.

"You can say that again," Ashes said.

"You didn't even walk anywhere!" Isaac said to the cat. "I wish *I* had somebody I could ride on."

Alice grinned, and scratched Ashes behind the ears. He rolled over and rubbed his head against her knee. Her eyes drifted closed.

"Alice?" Isaac said.

"Hmm?"

"What are you going to do if we win? If this First banishes the labyrinthine, and we get the others out. What then?"

Alice kept her eyes closed. She felt a pain in her chest, just behind her breastbone, and for a moment it was hard to breathe. She did her best to keep it out of her voice.

"I haven't really thought about it," she said. "Have you?"

"A little. The world will be changed, won't it? The magical world, and the human world."

"It will. And they're both the same world, especially now. There's no pretending otherwise anymore."

"I think people are going to need help," he said. "Humans and magical creatures are going to have to work together, like we did at Geryon's house."

She nodded. "That's going to be hard for both sides."

"We can help them, though. We might be the only ones who can." He sounded a little excited by the prospect. "You and I—and the others—we'll have to make sure they talk to each other instead of fighting."

*He's changed.* When Isaac had first come to Geryon's estate, breaking in to steal the Dragon book, he hadn't cared much about anything except himself and his master's orders. *But that's not quite right, either.* He'd worked with her when they'd been trapped in the Dragon's book. And he'd helped her in Esau's fortress. *He's always had a good heart. He just needed to learn to open it.*

"Yes," she said, forcing a smile despite the lump in her throat. "I think that's exactly what we should do."


"Have there always been paintings on that wall?" Isaac said.

Alice, who'd managed to doze off, blinked and sat up. Ashes was sound asleep in her lap. She followed Isaac's pointing finger, and in the rising and falling light of the flames, she saw that the black cliff behind them had a crude drawing scrawled across it in bright ochre pigment—upside-down V shapes that Alice assumed were supposed to be mountains and a standing woman with long, straight hair and a dress that hung to the ground.

She was barely more than a stick figure, but the artist had captured astonishing detail in only a few lines. The face was particularly expressive. In the slightest twist of paint, the artist had captured a raised eyebrow and a faintly mocking smile.

"I don't think so," she said, frowning. "We were tired when we got here, but I think we'd have noticed *that*. How did it get there?"

"I'm not sure," Isaac said. "It was there when I turned around."

"She looks like she's watching us," Alice said bemusedly.

"I hope not," Isaac said. "She doesn't look very friendly."

Something moved on the surface of the rock. As Alice watched, words scrawled themselves across the stone, stroke by stroke, as though an unseen painter were hard at work. The characters were unfamiliar, but as usual the meaning came through. It said:

"You don't look so good yourself."

"Um," Isaac said, taking a step away from the wall. "Okay. Alice?"

The figure was changing, too, very slightly. She uncrossed her arms, and the smile on her face widened. She didn't move smoothly, but rather in small jerks, as though she were being rapidly erased and redrawn several times a second. It looked a bit like the stutter of a malfunctioning film projector.

Alice got to her feet, tipping Ashes to the ground with a sleepy yowl of protest. She turned to face the rock and said, "Can you hear us?"

The message vanished, and another rapidly replaced it.

"OF COURSE I CAN HEAR YOU." The woman in the painting rolled her eyes. "I CAN SEE YOU, TOO. AND STAND ON MY HEAD! ALL SORTS OF TRICKS."

"Are you . . . What are you doing here?" Alice said.

"I LIVE HERE," the text replied as the woman put her hands on her hips. "A BETTER QUESTION WOULD BE, WHAT ARE YOU DOING HERE?"

"Why?" Isaac said, eyes narrowing.

"YOU'RE READERS, AREN'T YOU?" Her face had lost its smile, and she stared intently while the text wrote itself. "NO READER HAS COME HERE IN A VERY LONG TIME. BUT WE REMEMBER YOU."

"We're lost," Isaac said, glancing at Alice and raising an eyebrow. "And we want to leave your world. If you could direct us—"

"YOU'RE A VERY BAD LIAR," the text wrote. The woman covered a giggle with one hand. "BESIDES, I WATCHED YOU COME IN THROUGH THE GATE."

Isaac flushed, chagrined. Alice said, "The truth is that we could use your help. We're looking for another gate that leads back to our world, in a different place."

"To the Grand Labyrinth," the text wrote. "Readers went there once, long ago."

"Yes!" Alice said. "If you could show us the way—"

"When they came through, they destroyed many of our people," the text went on. The woman's eyes were hooded, her expression darkening. "Others were taken away and never seen again. It has been many years, but we remember."

*Of course.* Wherever the old Readers had gone, they'd used their power to take what they wanted, without regard to the misery they left behind. *Why should this be any different?*

The woman pointed to a distant band of dancing skeletons. "Should I call my Pact, then, to kill you?" the text wrote.

Isaac raised his hands, a threatening gesture, but Alice waved him down. "If you knew we were Readers, why haven't you done that already?"

There was a long pause. The letters disappeared, leaving only the woman, looking contemplative. Then, slowly, the invisible painter wrote:

"I WAS BORED. I HAVE HEARD STORIES OF READERS ALL MY LIFE, BUT I HAVE NEVER SEEN ONE. THERE ARE TALES OF STRANGE WORLDS BEYOND THE GATE, BUT WE CAN NO LONGER VENTURE THERE. I WANTED TO KNOW IF THE STORIES WERE TRUE."

*Okay.* Alice took a deep breath. "What's your name?"

"OSTRAVIKTRA-SUR-JORGHANSES FEDRE," the text scrawled. The woman laughed at the sight of Alice's expression, and the text added, "YOU CAN CALL ME OSTRA IF YOU LIKE."

"Ostra," Alice said thankfully. "I'm Alice, and this is Isaac." She reached down and picked up Ashes, who had been crouching suspiciously behind her legs, and put him on her shoulder. "This is my cat, Ashes."

"HELLO, ALICE, ISAAC, AND ASHES." The woman bowed, the mountains behind her drawn in for just a moment of herky-jerky motion.

"Probably most of the stories you've heard about Readers are true," Alice said. "But Isaac and I, and some more people like us, are fighting against the others. We want to undo the power of the old Readers. Open up the portals trapped in books, and bring things back to the way they used to be."

"That seems unlikely," the text wrote. "The Readers are very powerful."

"The Readers have been betrayed already," Alice said. "The labyrinthine have imprisoned them and are spreading their labyrinths to cover the world. We have to stop them, or the portals will be under labyrinthine control forever."

"The labyrinthine?" The text paused again. "They have freed themselves?"

Alice nodded.

"That would be a great change." Ostra looked pensive. "But I do not know if I can trust the word of a Reader."

"Do you have any contact with our world at all?" Alice said. "Anyone who has been there recently?"

"Some of the Pacts speak to travelers more regularly," the text wrote.

"Ask them," Alice said eagerly. "Anyone who has been to my world can tell you. The labyrinthine are running wild."

Ostra's expression became decisive. "I will ask," the text scrawled. "Wait here."

She turned away from them, walking "into" the cliff and becoming smaller and smaller. As she did, the painting gradually faded, until the last traces of ochre disappeared.

"That was . . . strange," Isaac said. He looked at Alice. "I never would have thought of that."

"Thought of what?" Alice said.

"Telling the truth." He scratched the side of his head. "I was trying to come up with a good excuse for our being here."

"It's something I learned when I went to the Palace of Glass, with Erdrodr and Flicker. The magical creatures hate what's been done to the world, the way the Readers have chained the portals up in books or put them behind guardians. And they don't like being abducted for use in prison-books either, obviously. If they believe us about what we're doing, they *should* be on our side." She smiled. "The truth can be useful, sometimes. Assuming you can convince people."

"That's a big assumption," Ashes said darkly. "She might come back with an army of skeletons."

"If she does, we'll figure that out, too," Alice said.

## CHAPTER TWENTY-EIGHT
# REVELATION

WHILE THEY WAITED FOR Ostra to return, Alice took out the Dragon's book, laid her hand on the cover, and closed her eyes.

She could see the Writing of the book hanging in darkness in front of her. It was an astonishingly complex creation, a shell wrapped around the Dragon itself to contain it, connected to the magical machinery that siphoned a creature's power and fed it to whoever had mastered the binding. Even the nature of the world inside the book was created by the nuances of the spell. Looking at it made Alice appreciate how much of the Reader's arts she hadn't even come close to learning—she felt like a primitive with a stone tool looking at the intricate inner workings of a Swiss watch.

Fortunately for her, she didn't have to replicate the spell—that would have been impossible—only manipulate what was already there. The section of it that contained the Dragon itself was relatively straightforward, although the tricky part would be tinkering with it without causing the whole structure to collapse. Alice toyed with the connections, feeling their relative strengths the way a musician might gauge the tension in a violin's strings. *I can do this. I hope.*

"Alice?" Isaac said. "She's back."

Alice opened her eyes. Ostra had returned, "approaching" from the mountainous distance inside the wall. There was a distant sound, too, a clattering, banging, metallic noise, quickly getting louder. Looking over her shoulder, Alice could see a troupe of black skeletons getting closer, still turning and whirling in a complex circular dance but definitely heading generally in their direction.

"Have you found anyone to confirm what's happening in our world?" Alice said

"I HAVE," Ostra's text wrote. "AND IT APPEARS YOU ARE TELLING THE TRUTH. TRAVELERS FROM SEV-

ERAL WORLDS WHO HAVE PASSED THROUGH YOURS REPORT THE SPREADING LABYRINTHS. BUT THERE WAS SOME DEBATE AMONG THE PACTS ABOUT WHAT TO DO WITH YOU."

"Why is that?" Alice said, trying not to look at the approaching skeletons. She felt Ashes' claws digging into her shoulder, and the thrill of power in the air as Isaac took hold of his threads.

"SOME SAID THAT IF THE LABYRINTHINE HAD OVERTHROWN THE READERS, WE OUGHT TO ALLY OURSELVES WITH THEM," Ostra's text wrote. "BUT THE OLDEST STILL RECALL THE TIME BEFORE THE READERS, AND SAY THAT THE LABYRINTHINE WERE EVEN WORSE IN THEIR CRUELTY. THEY DOUBT, HOWEVER, THAT ANYTHING YOU CAN DO WILL STOP THEM."

"What did *you* think?" Alice said, looking Ostra in her painted eyes.

"I SAID THAT WE MIGHT AS WELL LET YOU GO THROUGH," Ostra's text wrote. "IF THE LABYRINTHINE DESTROY YOU, IT WON'T BOTHER US, SO WHY NOT?"

"Not exactly a vote of confidence," Isaac muttered.

"I'll take it," Alice whispered back. She raised her voice. "And they agreed?"

"YES," Ostra wrote. "MY PACT IS COMING TO ESCORT YOU TO THE PORTAL."

Alice breathed out. She turned to face the approaching skeletons, who were quite close now. Seen clearly, they didn't seem to be entirely human—they had elongated skulls, with snouts like lizards or dogs, and long pointed teeth. Their ranks parted, smoothly, as though it were part of the dance, and then re-formed with Alice and Isaac at the center. Their bones were made of the same black metal as the enormous ruins, though untouched by rust.

"Thank you!" Alice said to Ostra, over the screech and clatter of metal that the whirling skeletons produced.

"FOR WHAT IT'S WORTH, I HOPE YOU SUCCEED," Ostra wrote. "I WOULD LIKE TO SEE YOUR WORLD, SOMEDAY."

The skeletons led them, always dancing their mad, capering jig, across the gray, smoky plain.

In spite of the fact that they were dancing in circles, the group as a whole could move quite quickly, and Alice and Isaac, in the center, were forced to walk fast to keep up. Alice was fascinated by the skeletons—there was no one calling the steps for their dance, and it changed constantly, but every member of the Pact had no problem keeping up. She wondered if they had to practice when they were young, or if they ever even *were* young, and what their relationship to Ostra was. Were there other painting-people?

*What would I do if we win, if I had the chance?* It wasn't something she'd allowed herself to think about much. Now, though, she got a brief flash of it. There was so much to *know*, world after world of beautiful mysteries to discover. The Readers had hacked their way through that complexity, enslaving the creatures they met and taking treasures for themselves. Alice only wanted to *explore*, to find out where the iron bones that littered the plain had come from and map the tunnels of Flicker's world. And the Enoki, Magda the bone witch, Lool the clockwork spider—each of them had come from a world just as rich in strangeness, too.

*It isn't likely to matter.* But, for a while, it was nice to daydream.

After a few hours walking, they came to a shore. The water looked foul, swirling with specks of orange grit, waves of rust washing up on the gray shore. There was a small island, about a hundred yards from the beach, and even from this distance Alice could see the shimmering, twisting light of another wild portal hanging above its

sandy beach. A line of the great iron ribs had been placed end-to-end to form a makeshift bridge.

"Thank you," she said to the Pact as its members split around them and brought their never-ending dance back the way they'd come. "And thank Ostra for us!"

"They were pretty friendly, for dancing skeletons," Isaac said, waving after them.

"If I've learned one thing," Alice said, "it's not to judge by appearances."

They took their time climbing the ribs out to the island, moving carefully in single file. The metal bones were wide enough to walk comfortably, but Alice wasn't eager to get dunked in that toxic-looking sea. Ashes was even less enthusiastic, maintaining a death-grip on her shoulder until she hopped off the last bone onto the orange-streaked sand of the beach.

The island was tiny, home to nothing more than the portal and a few black rocks. Alice sat down, put the Dragon book on the ground in front of her, and motioned Isaac to sit as well.

"Okay," she said, trying to ignore the rapid beating of her heart. "There's something I need to do, before we try this."

"Are you finally going to tell me why we had to get this thing?" Isaac said, settling down.

Alice nodded. "I'm going to unmake it. Unpick the spell, and give the Dragon its freedom."

There was a moment of silence. Ashes jumped down from her shoulder and circled the Dragon's book warily.

"Is that even *possible*?" the cat said. "I've never heard of such a thing. If a prison-book is *destroyed*, then the prisoner is lost forever."

"I can do it," Alice said, with a bit more confidence than she really felt. "Ending taught me enough about Writing to manage that. It's a matter of opening a way out without tearing the whole structure apart."

"If you say you can do it, I believe you," Isaac said. "You killed the Ouroborean, after all. But are you sure this is a good idea?"

"The Dragon hasn't always been the most helpful," Ashes added.

"I think it has been trying to do the right thing, in its own way. It's always allowed me to make my own choices." Alice brushed her mental grip over the Dragon's unyielding obsidian thread. "It might be able to help against Ending. But even if not, this is something I need to do."

"Maybe it would be a good idea to wait until afterward,

though," Isaac said. "If you free the Dragon, won't you lose your connection to the labyrinths? We might not be able to reach the Great Binding after we go through the portal without that."

"I won't lose my connection." Alice kept her grip on the Dragon's thread, knowing it could hear her, too. "Those powers never came from the Dragon to begin with."

Isaac's brow furrowed. "At first you thought they were a gift from Ending. Are you saying that's what they've been all along?"

She shook her head and took a deep breath.

"They weren't gifted to me or granted to me by anyone," Alice said. "They're a part of me, and always have been." She turned her attention to the Dragon's thread. "Because I am a labyrinthine. Aren't I?"

## Chapter Twenty-nine
# ORIGIN

For a moment she thought the Dragon was going to remain silent, even now. Then it spoke, echoing deep inside her mind. She saw Isaac stiffen at the voice, and she put her hand on Ashes' back, extending the thread to him so he could hear, too.

**"How long have you known?"** the Dragon said.

"I started figuring it out after I spoke to the First," Alice said. "She told me how the labyrinthine were created, that she'd combined a part of her essence with many different Earth creatures. If Ending was made from a cat, and Decay was made from a centipede, then I was made from a human." She shook her head. "I should have guessed sooner. You've been calling me 'little sister' since the very beginning."

"**I could feel the power in you,**" the Dragon said softly. "**Even then.**"

"The First has a *connection* to me," Alice said. "I saw her in the Palace of Glass, when I asked about my mother. She saved me there, and again when I was imprisoned in the void." Alice hesitated. "Do you know how it happened, how I was born? Is my father . . ." *Is he really even my father?*

"**Your creation was the culmination of a great deal of planning,**" the Dragon said. "**Your father was a carrier, one where the Reader talent lies just beneath the surface. The children of such people often have the talent themselves. When he was on a ship, passing close to the Grand Labyrinth, my siblings abducted him, and combined his essence with the sleeping First's to create you. Later the two of you were returned to his home, with his memory suitably altered.**"

"Why?" Isaac said. He'd been quiet up until now, and Alice hadn't dared look in his direction. "Why would they do that?"

"**It was the keystone of Ending's plan. The creation**

of a Reader-labyrinthine, a hybrid, who would be powerful enough on her own to maintain the Great Binding and who would help the labyrinthine rebel against the old Readers at last."

"I don't think her memory alteration worked," Alice said. "At least, not completely. My father remembered *something* about what happened. When Vespidian showed up and threatened to take me away, he got on the *Gideon*. I think he was trying to find my mother." Her eyes filled with tears. "He didn't know what had really happened, but he must have known there was a power somewhere along the path he'd taken, and he knew that it cared for me. He was trying to protect me."

**"I believe you are correct," the Dragon said. "After his death, Ending had no choice but to bring you under her protection directly, or else another Reader would have taken you for his own. It was sooner than she'd planned, but she had to hope your powers had grown enough to fulfill your role."**

"So Alice and I are related?" Ashes said.

"I think that makes us first cousins once removed," Alice said, smiling slightly.

"I don't know how to feel about that," Ashes said. "I've never been related to someone who wasn't a cat before."

"What was your part in all of this?" Alice asked the Dragon. "Why didn't you *tell* me?"

There was another long pause.

"Many years ago," the Dragon said eventually, "Ending and I had a disagreement. I had changed my mind, you see. We had made our bargain with the Readers and imprisoned the First and I began to believe that we had been wrong. The First wanted to take us home with her, and we were afraid. But she was right. This world would be better off without us.

"I tried to convince the others of this. I wanted to undo the Great Binding, and let the First return the labyrinthine to where we belonged. Ending, instead, offered her plan to free us from the Readers' domination. I challenged her, and I lost. When she told the Readers of my betrayal, they imprisoned me in this book.

"When I met you, Alice, I was . . . uncertain. Perhaps Ending had been right all along. You were so strong, but not cruel, as the other Readers were. I saw that they would all do their best to manipulate you, Geryon and Ending and the others, to twist that bright potential to their own ends. I swore to myself that I would let you choose your own path."

*Even the Dragon can be uncertain,* Alice thought. She cleared her throat. "Why didn't I hear from you after I imprisoned Geryon? You came to me in one dream, but that was all."

"I thought you had chosen your path," the Dragon said, "and you had picked Ending. If I tried to turn you from it, I would be no better than she was." It paused. "In truth, I was afraid. I did not know the right thing to do, and so I did nothing. But I did not know that Ending planned to imprison *you,* as well. If I had . . ."

"I believe you," Alice said.

"I am sorry," the Dragon said. "My kind have treated you poorly."

"You're willing for me to try to let you out?" Alice said. "We could use your help. But . . . there's a chance it could go badly."

"Please," the Dragon said. "I will take the risk. The time for inaction is over."

"All right."

Alice let out a long breath and let go of the black thread. She looked up at Isaac, who was staring at her as though seeing her for the first time.

*Now he knows I'm not human.* She'd wanted to tell him

earlier, but her courage had faltered. *I'm the same kind of creature as Ending or Decay. A maze-demon.*

He blinked, and cleared his throat. "How long do you think it will take?"

"What?" Alice said.

He gestured down at the book.

"Oh. Not long, I think."

"And then what? You have a plan?"

She nodded. "An idea, at least."

His expression was guarded. Alice couldn't tell if it was disgust she saw there, or pity. She swallowed hard.

"Then let's get started," she said.


Alice spent a long time drifting among the threads of the prison-book before she finally touched one of them.

As she'd planned, she applied her power only to the relatively simple part of the spell that actually imprisoned the Dragon. The key was breaking the prisoner out without setting up a catastrophic failure of the spell that would send everything in it tumbling into nothingness. It *looked* straightforward, but it was more complex than any Writing that Alice had attempted.

Bit by bit, strand by strand, she worked the threads of the prison loose from around the Dragon. It was like untying a very, very complicated knot of spiderwebs without ripping any of the pieces, or trying to get an egg out of its shell without breaking it, and if she failed, the Dragon could disappear forever.

All at once, without any fanfare, she succeeded. The essence of the Dragon, freed of the encumbering net of magic, popped free, and Alice hastily took hold of it and guided it back to reality with her. Even before she opened her eyes, she could feel its presence, a monstrous shape blocking out the light.

It had been a long time since she had seen the Dragon in the flesh. It took up most of the little island, curved around where Alice and Isaac sat, and even so its tail stretched out over the water. White scales reflected the glow of distant fires. It had eight legs spaced along its sinuous, reptilian body, and three eyes on either side of its massive head, shiny black hemispheres that belonged on an insect. Long fangs jutted from either side of its jaw.

In spite of all that—in spite of *everything*—Alice had never been happier to see an enormous monster. She got to her feet, her limbs aching from spending too long in concentration on the spell, and ran to wrap her arms around the nearest leg. The Dragon's tail curved across

her shoulders, a warm, dry weight, as it had once com-
forted her in Torment's treasure room.

Isaac, who hadn't seen the huge creature since he'd
fought it in the prison-book, was standing up very
straight. Ashes hid behind his legs, only the tip of his tail
peeking out.

"Thank you," the Dragon said. It was strange for Alice
to hear that bass voice through her ears, as ordinary
sound, instead of ringing in her mind. "I wouldn't have
blamed you if you'd left me in there, you know."

"*I* would have blamed myself," Alice said. "Besides, like
I said, we need your help."

"With what?" Isaac said. "We're just going to go
through and destroy the Binding, aren't we?"

"Ending will be waiting," Alice said. "Decay will have
told her that I've escaped. She knows what I'll be trying
to do."

"You think she's there?" Ashes poked his head out,
nodding at the wild portal. "Ready for us?"

Alice nodded. "She'll try to imprison me again."

"Then what can we do?" The cat's fur bristled. "You
can't fight her, Alice. You know that, don't you? Labyrinthine or not. She's much stronger than Decay. You
remember how she managed to hold off all the others put

together when they were attacking Geryon's library."

"I know," Alice said. She turned to the Dragon. "If we go into the Grand Labyrinth, you can open a path to any other labyrinth, can't you? The way Ending followed me and Ashes."

The great head nodded. "Unless there is a labyrinthine on the other side trying to keep me out. Then it would be very difficult."

"All right." Alice took a long breath and laid out her plan. The boy, the cat, and the Dragon all stared.

"It's a great risk," the Dragon said.

"Ending will be distracted," Alice said. "I'm the one at the center of all her plans. If I'm there, she'll be focused on me. Isaac, you need to keep your head down and stay out of it. Remember, she won't kill me. She needs me to keep the Binding going."

"Remember what Decay told you," Isaac said. "Just because she won't kill you doesn't mean she can't hurt you."

"I'll be careful," Alice promised. "Ashes, you go with the Dragon."

"What?" Ashes looked up at the enormous labyrinthine, his ears flattening. "Why?"

"The people back at Geryon's estate know you. If the

Dragon turns up alone, it'll take them too long to listen. You have to make them understand."

Ashes sighed. "Very well. If I'm once again to save the day."

"I know I can count on you." She looked at Isaac, again trying to read his expression, but his face was closed. "All of you."

"Of course," Isaac said. The Dragon rumbled agreement.

"Okay, then." Alice turned to look at the wavering, shimmering portal, and swallowed. "No percentage in hanging about."

## CHAPTER THIRTY
# RETURN TO THE GRAND LABYRINTH

A FTER THE USUAL MOMENT of dislocation, stepping through the portal brought them into a secluded cove, the curtain of light hanging above the beach of the Binding island. Tall cliffs stood behind them, and a little way along, a crude stairway led up to the center of the island. There was, Alice was glad to note, no sign of a black slab like the one Reaper had used. *This is going to be bad enough as it is.*

"Go," she told the Dragon. "Quickly. Ending will feel us soon."

She'd explained what she wanted them to do. Both

the Dragon and Ashes seemed dubious, but neither had voiced any objections. Now the tiny gray cat perched, absurdly, on the back of the enormous white monster, clinging between the twin rows of spines that ran down the Dragon's back.

"We will come as soon as we can," the Dragon said.

"Riding to the rescue," Ashes said, clearly getting into his role. "Come! Onward, mighty steed!"

Alice felt the fabric of the labyrinth warp around her, and the two of them were gone. She and Isaac were left alone on the beach.

Isaac turned to the stairs. Alice followed his gaze, and sighed.

"When this is over," she said, "I'm not walking anywhere for a week."

"A month," Isaac amended. "I'm going to lie in bed and make Ashes fetch my meals."

"I'm going to take two baths every day, just because I can," Alice said. "With extra bubbles."

"And I'm going to rub it in with Dex and Michael and Soranna that they missed out," Isaac said, looking slyly at Alice. "We'll have to invent a few extra adventures, obviously."

"Obviously." She gave him a weak smile. "But first we have to climb these stairs."

She *was* tired, Alice realized as they hiked up to the island's central plateau. There was a soreness in her muscles, but it was more than that. Some reserve, deep inside her, was on the verge of exhaustion. *Only a little farther,* she told herself. *This is the end, one way or another.*

Alice kept an eye out for hooded shadows at the top of the cliff, but there was only a narrow path leading inland over rocky ground. Isaac stayed behind her, hands in the pockets of his coat, silent. In the privacy of her own mind, Alice could admit it would have been nice to hold his hand, one more time. *Would he even want to hold hands with a labyrinthine, though?* She shoved the whole squirming mess of feelings down into her stomach. *It's not going to matter.*

There was the ring of boulders, just as she remembered it, each bearing a book leading to the fortress of a now-imprisoned Reader. In the very center was the standing stone, the characters of the Great Binding inscribed deep into the rock. Nothing moved, and Alice felt Isaac take hold of his threads.

"Maybe she's not as smart as you thought," he whispered. "Maybe she didn't realize you were coming here."

"She's here," Alice said wearily. "She just has a flair for

the dramatic." She raised her voice. "You might as well come out, you know!"

"Spoilsport." Ending's voice was a soft, velvety purr.

The standing stone wasn't big enough to conceal her, but she emerged from behind it nonetheless, slinking out of its shadow like it was a gateway to another place. Which it was, of course. Here in the center of the Grand Labyrinth, space was hardly an inconvenience for a labyrinthine. Her smooth, black fur rippled like dark oil as she moved, muscles bunching underneath. Huge yellow eyes like lamplights stared back at Alice, and her yawn showed long, ivory fangs.

"I was beginning to think you weren't coming," Ending said. "But you didn't disappoint me. You never have, really."

"Here's what I don't understand," Alice said. "Every other labyrinthine is an enormous version of the animal it was made from, isn't it? So why aren't I fifteen feet tall with six eyes?"

Ending laughed, loud and genuine. "That would have made you awfully hard to pass off as ordinary," she said. "We did our best to restrain the expression of our mother's physiology." She paused. "You've figured out everything, then?"

"More or less."

"I thought you might have," Ending said. "Of course she helped you escape. I should have anticipated that. She is, after all, the First Labyrinthine, and is not to be underestimated. And nor are you, it seems."

"I do my best." Alice flicked a glance at Isaac, who had broken away and taken shelter behind one of the boulders. *Good.* She stepped forward.

"Why go and bother poor Decay?" Ending said. "He's never been the brightest among us."

"We had to get away from you," Alice said with a shrug, not mentioning the Dragon. "It seemed as good a place as any."

"Don't think I don't see your friend hiding there," Ending said. "If he behaves himself, I'll take him home with me when we're done."

Alice took another step forward, saying nothing.

"Here's what *I* don't understand," Ending said, moving forward herself. "You knew I would be here, waiting for you. So why come at all? Why not hide? It would at least delay the inevitable."

Alice gave a wordless shrug.

"Surely you don't imagine you can *defeat* me," Ending purred. "You're smarter than that."

Another shrug.

"Sometimes," Alice said, "all you can do is try."

The two of them lashed out at the same instant.

Their first conflict was invisible, fought in the fabric of the labyrinth.

Alice threw all of her newfound strength against Ending, trying to twist space to move the labyrinthine away from the Binding stone. Ending, surprised by the onslaught, gave ground at first, and Alice saw the air shimmer. But it soon became clear which of them was stronger. Ashes had been right—Ending was nothing like Decay. Their power collided in waves, strange geometries rippling outward as the fabric of the labyrinth bunched and contorted. But Ending pressed the world flat again, in spite of every effort of Alice's to fold it, as easily as a grown man overwhelming a child.

*All right*, Alice thought, already sweating. *Something else, then.*

She reached for her threads. The Dragon's obsidian thread was gone now that it was free, an absence that felt as though she'd cut something out of herself, but she ignored that and reached for Spike's thread instead. She wrapped it around herself tight, feeling her body thicken and change, and started her run forward as soon as all four feet touched the ground. Alice lowered her head, quadruple spikes aimed directly at Ending.

The big cat didn't stand to receive the charge. Instead she pounced, vaulting lithely over Alice's horns and landing on her broad, scaled back. The impact pushed Alice off balance, and she staggered sideways a moment and then fell. The big cat lunged for the dinosaur's throat, fangs spread wide.

*Not yet,* Alice thought. *I'm not finished yet.*

She let go of Spike's thread and grabbed the Swarm's. Her dinosaur-body exploded, fanning out into a hundred tiny swarmers, *quirk*ing and bouncing as they ran in all directions. Ending's teeth snapped closed on one, and pain shot through Alice as its life was snuffed out. The huge cat pounced on another, trapping it under one front paw. The swarmer struggled, *quirk*ing madly, but the labyrinthine increased the pressure steadily until the little creature was squashed and broken against the rocky ground. Alice felt another stab of pain, and hurriedly brought the swarmers back together, across the ring of boulders.

"Must we play this out?" Ending said, padding forward. "I don't want to hurt you."

"Just lock me away forever," Alice said as she regained her human form.

"A fate you were more than happy to inflict on Geryon," Ending said, her lips drawing back from long fangs. "Besides, I have a new prison prepared for you. It will be just like going to sleep. You won't even know what's happened."

"And then everyone in the world becomes your toys?"

"That's the idea, yes," Ending said.

Alice took a deep breath and wrapped Spike's thread around herself. She wrapped her arms around the boulder next to her, as far as they would go, and dug her fingers into the bare rock. With a crunching, grinding sound, it shifted, raining dust and small pebbles as she lifted it over her head. Even with Spike's strength, the effort made her arms tremble, but she managed to take one knee-wobbling step forward and hurl the giant rock directly at Ending.

The huge cat reared up, paws flashing. She hit the boulder with both paws in midair, and Alice's spirits dropped as the stone was batted away as easily as a stuffed toy. It crashed to the earth, shattering with a *crunch*, and Ending dropped back to all fours and continued her advance.

"Everything you talked about," Alice said, backpedaling to the next boulder. "Wanting a partner. All of that was a lie?"

"Of course," Ending said. "We labyrinthine are at the pinnacle of the world by rights. What would I need with a partner?"

"But—"

"This is getting tiresome."

Ending bounded forward with shocking speed, a sudden pounce bringing her on top of Alice between blinks. Alice found herself pinned against the rock, one of Ending's enormous paws resting on her chest with just enough pressure to keep Alice in place.

"You *lose*," Ending hissed, her yellow eyes glowing bright.

"I know," Alice said, struggling to breathe.

The yellow eyes narrowed. "Then *why are you smiling*?"

"Alice!" Isaac's shout rang across the ring of boulders, and Alice's heart lurched.

*No! You brave idiot!*

"Oh dear," Ending said. "I hope *that* isn't your hope for rescue."

"No," Alice said. "This is between us. Leave him out of it."

"Interesting." Ending turned her head. "He doesn't seem to want to give me a choice. Stay put, would you?"

Ending contorted the labyrinth in a way Alice had never seen before. It clung to her wrists and ankles, tiny folds of space that bound her in place, giving her the strong sense that if she tried to pull herself free, she'd tear off her own hands and feet.

"Let her go!" Isaac shouted, charging across the circle.

"This should be entertaining," Ending purred. "Hit me with your best shot, *boy*."

Isaac was already pulling on his threads. Frost shot out from his feet as ice formed in the air around him, blasted directly into Ending's face by hurricane-force winds. Her fur went from black to gray as snow began to cling to her, and she squinted into the storm. A moment later there was a bright light, which Alice recognized as Isaac's salamander, and then a blast of scalding-hot steam washed over her and Ending. Alice hurriedly wrapped herself in the Swarm thread to toughen her skin.

Inside the swirling mist, Ending was barely visible, a dark shape turning slowly and emitting a rising growl. Off to the right, light flared again, and a wave of fire washed over the labyrinthine. Ending spun back, snarling, and lashed out with one paw, but Isaac had faded back into the mist. Another blast of flame came from the other direction. Ending's fur was starting to smoke.

"Clever," the labyrinthine growled. "I have to admit." Her tail lashed. "But I don't need to see you . . ."

The yellow eyes closed. Alice felt Ending's touch on the fabric of the labyrinth, and realized what was happening a moment too late—the labyrinthine could sense Isaac that way, even if her vision was clouded. She opened her mouth to shout a warning just as Ending pounced. Alice heard a cry, abruptly cut off, and a thud.

She threw her powers against the bonds holding her, unraveling the twisted space that Ending had wrapped her in. It gave way, but frustratingly slowly. By the time she had her arms free, the cloud of steam was dissipating, and Ending's dark shape was fully visible, slinking back toward her with something dangling from her mouth.

It was Isaac, hanging limp from her jaws by his battered coat. Ending dropped him in a heap at Alice's feet. The big cat's tongue licked out, cleaning a dark spatter of blood from her muzzle.

"Isaac!" Alice shouted. She couldn't see much of him under his long coat, but he wasn't moving. She was suddenly back in Esau's fortress, watching as another labyrinthine casually tore out Jacob's throat. "*Isaac!*"

"You want him to live?" Ending said. "Is that it? Stop fighting me, and I'll grant you that, at least."

Alice struggled to free her legs. "I'd never trust you," she spat.

"You don't have much alternative." Ending yawned. "I might as well keep him alive, if you cooperate. He's no threat to me. Not like you are."

"If you've . . . if you've hurt him, I'll kill you," Alice said, breathing fast. Her right leg came free. "I don't care what it takes."

"You won't, you know," Ending said, looking on with interest. "This isn't some stupid storybook where the underdog wins in the end. This is the real world. The strongest do what they want, and everyone else has to live with it. Or"—she glanced significantly at Isaac—"not."

Alice finally got the last knot in space undone. She was free, but Ending was standing right in front of her, as though daring her to make a move. Isaac lay motionless between them.

"You know me," Alice said. "You know I won't give in."

"And *you* knew from the start that you couldn't beat me," Ending said. "So what are you doing?"

Alice felt the fabric of the labyrinth shiver as someone twisted a pathway from *here* to *there*.

"Buying time," she said.

## Chapter Thirty-one
# ONE LAST TIME

Ending spun as an enormous portal shimmered into being. There was no doorway, no convenient corner to hide the twist of space. Just the utter impossibility of it, a place where one that could take you from this desolate island—

Back to Geryon's library, with its toppled shelves and book-strewn floor.

In the center of the circular hole in space stood the Dragon, towering above Ending. Its head snaked through the portal, followed by one foot.

"Sister," the Dragon said.

"Brother," Ending snarled. "So this was her gambit."

"Yes."

"You know it won't be enough." Alice felt Ending's energy ripple through the labyrinth. "However large you are, your power is no match for mine. You couldn't beat me when I locked you away the first time, and I am so much stronger now."

"Nevertheless." The Dragon took another step forward.

Once again, two labyrinthine fought, their colliding energies shaking the fabric of space. Alice ignored them for a moment and ran to Isaac, rolling him onto his back and pulling his coat out of the way. She was relieved to find him breathing, though his eyes were tightly closed. There was blood on his shirt, but the cuts beneath didn't look serious.

"This time," Ending grated, "I'm going to find a more unpleasant world to lock you in."

Alice looked up and saw the air between the maze-demons shimmering. Ending was right. The Dragon's influence was shoved back, step by step, and bonds of folded space wrapped themselves around its legs, pinning it halfway through the portal. It was all the huge creature could do to maintain the link between the library and the island.

Alice got to her feet, her legs shaky, ready to add her scant remaining strength to the battle. The fact that Isaac was all right gave her a kind of peace. *I'll do everything I can.*

Someone else emerged from the portal, stepping around the Dragon. It was an Enoki girl, not much older than Alice, with purple toadstools growing in her hair. She carried a long spear, little more than a straight stick with a sharpened end. Her eyes were wide with terror, but she managed to move a few steps forward and lower the spear in Ending's direction.

The huge cat stared at this defiant display, then looked over her shoulder. She chuckled, then began to laugh, pawing at her ear.

"Really?" she said, between breaths. "*Really?* I expected better of you, Alice."

"It's Gulitheps, isn't it?" Alice said, loud enough to carry over the labyrinthine's mockery.

"Y . . . yes." The mushroom-girl's voice was nearly inaudible.

"Thank you for coming." Alice got to her feet.

Two more Enoki, a man and a woman, stepped through the shimmering portal. They also carried spears, and they took up positions on either side of Gulitheps. The woman put a reassuring hand on the girl's shoulders, and she steadied a little. Another half dozen of them were

close behind, forming a line of sharpened points in front of Ending. Next came Coryptus, the old man who led the Enoki, with at least two dozen of them. He waved cheerily to Alice, the fungal growths on his back shaking.

Magda the bone witch was right behind him. Her long coat, made of sewn-together bones, was fully animated, dozens of skeletal limbs rising around her.

"By Ushbar, it's good to see you!" she called to Alice.

"You too," Alice said. She felt strength returning to her exhausted limbs.

More of the magical creatures of the library filed through. Sprites of every description, multicolored hair sparkling, all carrying swords or spears or bows and arrows. Lool, the clockwork spider, had equipped herself with what looked like an enormous circular saw. Ephraster the harpy-girl flapped above the rest, her talons outstretched.

Alice almost missed Jen in the crush of people. She fought free of the press and ran toward Alice. Ashes, Alice saw, was riding on her shoulder.

"Is that Isaac?" Jen said.

"He's all right," Alice said. "Are *you* okay?"

"Much better," Jen said. "Magda says I'm back to normal, more or less. But Michael—"

"We're going to get him back," Alice said. "Right now."

Still more creatures were coming through the gate. People Alice didn't recognize—lithe, elegant figures in white masks and black tailcoats, stumpy three-legged monsters with long, waving tentacles, a great clanking knight in rusty armor with a sword as tall as he was. A blaze of orange and red light marked a cluster of fire-sprites, and Alice recognized Actinia at their head. Bringing up the rear was a phalanx of ice-giants, huge women in armored blue steel and bearing enormous double-headed axes. Erdrodr and her mother, Helga, were leading them.

"There's so many," Alice said. "Ashes, how did you do it?"

"I'd like to say it was all my own talent, but cats are naturally modest," Ashes said. "They barely needed any convincing. Once I said you needed help, they started spreading the word, across the library and into the books."

"They believe in you, Alice," Jen said. "We all do."

Alice blinked back tears. "I don't . . . I can't . . ."

"I think that you should take charge," Ashes said quickly. "Before Mother does something drastic."

Ending was no longer laughing.

Alice pushed her way through the throng of creatures,

with Jen by her side. A shout went up, so many voices at once that she couldn't understand them. She nodded, eyes blurred with tears, and they parted to let her through.

Actinia, at the head of the small band of fire-sprites, was waiting near Helga, Erdrodr, and the other ice-giants. He handed off his spear and ran to wrap Alice in a hug, while Erdrodr, looking formidable in gleaming armor, gave a hesitant wave.

"When Flicker didn't come back, I wanted to go after him," Actinia said. He'd been one of Flicker's closest friends in the fire-sprite village. "Pyros wouldn't let me, so I asked Erdrodr to help convince him. When word came that you needed us—"

"It ended the argument," boomed Helga, Erdrodr's mother. She had a massive double-headed axe in either hand. "I told that fussy old man that you had earned our faith."

"Thank you." Alice gently separated herself from Actinia. "Flicker's alive. We'll get him back, I promise."

"Of course we will," Actinia said. His glowing hair flamed a bright orange-red.

The front rank of magical creatures had their spears lowered, a wall of sharp points that Ending regarded with slitted eyes. Alice had feared she'd attack at once, but she was outmatched and she knew it. If Alice and the Dragon could keep her space-warping power at bay, even Ending couldn't fight an army.

Alice stepped between spear points, and once again stood facing the labyrinthine.

"The strongest don't always get what they want," she said to Ending. "Not when the weak can work together."

"Very touching," Ending said. "You know that if we play this out, a lot of those people are going to die."

"Do you think I don't know that?" Alice said quietly. For a moment, she saw Reaper's hovering shadow again, and shook her head. "Do you think *they* don't know it?"

Ending's eyes narrowed further. Then she sighed and sat back on her haunches.

"I underestimated you," the big cat said. "A hard mistake to admit. I should have known better."

"Don't make us fight you," Alice said. Her throat felt tight. "You can't beat us all."

"You're right." Ending yawned theatrically, her tail whipping. "You win. How does this sound? You get the library, and my siblings and I agree to leave you in peace for a reasonable period. You can be included in our councils if you like; it's your birthright as a labyrinthine. We can even find some territory for my fool of a brother over there."

"No," Alice said.

"I wouldn't get too pushy, if I were you," Ending said. "You may have me at a disadvantage, but you still have to deal with the others—"

"I mean no terms," Alice said. "I'm going to break the Great Binding. Stand aside."

There was a long pause.

"You're serious," Ending said.

"Of course," Alice said. "You thought I was doing this for . . . for *territory*? For power?"

"I thought you were upset that I imprisoned you in the void," Ending said. "That would be reasonable. Freeing the First is *not*. Do you have any *idea* what would happen?"

"She would return home," Alice said. "Taking the labyrinthine with her."

"It's one thing to try to win the game," Ending said. "It's another to set the board on fire!" She was speaking quickly now. "I know I've hurt you, Alice, but—"

"It's *not a game*," Alice said. "Don't you understand? There are people out in the real world, in the libraries, and the books, and you're hurting all of them." She took a deep breath. "Geryon killed my father, and I hated him for it. But it wasn't just my father he hurt, it was *everyone*. Everyone he touched. All the old Readers were the same. And so are the labyrinthine."

Another, longer silence. When Ending spoke again, all the humor was gone from her voice, replaced with a low, dangerous growl.

"You were a mistake," she said. "I should have known. I wanted a labyrinthine with the powers of a Reader, and I got one, but I left it to be raised by *humans*." Her lip curled back. "We're hurting people? *So what?* People hurt each other all the time, every day. We're just *better* at it."

"Get out of the way, Ending."

"So that you can destroy us all?" She drew herself up to her full height, fur bristling. "No. I'll send every one of you to the void if I have to." Her voice rose to a full-throated roar. "Let's see you get out this time!"

Alice blinked, and for a moment her head swam. The fabric of the labyrinth, of space itself, shuddered and began to *tear*. Alice looked around wildly, and saw rents appear in the world, brief glimpses of the blackness that lay beyond. The magical creatures saw them, too, and there were shouts of alarm. Some of the Enoki surged forward, spears jabbing, and Ending twisted lithely away, baring her fangs.

Alice concentrated, throwing her own strength against Ending's, trying to calm the storm. It wasn't enough. The fabric frayed further. Alice felt as though she were on the edge of a tabletop, scrabbling to hold on as it was tilted further and further, tipping her into nothingness along with everyone else.

"Enough." The voice was a deep, bass rumble. "Tantrums ill become you, sister."

The Dragon stepped all the way through the gate, and let it fade into nothingness behind it. In her rage, Ending had abandoned the twists of space that kept the huge creature pinioned. Alice felt its power flow around hers, stabilizing the world, pressing back against the raw force of Ending's strength. The magical creatures parted ranks to let the Dragon through.

"Brother!" Ending hissed, back arched. "How can you take her side?"

"Because she is right," the Dragon said.

Its head snapped forward, jaws spread wide. Ending tried to dodge, but the Dragon was as fast as a snake, and it gripped her in its teeth and lifted her off the ground. She *yowled*, the whine of a cat in deep trouble, and scratched wildly at the side of the Dragon's face, but her claws only drew sparks from its scales.

"Now cease your struggling," the Dragon said, its voice unaffected by the fact that it had a mouth full of angry cat. "If you wish to remain a witness to the proceedings."

Ending's assault stopped abruptly. Alice let out a deep breath and let go of the fabric.

"Are you all right?" Jen said. "What just happened?"

"I'm fine." Alice glanced up at Ending. "We'll all be fine. I just need to do what I came here to do."

Jen clapped her on the shoulder and grinned. Wearily, Alice turned to the binding stone, just beyond where Ending had been standing.

"Don't be a fool!" Ending shouted, from where the Dragon held her high overhead. "Alice!"

Alice stepped forward.

"The First will take *every* labyrinthine home with her," Ending said, her voice cracking in desperation. "That means Ashes. That means *you*."

## Chapter Thirty-two
# ALICE'S SACRIFICE

ALICE'S STRIDE DIDN'T EVEN falter. But another figure stepped in front of her as she approached the binding stone, a boy in a long, ragged coat, one hand pressed to a fresh cut in his side, his face white under the grime and streaks of blood.

"Isaac," Alice said. "Are you—"

"Is it true?" Isaac said.

"You should get Magda to—"

"*Is it true? You're leaving?*"

There was a long pause. Finally, Alice nodded. Isaac took a step backward, slumping against the binding stone.

"How long have you known?" he said.

"Since I figured out the truth about what I am," Alice said. "I was going to tell you, but..."

"But what?"

Alice swallowed and squared her shoulders. "I was scared."

"Of me?"

"That if you knew what would happen when I set the First free, you wouldn't—"

"Wouldn't help you kill yourself?"

"I'm not killing myself!" Alice said. "The First is taking the labyrinthine *home*. It's just another world."

"No it isn't," Isaac said. "You have no idea what it will be like! Whether you can even *live* there. And you won't be able to come back, will you?"

Alice found she couldn't lie, not now. She shook her head. "I don't think so. The First only got here by luck. I don't think she expects any of us to come back again."

"So don't act like you know what you're doing, then!" Isaac said. "Please, Alice. There has to be another way."

"You think I haven't thought about it?" Alice felt herself tearing up again and blinked furiously. "You think I *want* this? I don't have a choice. It's either free the First, or let the labyrinthine take over the world."

"You're a Reader," Isaac said. "You always have a choice.

You could leave this world behind and find another one, far away from the labyrinthine, far away from *every-thing*." His voice sank. "I would go with you."

"I can't." Alice stepped forward. She reached out and touched Isaac's cheek, gently. Tears were cutting a clean trail through the grime on his face. "You know I can't."

Isaac swallowed. "After Evander . . . after he left, I was alone. I did what my master commanded. I told myself that had to be enough. Then *you* came . . ." He closed his eyes. "Now you're going to leave me, too."

"The others will still be here. Dex, Michael, Jen, Soranna. They need you." Alice could barely speak past the lump in her throat. "There'll be a lot to do. There'll be people who need help."

Her hand slipped down his arm, and their fingers intertwined. Isaac squeezed so tight, she thought her bones might break.

"If you can find a way back," he whispered. "If there's *any* way. I'll be waiting."

Alice nodded, and laid her hand on the binding stone.

It wasn't like freeing the Dragon from its prison. This spell was much simpler, and the prisoner was so much greater than anything that could have been bound into a book.

Even with all the power of the Great Binding, the First Labyrinthine strained in her sleep, pushing at the restraints. Her dreams leaked out, she said, to touch the world.

Freeing the Dragon had been like carefully cutting a single leaf from the center of a thorn bush. This was more like snipping the string on a helium balloon, and watching it bob upward into the sky.

Alice broke the Great Binding.

Power surged through her, and she felt a moment of giddy euphoria. It was the energy the binding had been draining from her to maintain itself, now freed.

"What happens now?" Isaac said, wiping at his nose with the sleeve of his coat.

"I don't know." Alice stepped away from the binding stone, pulling Isaac with her. "But I think we might want to stand back."

They retreated a few more steps. The crowd of creatures followed suit, shuffling outward. The Dragon stood watching, Ending still in its mouth.

The ground shook. A light tremor at first, enough to make everyone sway on their feet. Then a hard, constant vibration, as though a dozen jackhammers had started up at once. Then there was a tremendous *crack* as the binding stone split down the middle. With a rumble, the split continued outward, a zigzagging line stretching across the ground from the stone. Dust rose into the air.

"Stand back *a bit* farther," Alice said.

The crack stretched on, and began to widen, the earth pulling apart like a great mouth yawning wide. The resulting crevasse was steep-sided, its edges crumbling as rocks were shaken loose and pattered into the abyss below. The ground was shaking so hard, it was difficult for Alice to keep her balance, and plumes of dust and smoke shot into the air.

"Alice!" Isaac shouted. "Are you *sure* this was a good idea?"

Something rose about the lip of the crevasse. It was an eye, as big around as Alice was tall, with a cat-like pupil and silver iris. It was supported on a long, flexible stalk of greenish flesh, turning slowly to take in the assembled creatures. At the sight of it, Ending let out another yowl.

Alice squeezed Isaac's hand.

"Yes," she said.

The First Labyrinthine rose out of the pit, pulling herself up the rocky wall with a dozen long, ropy tentacles. She was huge, nearly as big as the Dragon, and seemed to be composed of a mass of contradictory features, as though someone had set off a bomb in a seafood kitchen and stitched together everything they'd found afterward without knowing where it had come from. Each tentacle was a different length and color, some slimy with mucus, others the dry, pebbled texture of an elephant's trunk. They were tipped with claws, or horns, or tiny, perfect hands. More appendages unfolded as she moved, enormous crab-like pincers, long, thin strands that might have belonged to a jellyfish. And above them all was the single eye, lidless and piercing. It focused on Alice, pupil shifting and narrowing.

Alice had never seen a more hideous creature in all her life. But, under the lambent silver gaze, she felt no fear. She unlaced her fingers from Isaac's and stepped forward. Tentacles stretched toward her, hovering around her and above her head without coming close enough to touch. Just in front of her was one of the dry, trunk-like limbs, ending in a long point that might have been a stinger. Alice reached out, slowly, and ran her hand along it. Tiny stiff hairs tickled her palm.

"Hello," she said. "You're my mother, I think."

"**I am**," said the First. Her voice echoed in Alice's mind, and—judging from the startled looks she saw—in the minds of everyone present. It was a measured, reassuring voice, with a touch of humor, the hint of a smile that the

First's body couldn't offer. "Though I must say you get your looks from your father's side of the family."

Alice grinned shakily, and let out a breath that she didn't realize she'd been holding.

"You are *all* my children," the First said, looking at Ending hanging in the Dragon's jaws. "And you have misbehaved, I think."

"You can't," Ending said. It hurt Alice a little to hear her proud voice turned to a whimper, even after all that had happened. "Please."

"You are afraid," the First said. "I understand. You were born on this world, and have never known your true home. But the time has come for you to find out. Our time here is passed, my daughter. We have long since overstayed our welcome."

Ending shrieked, a long, ear-splitting yowl. In the back of Alice's mind, she heard dozens of similar cries, resonating through the fabric of the labyrinth. All over the world, the labyrinthine realized what was happening, and they screamed their fear and desperation. For just a moment, she saw Ending *twist*, as though rotating into a set of dimensions beyond the usual three. Then she and the others were suddenly gone, their cries still ringing in Alice's ears.

"**The labyrinths will fade away, in time,**" the First said. "**The world will restore itself.**"

Alice nodded. The First's gaze shifted, and she followed it, looking up at the Dragon.

"Mother," the Dragon said. "I am sorry."

"**You did not join them, when they imprisoned me.**"

"No," the Dragon said. "But I stood aside."

"**Then I forgive you.**" A long, glistening tentacle reached out and caressed the Dragon's cheek, just below its three jet-black eyes. "**Come home to where you belong.**"

"Thank you." The Dragon bowed its head. "And thank *you*, Alice. More than I can say. I will see you soon."

Alice waved, swallowing a knot in her throat. The Dragon's huge form twisted, as Ending's had, moving in a direction that the eye couldn't quite follow. Then he was gone, too.

"**And now, daughter?**" The First's single-eyed stare shifted back to Alice.

"My friends," she said. "They're still in the void." She hesitated. "And the Readers, too. We can't just leave them there."

"**Indeed.**"

Alice felt the First's power *thrum* through the labyrinth, greater than anything she'd sensed before. Space twisted, opening up like an origami flower. A black shadow flitted across the rock, and when it passed, Dex, Michael, Soranna, and Flicker lay on the stone, with Cyan curled into a tight ball at Michael's feet.

"**They are asleep,**" the First said. "**It will be easier for them, this way.**"

"Oh." Alice looked down at Dex, who was grinning, as though she were having a good dream. "I . . ." *I wanted to say good-bye.* But it was better this way. *How can I explain what's happening, and why I have to go?*

Isaac stepped beside Alice. He was trembling slightly, but he looked up at the monstrous bulk of the First and coughed.

"**Yes?**" the First said. Alice had the sense of another amused smile.

"She has to go?" Isaac said. "There's no other way?"

"**It is her home,**" the First said gently. "**When I leave this world, no labyrinthine can remain behind.**"

"Will she be okay?" Isaac said. "On the other side. On your world, or whatever it is. Will Alice be all right?"

"**She will,**" the First said. "**She is my daughter, and I will be with her.**"

"You can promise me that?"

"I promise."

Alice put a hand on Isaac's shoulder. He looked at her, eyes shining, then stepped away.

"I don't suppose you can tell me what it will be like," Alice said. Her heart was beating very fast.

"**It is difficult to explain,**" the First said. "**It will be easier to show you.**"

"All right." She looked around, one last time, at her sleeping friends, at Jen and Ashes, at the crowd of creatures, Erdrodr and Actinia and the others. At Isaac. "Then—"

"**But I must say,**" the First interrupted, "**I am *very* tired.**"

Alice blinked. "What?"

"**It's a long way home, after all.**" She gave a yawn, which echoed in Alice's mind. "**Perhaps a nap. Yes, I think a nap first will be just the thing.**"

"A . . . a *nap*?" Alice shook her head.

"**Just a short one.**" While the huge eye didn't move, Alice got the mental image of a wink. "**A hundred years, perhaps.**"

"A *hundred years*?" Alice said.

"**Lazy of me, I know. But, on the other hand, what's the rush?**"

"You mean—" Isaac began.

**"She'll have to come home with me, when I'm ready."** The First's stare shifted between the two of them. **"I trust you can amuse yourself until then?"**

"I think so?" Alice said. Her voice was a tiny croak.

**"Good."** The First's voice softened, and Alice had the sudden certainty that the labyrinthine was now speaking to her alone. **"Live your life, my daughter. Enjoy your world. And then I will show you what lies beyond it."**

## Chapter Thirty-three
# WHAT COMES AFTER

FOR A WHILE, EVERYTHING was a confusion of cheers, shouts, handshakes, hugs, and the relieved, excited babble of a hundred creatures from almost as many different species. Alice was crushed in an embrace by Erdrodr, warmed by Actinia, and alternately scratched, moistened, or crusted with mud by the other sprites.

Somehow, in the midst of all these congratulations, Alice managed to collect enough presence of mind to open a way back to Geryon's estate. She could feel the labyrinth there fraying, especially at the edges where it had most recently grown, but the core of it would take a long time to erode. The fabric was still solid enough that she could create a portal as the Dragon had done, and herd everyone back through.

The First herself had climbed back into her crevasse, her huge eye gazing at Alice until it slipped out of sight below the ground. Napping or not, Alice could still feel the hum of her mother's immense power, and she suspected that the Grand Labyrinth would now be totally closed to outsiders. *A good thing, I suppose. We wouldn't want any ships blundering into it.*

After their return, the milling, chattering group congregated on the lawn outside Geryon's library. When no one showed any signs of leaving, Alice found Emma down in the house storeroom and asked her to bring out food and drink from the kitchen. Soon the invisible servants were working overtime, supplying the needs of so many disparate creatures. Alice herself drank several jugs of cool, clear water and gobbled down a sandwich and a half before her stomach began to protest. *Anything but apples. If I never see another apple again for as long as I live, it'll be too soon.*

Isaac waved at her from where he was sitting with the rest of the apprentices. Dex was sitting up, and the others were beginning to stir. They'd carried their sleeping forms back through the portal and laid them out on the grass, where most of the creatures gave them a wide berth. In spite of the First's assurances, Alice had asked Magda to look her friends over. The bone witch had proclaimed that all was well, and had wrapped Isaac's side thoroughly in a clean bandage.

Grabbing two more jugs of water, Alice hurried over. Dex drank, coughed, and drank some more, and Soranna moaned and rolled over in her sleep. Jen was by Michael's side. It was a few minutes more before everyone was fully awake, sitting in a rough circle on a patch of undamaged turf in between the craters and burn scars.

There were, of course, a thousand questions all at once. Alice did her best to answer them, with Isaac filling in a few missing parts to her halting explanation.

"So we all got caught by the labyrinthine," Dex summarized, "but it's okay, because you beat them before we even woke up?" She pulled a face. "Sister Alice, you're not leaving us a very heroic role in this story."

"Sorry." Alice grinned. "If I could have had you around to help, I'm sure things would have been a lot easier."

"She had *me*," Ashes said, back in his usual place on Alice's shoulder. "That was obviously enough."

"I knew you would succeed," Soranna said, beaming.

"I can't believe Actinia managed to get old Pyros to let him come help," Flicker said. "There's going to be some harsh words at home after this."

"Why don't you go talk to him?" Alice said. She'd noticed Actinia shooting shy glances at Flicker since he'd woken. "And Erdrodr's here, too. She'll be happy to see you."

The fire-sprite looked around the circle, then back at Alice. He nodded and climbed to his feet, a little shakily.

"Why send him away?" Jen said, looking after him. "Something you need to keep secret?"

"There's something we need to talk about," Alice said, looking around the circle at the five who remained. "The Readers."

She could see it strike them, one after another. The six of them, in this circle, were all the Readers left in the world.

"I hope no one is suggesting that *I* go anywhere," Ashes said. Alice scratched him behind the ear reassuringly.

"So what is it we need to talk about?" Jen said.

"What happens next," Michael said, fingering his spectacles.

"That seems clear," Soranna said. "Alice is in charge, isn't she?"

"In charge of what?" Isaac said.

Soranna waved her arms vaguely. "Everything, I suppose."

Dex cocked her head, her expression thoughtful. "Well, Sister Alice? Will you now rule the world?"

*I could,* Alice thought. *I really could.* Not only was she among the last of the Readers, she was the last labyrinthine, not counting the sleeping First. She was the only one left who knew the secrets of Writing magical books. She could be a singular power in a way that the squabbling, feuding old Readers never had. *I could . . .*

"Of course not," Alice said. "I don't want to rule anything." *The First gave me a hundred years. I'm not going to waste them.* "But there are things that need to be done, and I could use your help."

"The last time all the Readers met like this, they divided up the world between them, and then fought over the pieces," Isaac said. "We're not going to do *that*, are we?"

"No. We can't, and that's part of the point." Alice took a deep breath. "First of all, no one will be *able* to be as powerful as the old Readers were. They could only collect and contain the books that they did because of the labyrinthine. Without them, the labyrinths will break down, and the books will go wild."

"It's true," Ashes said. "Get too many books in one place, too much magic leaks through, and things go mad."

Alice nodded. "*That* is the job for the Readers. Someone is going to have to deal with the libraries before they go wild, and we're the only ones who can."

"Deal with it how?" Isaac said. "Separate the books from one another?"

"No," Dex said, eyes going wide. "Sister Alice wants us to *undo* the bindings in all the books. Isn't that right?"

"Yes," Alice said. "I want us to free every prisoner and unlock every portal." She looked over her shoulder at Flicker. He'd told her once that binding the portals had hurt the worlds beyond them, dimmed the fires his people relied on. "The old Readers and the labyrinthine distorted the world. Our purpose is to set things right."

"That will take a very long time," Michael said. "There are a lot of books. Tens of thousands."

"I know," Alice said. "And there's more. The old Readers left wards and spells all over the world that need to be taken down before they hurt somebody. And as for people they've already hurt"—Alice pointed at Emma as she went by—"we can see if there's anything we can do for them."

"For that matter," Isaac said, "we may *not* be the only

ones left. The old Readers had more apprentices. The labyrinthine may have gotten to some of them"—he grimaced—"but some may be hiding, or trapped."

"What about the old Readers themselves?" Jen said. "They're still trapped, aren't they?"

"I want to set them free," Alice said. "But we need to make sure it's safe, first. Once the books are unbound, without labyrinthine, the old Readers will be powerless and we can release them."

"If we undo all the books," Michael said, "*we* will be powerless."

"Not necessarily," Alice said. "Prison-books capture a creature against its will and steal power from it. But if you could make a *contract* with a *willing* creature, you might still be able to use its power without locking it away." She shook her head. "It will take a lot of negotiation and time, but—"

"We'll figure it out!" Isaac and Ashes chorused along with Alice.

"There's another problem," Dex said. "If we undo the bindings on the portals and the prison-books, then all the doors will be open again, as they were in the days before the Readers. Magical creatures are going to come through, and ordinary humans will find out."

"I know," Alice said. "And that's the other thing we're going to have to do. There's no going back to the way the world was; the labyrinths have seen to that. Now ordinary humans and magical creatures are going to have to live together. I thought we might be able to help them do it. Or guard one side from the other, if it comes to that." She blew out a long breath, looking around at their faces. "When I put it all together, it sounds impossible."

"Impossible or not, Sister Alice, it is a worthy goal. Not to rule over the worlds, but to protect their people," Dex said. "You have my aid for as long as you need it."

"I'll do whatever I can," Soranna said.

"I'll help," Jen said abruptly. She looked down at Michael, and frowned at his quizzical expression. "What? It's the right thing to do."

"It is," Michael said gravely, then grinned. "I'll help, too."

"The whole thing sounds like it would interfere with my napping schedule," Ashes said, and yawned. "But I could be persuaded to come along, just to keep you kids out of trouble."

Alice looked at Isaac, who was looking at the ground, hands in the pockets of his battered coat.

"Come," Dex said, getting to her feet. "We should see how Flicker and the others are doing."

Soranna followed, then Michael.

"What?" Jen said. "Why—*ow!*" Michael had elbowed her in the side. "Fine, fine. I'm coming."

"Your presence would be useful as well, Master Ashes," Dex said.

"Oh, very well." Ashes hopped down from Alice's shoulder. "I like the look of that roast chicken they just brought out anyway."

And then Isaac and Alice were alone, on a quiet corner of the lawn. Behind them, the party continued, all noise and excitement. In front of them was the forest, gloomy in the gathering twilight.

"Well?" Alice said. "Are you going to help me fix the world?"

"It's too big for you," Isaac said. "For all of us, probably."

"I'm going to try anyway," Alice said.

"I know." He sighed. "Of course I'll help."

There was a long, awkward silence.

"Look—" said Alice.

"The thing is—" said Isaac simultaneously.

They paused, and there was another, even more awkward silence.

"You first," Isaac said.

"I'm a labyrinthine," Alice said. "I'm not really human. You saw the First. She's my *mother*."

"I know." Isaac shook his head. "Like you said. If I've learned one thing, it's not to judge by appearances."

"You don't care?" Alice's chest felt tight. "You're not worried I'll turn out like Ending?"

"I know you won't." Isaac stepped closer. "You could never be like her."

"I wish I was so certain."

Isaac took her hand and squeezed. "I'll talk some sense into you if you do. I promise."

Alice felt herself blush. She grinned. "All right. Now, what were you going to say?"

"I don't remember," Isaac said. "Probably nothing."

"Come on."

"I just . . ." He sighed. "When I thought you were going to leave with the First, I realized . . . I don't know." His brow furrowed, and now he was blushing, too. "Why can't I say this right?"

Alice's heart was beating very fast. She swallowed hard. Isaac was suddenly very interested in his shoes.

"Isaac."

"Look, never mind," he said. "We can talk about it later."

"Remember when you came to steal the Dragon?" Alice said.

"We kissed," Isaac muttered. "It was part of the spell."

"I know." Alice closed her eyes, blew out a breath, then opened them again. "Now that it *isn't* part of any spell, would you mind very much if we did it again?"

"That would . . . be all right." Isaac's cheeks were a flaming red, but he managed to look her in the eye. "I guess."

Alice leaned forward.

Ashes, eavesdropping from the branches of a nearby tree, listened to the pair of them circle around and around what they actually wanted to say.

*Humans,* he thought, and yawned. *Why do they have to make it all so complicated?* Ashes licked one forepaw delicately, and swiped it over his ear. *Cats have everything worked out.*

# THE END

# Acknowledgments:

I feel like I'm in a strange place, writing this. For the first time, I've actually made it all the way to the end of a series, and reached the conclusion I imagined what feels like a million years ago. It's been a wonderful journey, and my heartfelt thanks to everyone who's made it with me. I hope you've enjoyed reading Alice's adventures as much as I've enjoyed writing them.

My early readers for this volume were Robyn Murphy and Carl Meister, who in addition to their invaluable commentary helped keep me sane. Thanks so much, to them and everyone who read a draft throughout the series.

My agent, Seth Fishman, helped bring this series to life when I brought him the very first draft and said, "I wrote something strange, what do you think it is?" Not only did he have the answer, he knew what to do with it, and I'm forever grateful. Thanks as well to the team at The

Gernert Company: Will Roberts, Rebecca Gardner, Ellen Coughtrey, and Jack Gernert, as well as my UK agent, Caspian Dennis.

My editor, Kathy Dawson, believed in the series from the start, and helped me bang it into shape when I had no idea what I was doing. My eternal thanks to her, her assistant Claire Evans, and everyone at Kathy Dawson Books who helps give these words a physical reality.

Alexander Jansson's covers and artwork have truly brought the series to life, starting at the very beginning. My thanks for all the beautiful work.

It's been a lot of fun, everyone. I'll see you next time around!